Holding hands, they made their way carefully across the room until his knee struck the iron cot and he staggered. She took his weight for a moment, then staggered herself and landed on the thin mattress, Gideon falling on top of her. . . .

His breath was warm on her cheek. Instinctively, Amelia turned in to that warmth and her lips met his in a kiss that at first was as light and innocent as a butterfly's wing. Then she angled her mouth against his as if she had been doing it for years. No, she had only wanted to do it for years. Their mouths fit together perfectly. . . .

By Martha Schroeder
Published by Fawcett Books:

LADY MEG'S GAMBLE
GUARDING AN ANGEL

GUARDING AN ANGEL

Martha Schroeder

FAWCETT CREST • NEW YORK

A Fawcett Crest Book
Published by The Ballantine Publishing Group
 Published in the United States by The Ballantine Publishing Group, a division of Random House, Inc., New York, and simultaneously in Canada by Random House of Canada Limited, Toronto.

http://www.randomhouse.com

Library of Congress Catalog Card Number: 98-93318

ISBN 0-449-00342-6

Manufactured in the United States of America

First Edition: November 1998

10 9 8 7 6 5 4 3 2 1

Dedication

To Susan and Miranda, the dynamic duo that, between the two of them, cover all the bases from cookie-baking mom to romance superstar.

To both of you, thanks for the endless conversations, the sage advice, the dead-on perceptions and, most of all, for the warmth of your friendship.

Chapter One

"I cannot understand why you are making such heavy weather of this, Gideon," Lady Amelia Bradshaw said. "Eustace is not going to kidnap me and wed me at pistol point, you know."

"You think not? He's a damn—dashed loose screw, Amy. And rumor is that he's so deep in debt, he must either marry a fortune or flee to the Continent to escape his creditors."

"Well, he is the Duke of Doncaster, after all. Even for Eustace, marrying money should not be too difficult now." Amelia tried and failed to smile. Until four months ago, the title of Duke of Doncaster had belonged to her father, a man Society loved for his good looks and sporting skill and admired for his many charitable works. Amelia had loved him, revered him, and devoted her life to helping him in his work.

Though Gideon seldom spoke of his feelings, Amelia knew his love and gratitude for her father were boundless. During a time when she found it difficult to speak of a loss that was so profound and so new, she had turned to Gideon in part because she knew he shared her sense that the world had somehow been tipped off its axis by the duke's death.

Her father's title had descended—the perfect word, Amelia thought—to Eustace Mannering. And while Eustace appeared to be merely an affected and useless dandy, as harmless as he was silly, Amelia knew her father had never trusted his heir.

"Has he tried to take possession of any of the estates?" Gideon asked, unconsciously clenching and unclenching his hands. He was not used to having difficulty controlling his temper. But from the very first day they met, the urge to protect and defend Amelia burned in his breast. He would have disliked anyone who took the duke's place, and in effect drove Amelia from her home. But he had always despised Eustace. It was all he could do to refrain from driving his fist through the library wall at the thought of the new duke.

"Well," Gideon said again, his voice as hard as iron, "has he?"

"He has informed me that he has no wish to inconvenience me, but he will establish himself at the Abbey after the first of the year. He and his mother will be spending Christmas here." Amelia's voice was colorless, and she sat quietly, pale and steadfast in her black woolen gown. But her eyes, stormy with emotion, betrayed her.

Gideon knew that the idea of Eustace taking over her father's title and estates must be gall and wormwood to Amelia, but she gave no outward sign, except for those passionate eyes.

"He is going to spend Christmas here? With you?" Gideon demanded. "With whom for a chaperon? His mother? That archwife!" He surged to his feet and went to stand in front of the fireplace, where he kicked the logs until they fell apart in a shower of sparks.

"Please, Gideon, it does no good at all to rant and call names."

Her tone was one of a nanny scolding a recalcitrant charge. Instead of resenting it, Gideon gave her a lopsided grin. She had always scolded him that way. It was difficult for some people to take Lady Amelia Bradshaw altogether seriously. She was tiny, with a curvaceous figure and a wealth of sunshine-colored curls. Her eyes were large and sky blue. She even had dimples. Gideon, however, had learned early in their acquaintance that she had a will of iron and a formidable intelligence.

"You still talk to me as if you harbored no hope at all that I would ever reform and curb my temper!" he said with a chuckle.

"And indeed I do not." She tried to smile at him. "I only want you to see that I am not going to weep and faint and fall into a decline because of Eustace. Papa would never forgive me if I were to do so."

"As if you could ever do anything so poor-spirited! No, no,

Amy, I am angry with the fates, not with you! But I think you are oversanguine about your cousin."

"Second cousin," Amelia reminded him.

"Thank God. The farther removed from you he is on your family tree—and in your life—the happier I will be. Can you not go to one of your friends in the country for Christmas?"

"I have been invited to a few of the quieter house parties. Most people do not want a woman in deep mourning at their gatherings. Besides, if I left London, I would not be able to spend the day with you, Gideon." Amelia's smile was brave. "And I was looking forward to it. It is the first time in so very long that you have been in England at Christmas. It would feel almost like the old days."

Gideon took her hand. "I remember those Christmases, too. We will both be missing the duke. But we will have each other. I'll make sure I spend Christmas Day with you if I have to take French leave to do it."

Amelia's answering smile went a little awry. "Oh, dear, Gideon, I had not meant to weep all over you, but you are my dearest friend and my closest link to Papa. You remember him as well as I do."

"Indeed, I do." Gideon rallied her. "I began by being terrified of him, but he gave me a gold guinea and told me that I could always run away again so long as I had it." He released her hand, but only so he could embrace her shoulders and pull her close against his side. She felt so small and vulnerable that Gideon gave her shoulder a reassuring squeeze. "I have it still, you know. It gave me such a sense of freedom and power just to have money of my own."

There was a silence between them for a few moments. Then Gideon said, "You are not going to stay here for Christmas, are you, Amy? Not with Eustace and his mother in attendance, lording it over the servants and counting the teaspoons."

"No, the teaspoons are mine," Amelia reminded him. "You know that. Papa left all of the money and unentailed property to me. That is why Eustace must hang out for a rich wife."

"So he did. The duke always knew what Eustace was."

Gideon smiled reminiscently. "Do you remember that first Christmas when you brought me here?"

Amelia sighed a little and pulled out of the protection of his arm so that she could see his face. "Indeed, I do. I was so proud of myself and so sure that Papa would commend me for saving you."

"Instead, we encountered the entire staff at the front door, sure that you had met with an accident or suffered some other catastrophe." Gideon remembered that day, eighteen years earlier, when he had come to the duke's household as the day of his rebirth. He never forgot, however, that it could just as easily have been the day of his death.

Gideon had a double view of life—he always saw it as it was and as it might have been. Luck had played an enormous part in his life. Up to the time Amelia found him, it had all been bad, and he had already acquired the bone-deep cynicism that was still his hallmark. He knew only too well that much of life depended on luck. If yours was bad, the world would make you suffer for it and you could do nothing but endure until the luck changed. And if it was good, it behooved you to temper your joy with the certain knowledge that it could change again without notice. And the world's estimate of you would change just as quickly.

"They tried to hustle you off to the kitchen, I remember." Amelia was still reliving that red letter day.

"And you clung to me like a limpet." Gideon's smile was warm. Two people were exempt from his jaundiced view of mankind—Amelia and her late father. They had saved his life, and from that day forward Gideon had sworn that he would lay down his life for them, should the need arise.

He had read of King Arthur and the Round Table when the duke had sent him to school, and he immediately recognized their code as his, and Amelia as his lady. He would stand in the background of his lady's life, never giving the slightest thought to actually possessing her. No, he would guard, he would protect her with silent devotion. Although he later laughed at himself and his grandiose notions, which were very out-of-date in these modern times, he had never forsworn his vow. He remained, in silence and in secret, the last knight of the Round Table.

"Yes," Amelia continued, "I was determined that Papa should see what a wonderful deed I had done. I knew he would recognize you."

"Recognize me?" Gideon raised his dark winged eyebrows in his typical expression of amused doubt.

"Yes, of course. I knew you were going to be special. I could tell the minute you opened your eyes."

Amelia had insisted on this at the time, Gideon remembered. When Somers, the butler, had tried to lead the dirty little urchin into the back of the house—and from there, Gideon was sure, right out the door and back onto the street—Amelia had resisted.

"No, he must stay here. Papa must speak with him. He is not to be simply fed and sent away." Even at six, Amelia had a will of iron. And when that did not suffice, she gave the world a melting smile and a limpid gaze. That card always took the trick.

So Gideon had stayed in the drawing room, delighted that he had won out over the starched-up old stick, as he'd thought of Somers then. He remembered being too afraid to sit down.

"You were the most intrepid little thing," he said, amazed as always at the lion's heart hidden beneath the kitten's surface. His memory of the little girl tended to superimpose itself on the reality of the woman. When he looked at her, he was sometimes unsure of which he was gazing at.

"Gideon." The sound of Amelia's voice did not immediately draw him from his reverie. For a moment he was suspended between past and present, some of the emotions of each swirling in his heart and brain.

"Look, Cook has made you your favorite currant scones, Gideon."

Their homey fragrance drew him back to the present. He smiled apologetically at Amelia and sat down opposite her, watching as she poured his tea. "You reminded her to do so, Amy. Cook always swore I would eat the duke out of his dukedom." He grinned at her. "It would be porridge for me and not too much of that if not for you."

"In any event, here they are and you must eat several so as not to hurt her feelings." Amelia handed him his cup and prepared to give him a scone as well.

Gideon was just taking his first sip when the knocker at the front door sounded. Somers appeared in the doorway moments later. "Mrs. Mannering has called, my lady."

"Oh, never mind." The shrill voice came from the doorway as well. "As if she would not want to see me! Really, my good man, you take a great deal upon yourself, indeed you do."

With those words, Hortense Mannering, the new Duke of Doncaster's mother, swept through the door. She took in the cozy room with its well-worn carpet and walls of books and dismissed it with a glance. Her eyes were cold as agates, and Gideon could see her add up the value of everything in the room in less than a minute. Ignoring Gideon as beneath her notice, she smiled at Amelia and bustled over to kiss her effusively. "My dear girl, it is so sad to see you here, all in black, with no one but servants and hangers-on!" she said, her voice dripping honey. "How glad I am that Eustace and I will be able to bear you company for the holidays! I told him that I simply could not bear thinking of you with no family about you at such a time." Hortense patted Amelia's hand. "All alone as you are, my poor dear."

Amelia's eyes met Gideon's for a moment of shared, silent laughter. "Have you met Captain Gideon Falconer, Cousin Hortense?" Amelia said sweetly.

"Why, yes, he was at your dear father's obsequies. Indeed, I believe the captain received a bequest in the late duke's will." At the thought of the document that had deprived Eustace of the fortune that should by rights have been his, Hortense's lips tightened.

"Mrs. Mannering." Gideon, who had risen when she had entered, gave her a bow. "How pleasant to see you again."

"Gideon comes as often as his duties permit him to do so." Amelia smiled gently. "And, of course, my friends have been everything that is kind. I have not been alone, you see."

Hortense gave her another bright, meaningless smile, and sat down in one of the tapestry-covered armchairs that flanked the tea table. "But none of them are your *family*, my dear Amelia. Eustace and I want you to know that we will be only too happy to devote ourselves to your welfare. We want you to consider both the Abbey and this house as your homes."

"Thank you, Cousin Hortense." Amelia's voice was colorless, but Gideon noticed that the hands clasped in her lap showed white at the knuckles. "May I offer you some tea and scones? Cook makes excellent ones."

"Yes, my dear, I'm sure your cook is all very well for plain fare like scones. But, really, in a house of this stature, you should have a French chef who knows how to make those dainty little iced cakes."

"Petits fours," Gideon said politely.

"I beg your pardon?" Mrs. Mannering's tone was icy.

"The little cakes. They are called petits fours." Gideon's face was without expression. Only his dark, hooded eyes, as bright as a falcon's and as unforgiving, gave any hint of the murderous anger that consumed him.

Amelia, forced to put up with this spiteful, vulgar woman and her man-milliner son! Cook, who had been with the Bradshaw family practically since her birth, to be fired! He set his teeth and vowed to keep his temper. Usually he had no trouble doing so. His sangfroid was legendary in his regiment, but he had a strong desire to run Hortense Mannering through with a sword, or lacking that, any sharp instrument that came to hand.

"And"—the odious woman was still talking—"we insist that you spend Christmas here, with us! It is only fitting, now you no longer have the right to be here, that we make you welcome."

Gideon clenched his hands, automatically reaching in his pocket for the small iron ball he habitually fingered in moments of high emotion. Talking as if Amelia were some penniless relation! There were no sharp instruments handy, dammit, but he could always hit her over the head with the fireplace poker. Anything to still her tongue.

"That is very kind of you, Cousin Hortense." Amelia's

cheeks were pinker than usual, and her blue eyes held a dangerous look, if one were wise enough to recognize it.

Hortense Mannering was not. "Oh, my dear, we do not want you to feel that you have been . . . supplanted. You are welcome to remain here until you marry. And, indeed, perhaps afterward as well." She cast a simpering look at Amelia. "If you take my meaning."

Amelia ignored her. Gideon's sharp eyes noted that her cheeks showed a deeper flush, but her tone was polite, her voice quiet. "I thank you. But, as I was about to tell you, I will be removing to my friend Jane Forrester's home until I can arrange for my own house here in London."

Cousin Hortense protested loudly. "But, my dear Amelia, you cannot live by yourself! A green girl like you! It is unheard of. Preposterous. People will think we did not offer you a home. You cannot. Indeed, you must not."

For once, Gideon was inclined to agree with Mrs. Mannering. Young, unmarried ladies did not hire their own houses in town. They might, under unusual circumstances, live quietly in the country with only old family retainers as long as they did not entertain. But in London? Never. Gideon, however, knew Amelia a good deal better than Mrs. Mannering did, and held his tongue for the time being.

"I do not intend to live alone." Amelia's voice had frozen. Her tone brooked no further questioning of her purposes.

"Oh" was all Mrs. Mannering had to say. Something in the militant sparkle of Amelia's eyes must have communicated its message to the duke's mother. After a few more random comments on the joys of spending Christmas with one's family, she took her leave.

Gideon drew a deep breath. It might not be any of Hortense Mannering's business where Amelia was going to live, but as her oldest friend he thought it damn well was his. He looked at his hostess. She had sunk into a chair and was contemplating her untasted cup of tea with an absent look in her eye.

"Amy," he began.

"Do not start a lecture on the strict chaperonage required by my unmarried state, Gideon, unless you want the tantrum I spared Cousin Hortense." A half smile touched her lips, but he knew she was serious.

"Very well, Amy. I know you have been sorely tried this afternoon, and I will keep my opinions to myself for the time being." He bent down and brushed a kiss against the bright softness of her hair. "But be warned! As the next thing you have to a brother, I am not going to keep silent forever."

"No, I never supposed you would, my friend." Amelia sighed. "But I shall treasure my peace for as long as you do."

"Poor Amy. I shall leave you alone to bask in it, then. Remember, my dear, you have only to send word and I can be here at any time. For any reason. If I do not hear from you, I shall call again tomorrow."

Chapter Two

Eustace Mannering, the Duke of Doncaster, lounged in a sagging wing chair and looked around the shabby, furnished house with profound dislike. His full lips pouted, and he reached for another bonbon.

"Really, Mama," he said, his high-tenor voice more querulous than usual, "I do not see why you could not bring our dear cousin to accept your most flattering invitation."

"In the ordinary way of things I am sure she would have accepted, my dear. After all, where else can she go? But that odious Captain Falconer was there, sneering and glowering and generally making himself most disagreeable."

"Confound the man, Mama! I am sure I could cut him out with her if only I had the chance!" Eustace clenched his hands and stared into the meager fire. Succeeding to the title should have made all his dreams come true. He had looked forward to nothing else his entire life. The duke had limited his contact with his heir to a dinner once or twice a year in London, after that unfortunate affair with the housemaid at the Abbey.

Eustace grimaced. Tiresome old bore. Even in death the duke had managed to cheat him! All the money—and there was so much money—to go to that tiresome little chit. She was as mealy-mouthed and methodist as her father. Pretty little morsel, but so good and pure it made one positively queasy! Nevertheless, there was nothing for it but to swallow his distaste and marry her. The Mannerings' need for money was acute, and only an advantageous marriage would save them once his creditors discovered that the title, a town house, and some moldering old pile in Devon were all the inheritance Eustace had received.

Damn the old skinflint! Eustace couldn't bear any more fruitless reflection. "I think I'll just toddle along to the club, Mama," he said, rising from his chair and smoothing the ruffles on his shirtfront.

Hortense frowned. "Don't go losing any more money, lovey. We'll be all right once we remove to Doncaster House. There must be all sorts of little things lying about that we can sell to tide us over. But until then you'd best keep up the idea of coming into money."

"Did you tell Cousin Amelia that we'd be moving in soon?"

"Oh, my, yes. And asked her to stay for Christmas. Offered a home with us, just as we decided, dear."

"All right, all right. I know." Eustace slid into his overcoat and waved good night to his mother. "I must marry the girl, but there is no use talking about it tonight."

At the same time, in Colonel Sir Richard Sinclair's snug bachelor rooms, that gentleman sat in a leather armchair in front of a cheerful blaze and stretched his long legs out with a sigh of exquisite comfort. His cravat was loosened and his straight dark blond hair was disheveled. It had been a long day, and Sir Richard was looking forward to a brandy and a complete absence of thought.

There was a sound that might have been a knock, which Sir Richard ignored until his man, Hoskins, entered and quietly announced, "Captain Falconer requests a word with you, sir."

With a sigh the colonel rose and turned to greet his young friend and protégé. "Gideon," he said with a smile that was only slightly forced.

"I am sorry to disturb you so late, sir," Gideon said, his face grave. "If you would prefer, I can wait until tomorrow. It is only a trifling personal matter, nothing that you should be bothered with. I am sorry I even thought of coming."

Sir Richard gave a short bark of laughter. "Oh, come, Gideon, cut line. Humility doesn't become you. You are here, and you will sit down and take a brandy with me."

"Thank you, sir. It is good of you to admit me at this hour." He stood for a moment and looked around the cozy apartment. It was filled with books, pipes, and newspapers. Gideon had never before called upon the colonel and was somewhat apprehensive.

His life in the army had been essentially very simple and very solitary. He had lived for his work, determined to make the duke proud of him. The fact that a commission had been purchased for him, not in a line regiment but in the cavalry, the elite of army services, had inspired Gideon with a determination to excel.

Gideon not only did not participate in the social life, which for most was the reason to choose the cavalry, he ignored it totally. He was concerned only with horses and tactics. He made no friends—though he made no enemies, either. There was something in his single-mindedness that kept envy as well as friendship at bay. The other junior officers regarded him as an eccentric, but a harmless one. They rather liked the dour, humorless young man with the mysterious past, particularly since he turned into a hell-for-leather dervish once the fighting started.

Sir Richard was a ranking officer whose knowledge of the history of cavalry was formidable. Gideon had first come to his attention when he had asked several penetrating questions regarding Cromwell's innovative use of cavalry in the Civil War. Sir Richard had noted with some amusement that the other young officers, all sprigs of the nobility, had not taken kindly to a respectful discussion of the Great Regicide's military genius. Later Gideon had told him what had sparked his interest.

"He had no formal training. It was all intelligence and necessity that guided him. He was a nobody." Gideon had not added *like me*, but Sir Richard knew a little of his history and he guessed the kinship Gideon felt.

For some reason, the dark-haired young officer had sparked an interest in Sir Richard and he had taken Gideon under his wing. When, on the Peninsula, Gideon had taken a saber cut intended for the colonel, a friendship had grown and flourished.

"Sit down and drink the brandy Hoskins has supplied you with, and tell me what is on your mind this evening."

Gideon remained standing in front of the fireplace. "Sir, I hardly know why I have come. I need advice but I'm not sure if you can help." He ran a hand distractedly through his hair.

Sir Richard raised his sandy brows in a silent question.

"Yes, I know I am not being very clear. But I am not precisely sure why I am worried."

Again, Sir Richard said nothing, gesturing him to continue. Gideon took a large sip of brandy and said, "It concerns the late Duke of Doncaster's daughter. Lady Amelia."

"Ah." Sir Richard nodded, as if Gideon had said something very significant. "The duke was your sponsor, was he not, and the lady is an orphan now, if I am not mistaken."

"Yes, and she has no relatives except the new duke and his mother, and I do not trust them." Gideon kicked the log, sending up a shower of sparks. "I fear what they may do."

"Why? Why should they do anything?"

"Money. The duke left all his money to Amy—Lady Amelia. And from what I have managed to learn, Eustace and his mother are very hard up."

"You, listening to gossip? I am amazed, Falconer."

"Yes, sir, so am I." Gideon smiled a little sheepishly. "But I would do anything to protect Lady Amelia." The smile faded, and a grim look replaced it. "Anything."

Sir Richard motioned Gideon to sit down. "The duke arranged for your commission, did he not?"

Gideon sat down in the other chair that flanked the fireplace. "He did more than that. He bought it for me." He looked at Sir Richard but said nothing for a long moment. "Everyone knows I was a foundling. I have never made a secret of it. I have no idea who or what my parents were. I ran away from the man who owned—whom I worked for."

Gideon got up and went to stand, looking out the window at the rain coming down in the darkness outside. "It was winter, and I had been on the streets for a few weeks, I think. Anyway, to make a short tale of it, Amelia and the duke found me, and she convinced her father to let me stay and to send me to school.

She saw something in me, something worth saving. I owe her my life."

There was silence for a moment while Gideon drank the last of his brandy. He had never told anyone this much before, but his concern for Amelia compelled him to reveal his shameful past. Sir Richard had to understand why he cared for her—and that she had no one else to turn to.

"I can see why you feel that you must do everything you can to protect the lady. It is what any foster brother would feel."

"I am not her brother. The duke never adopted me. I was only one of the many boys he helped."

"The solution seems obvious. Once the lady has married, she will have a protector and your sense of responsibility will subside."

"Amelia says she has no interest in marriage."

"Absurd. Every woman is interested in marriage, even those who profess the contrary." Sir Richard reached for the pipe conveniently placed amid the clutter on the table at his elbow. "A clutch of them have tried to marry me over the years. As I recall, Lady Amelia is a taking little thing. She should have no trouble bringing any number of eligible males up to scratch."

It was well-known that Sir Richard took a dim view of the fair sex. Succeeding unexpectedly to his brother's title and expectations, he had gone overnight from being just another younger son in the military to a very eligible *parti*. Gideon wondered why he had come. He'd wanted to talk to someone, share his worries, get advice from an older and wiser head. He should have remembered Sir Richard's reputation. No one as cynical as the colonel could be expected to understand Amy.

"She is not like other women."

"Of course, you would think so." Sir Richard rose and joined Gideon in front of the fireplace. He reached in with a long taper and carefully lit his pipe. "But where the important things of life are concerned—husbands and babies and re-covering the chairs in a man's library—believe me, Captain, they are all alike. You will see."

"Not Amy." Realizing he'd spoken too quickly to be polite,

Gideon added, "Although I do not know her attitude toward chairs."

Sir Richard smiled, his hazel eyes disbelieving. "Well, my friend, short of marrying her yourself, I do not see that there is much you can do. You are not the young lady's guardian, are you?"

"Amelia is twenty-four, sir."

"Good heavens. If I remember her correctly, she looks much younger. She is the small blonde with the big blue eyes? I am sure I have seen her occasionally at a musicale or the theater."

"Yes, that describes Amelia. Lady Amelia," Gideon amended, remembering too late that he had referred to her without her title several times.

"A taking little thing. And a considerable heiress? Hmm." Sir Richard rapped his pipe smartly on the marble mantel. Ashes fell on a hearth already thickly scattered with them.

Gideon felt he had to explain just why Amy was so different from other women. "Lady Amelia is following in her father's footsteps. She is continuing his work with children and has decided to found a school for orphan girls. She is devoting her life to charity."

"What a waste!"

Gideon's anger at his mentor's cynical dismissal of the systematic kindness that had saved his life was hotter than he expected. He beat it down. Amelia and her father had saved a number of boys like himself. In later years he had helped them in their work, and his admiration for the rich and well-favored Bradshaws, father and daughter, who could have spent their lives in pursuit of pleasure, in elegant salons with people as elegant and attractive as they themselves, was boundless. His disgust at those who belittled them was equally vast. He hated to feel that way about Sir Richard Sinclair.

His host's shrewd eyes took their time taking in his rock-hard jaw and thin lips. Gideon knew his eyes were black and stormy—they always were when his temper got the best of him. Fortunately, he had so far managed to keep his mouth shut.

"I am sorry, Gideon." The colonel's words were quiet, but Gideon could tell that they were heartfelt. "I did not realize quite how much the lady meant to you. I believe that we can find a way to keep her out of the grasp of fortune hunters, Mannering included. Sit down, and tell me about Lady Amelia's work."

Gideon's anger seeped away. "Thank you, sir. I would appreciate your advice." He raised his glass and prepared to share still more of his life with a friend. It was a new feeling, but he thought he might grow to like it.

"Amelia, my dear, what in the world are you doing here? Oh, I didn't mean that the way it sounded!" Jane Forrester greeted her friend with the quick laugh and good humor she used to confront a world that was not always kind to spinsters of slender means. "Of course, I am delighted to see you anytime you can break free from those ton parties that occupy your evenings."

Jane put her arm around Amelia and led her into the small parlor. A woman of indeterminate years, Jane was too tall for beauty, though her glowing topaz eyes and wealth of chestnut hair could have made her seem beautiful. Jane Forrester had confronted and prevailed over circumstances that would have felled others. The only child of improvident artists, Jane had been the practical member of the household. From a very early age, she controlled the purse strings and managed everything except her parents' painting. In her teens she had nursed both her mother and father through their final illnesses, to find herself alone in a world that placed a low value on the managerial skills she had in abundance and set a great price on wealth and family connections, of which she had none.

In her usual blunt, straightforward fashion, Jane had tried to use her talents to help others. She had begun as a teacher in a London girls' school, and at the end of three years was its headmistress. Amelia met her when she was trying to expand the duke's charities to include girls as well as boys. Jane's school took a certain number of poor girls, and she worked hard to get the money to take in even more.

Now Jane offered her friend tea and sat on her shabby sofa,

her feet curled under her. "You're frowning, my dear, and staring into your cup. 'Fess up, Amy. Tell me what's wrong."

Jane's comforting voice, the tea, the cozy surroundings made Amelia's eyes sting. She'd never known her mother, but Jane, though only a few years her senior, was as warm and welcoming as any mother could be. No wonder the school administrators chose her instead of a learned lady to head their institution, Amelia thought. Jane could smooth problems and ease hearts—much more necessary for young girls than mere knowledge.

"Ah, Jane, you know me too well. But I did not come here to complain. It seems I have done nothing but burden you with my grief ever since Papa died."

"Nonsense, Amy. You have continued the duke's work almost from the day of the funeral. In fact, I thought that you were to attend some musicale this evening, hoping to corner that wealthy nabob and wring a few groats from him." Jane laughed at Amy's indignant look.

"Calumny, vile calumny!" Amy chuckled, too. Hostesses who were pleased to entertain a duke's daughter often found that they and their guests paid for the privilege with a subscription to one or another of Lady Amelia's favorite charities.

"I simply offer the ton the means to balance their frivolities with the gift of some necessities for others."

"Ah, of course." The door opened, and a bright childish face looked in. "Yes, Opal?"

"Excuse me, Miss Jane, but you telled me to read my chapter and now I done it." Opal, a small, thin child with bright eyes shyly cast down before her schoolmistress's elegant friend, sketched a curtsy.

"You may ask Cook for a glass of milk before you go to bed. You remember Miss Amelia, do you not?" Jane rose and went to put her arm around the little girl, who smiled up adoringly.

"Yes, ma'am. Good evening, Miss Amelia. Good night, Miss Amelia, good night, ma'am." Having taken care of the polite formulas in a few words, Opal slipped back out the door.

"Does she live with you now?" Amelia asked. "I remember seeing her at the school."

"No. I take one of the scholarship girls home with me each month, so that they can learn how to go on. That way, when they are employed in a genteel household, they will fit in."

"What a splendid idea. I must talk to Gideon about doing the same thing with the orphans in our school." Amelia made a mental note. "I can have them stay at Doncaster House and—" She broke off as memory returned. "No, I cannot. I forgot. I will not be taking anyone to Doncaster House anymore. Hortense called this afternoon to announce that she and Eustace will be moving in shortly. In time for Christmas." Amelia leaned forward and clasped her hands tightly. "I thought I was prepared for this, but now that it has come, I find I am not. Even though Papa left the contents of the house to me and the rest is just brick and mortar, the thought of leaving—is difficult." Amelia's throat constricted, and she clenched her hands more tightly. She hated the very idea of crying. She should be done with all that by now. Papa would not wish her to mourn, but to carry on his work.

"Of course it is. Especially since it is that toad Eustace who has inherited it. Where are you going to go?"

Amelia looked up. "I was rather hoping you would take me in for the holidays. I can earn my keep, you know. If Cook wants to return home for Christmas, I can replace her. Or any of the teachers. Except music, of course. Or drawing. I was terrible at those, but I can keep up with almost everything else."

Jane shook her head. "You are welcome here anytime you wish to come, Amy, you know that. You do not need to do any more than you already have." She reached out her hand to her friend.

"I simply hadn't thought about Christmas. Or rather I had planned to fill the house with you and the children. And Gideon of course since he's at Horse Guards for the time being."

"This house hardly compares to Doncaster House, but we can certainly squeeze Captain Falconer in. Perhaps he might consent to pass out the presents. If he wore his regimentals, the children would be most impressed."

The idea of Gideon surrounded by little girls amused Amy. He spent most of his spare moments at the orphanage the duke had established on a farm not far from London. There it was clear that Gideon had a gift for talking to small boys. And he could talk to men in the military or politics about their professions, or indeed anyone who had an interest besides amusing themselves. He had encountered many such men at the duke's masculine dinners. But Amy knew he avoided dandies and sportsmen, lapsing into a brooding silence on the few occasions he had encountered them in her presence.

But she had never been aware of exactly how Gideon related to women other than herself. Why was that? When she gave it a moment's thought, she realized Gideon avoided ton parties. Occasionally he would escort her to the theater or the opera, both of which she adored, but never the normal events she attended.

"I do not know if he will come," she said slowly to Jane as her mind assimilated this startling fact. "I find I know practically nothing of his social life. I suppose it is because he has been away with the army, and we have grown apart. I used to understand him so well."

For a horrified moment Amelia felt tears clog her throat for the second time that evening. She could not bear the thought of embarrassing herself again. Hurriedly she rose to her feet and held out both her hands to Jane. "I must go. Thank you for giving me carte blanche to impose on your hospitality. I may have to take advantage of it sooner than I would wish. I have the feeling that Eustace and his mother are going to spare no effort to keep me at Doncaster House for Christmas."

Chapter Three

Amelia was more prescient than she knew.

After a long discussion with his mama, Eustace presented himself at Doncaster House the next afternoon. It was Wednesday, Amelia's day to receive callers. As he intended, he was the first to arrive. He greeted her with an effusion of compliments carried on a wave of scent. It was all Amelia could do not to back away in revulsion.

"My dear cousin, how lovely you look. Black becomes you. You should always wear it." When Amelia remained silent, Eustace seemed to realize how unfortunate that remark was. He hastened to make amends. "Of course, one does understand that you wear it not for fashion's sake but to honor your dear papa. Such a loss to everyone. I myself was devastated, truly. That was why I did not attend his funeral. It was simply too painful."

Here, Eustace put his hand over his heart, and Amelia had to suck her breath in sharply to keep from telling him exactly what she thought of his supposed grief. *You managed to overcome your grief enough to come to hear his will read,* she thought wrathfully. *You odious toad!*

If Eustace noticed the dangerous sparkle in her narrowed eyes, he ignored it. Other callers arrived just then, and he had no further opportunity for private conversation with Amelia. Since he hoped to further his suit and reinforce his mother's invitation to spend Christmas with them, he determined to stay until everyone else departed.

Those hopes were dashed when Gideon Falconer entered the drawing room a few minutes later. Eustace noted that the cavalry captain lacked his own ease of address. Falconer stood stiffly, holding a glass of sherry but never drinking from it and looking around with an unsmiling mien. Enough to frighten most guests into leaving immediately. The icy look he gave Eustace left the duke in no doubt as to his feelings. Eustace shrugged. A nobody. A captaincy purchased by the old duke—more money wasted, damn him. Who would have Gideon Falconer now that his patron was dead? His dark, brooding looks might remind women of Lord Byron, but with no family and no fortune, he would be lucky to find himself a provincial miss with a mustache and a modest dowry.

Amelia watched Eustace preen. *He's looking at Gideon as if he were beneath contempt!* she thought. *Give a man like Eustace a title, and he prances about the world as if he owned it!* She turned away in disgust and crossed the room to greet Lady Maltby, one of her father's oldest friends.

"Amelia, my dear, it is so nice to see Eustace here," Lady Maltby said. "I am happy there will be no rift in your family. I do deplore such feuds."

Eustace had followed Amelia across the room and overheard the remark. "How right you are, Lady Maltby. Mama and I are determined that our dear cousin will not only spend Christmas with us here but will remain for the indefinite future. We wish her to make her home with us!"

"That is very generous of you, Eustace," Amelia said, managing to keep her voice even and pleasant. "But as I told Cousin Hortense, I plan to stay with friends over the holidays and move into a new house soon after the beginning of the year."

"Nonsense, Amelia," said Lady Maltby. "Eustace is very right. Christmas is for families. I myself always spend it at the home of my eldest daughter. She and I have never gotten along, and her children are insupportable. Nevertheless, every December I hie myself into the wilds of Scotland to suffer through Christmas with them. Family!" she barked, sounding very like an aging sergeant major. "Tradition!"

Amelia fought a losing battle with a smile. She took the older woman's arm and guided her to a comfortable wing chair. Once she had her guest installed, she sat herself. There were no other chairs nearby. She hoped to discourage Eustace from lingering in her vicinity.

Offering Lady Maltby a dish of comfits, she said, "Scotland and insupportable children! What fortitude you must have, ma'am. I am not so intrepid, and will slink off to visit friends in warmer climes." She was not actually misleading Lady Maltby—London was warmer than Scotland! If she and Eustace believed that Amelia was traveling some distance for the holidays, so much the better. "I believe the children who live with my friends may be somewhat less troublesome as well, though I am by no means an expert on the subject. You are more than welcome to remain and pass Christmas with us."

Lady Maltby gazed fondly at Amelia's mischievously smiling face. She had known Amelia since babyhood and had often bemoaned the fact that her own daughters were not half so pretty or charming. She hated the thought of Amelia spending Christmas somewhere other than her own fireside. Not that Amelia had her own fireside anymore. "You must marry, my dear girl!" she said, still in her sergeant-major voice. "Then you will always have a place to go for Christmas."

Eustace, who was hovering around Amelia's chair, pounced upon the remark. If he could not maneuver a private meeting with Amelia, he would do his best with the public forum that was available to him. "Just what I have been telling my cousin, ma'am," he said enthusiastically, lowering his voice in what sounded to Amelia like a horrid parody of sympathy. "She needs a strong arm to lean on, a hard head to handle her business affairs, and"—he sighed deeply—"a tender heart to care for her. Such a small, helpless creature." Amelia longed to punch her cousin in the stomach and have Frederick, the footman, frog-march him off the premises.

"Such fustian!" she exclaimed. "I need no such thing. I have a strong arm of my own and likewise a hard head. I do not need a man to come along and rescue me!"

Glaring at her cousin, she picked up a glass at random and drained it. Only when she felt the fiery liquid burn its way down her throat did she realize she'd gotten some gentleman's brandy glass by mistake.

Her eyes watered, and she began to sputter. Before Eustace or Lady Maltby could take action, Gideon crossed the room in two strides and thumped her sharply on the back. He sniffed the air appreciatively. When she stopped coughing, he looked down into her rosy face and said, "When did you take up brandy, Amy?"

Eyes tearing, she grinned up at him and gasped, "It certainly has a greater effect than tea. I can see why you gentlemen prefer it. Unfortunately, I drank it too fast. Thank you for that mighty blow." She turned to Eustace, still standing and staring. "I suppose I must grant that you are right, Eustace. I do sometimes need someone with a strong right arm to rescue me." She gave him what she hoped was a friendly smile, but Eustace did not respond. He continued to stare at her and Gideon, his eyes dark and unblinking.

"Mama and I would like to move into Doncaster House next week," he said, his voice harsh. "If that would be convenient, of course," he added, clearly as an afterthought.

"It might be better to discuss this in private, Eustace. Perhaps you and Cousin Hortense will call on me to discuss it."

She felt Gideon move to her side, his arm protectively at her back. The way he would stand with a comrade in arms, she thought, warmed by that status.

"Mannering," he said, his deep voice resonant with warning.

"Doncaster," Eustace responded. His face was a mask, only the eyes betraying emotion. They were molten with fury. "I am the Duke of Doncaster, Falconer—or whatever your name may be."

"I will expect you and Cousin Hortense," Amelia said.

Though Eustace opened his mouth, Amelia's air of quiet command stilled his protest. With Lady Maltby staring at him, obviously amazed that he would discuss such private family business in front of callers, and with Gideon glaring at him, he was left with nothing to do except to agree and bow himself out.

Gideon waited until the last of the visitors had been shown out. Then he came to Amelia and took her by the arm. He led her, unresisting, to a comfortable settee.

"Sit here and rest your mind for a few minutes," he said, concern for her apparent in the deep quiet of his voice.

"It's not my mind, it's my feet that need rest," she replied. With a sigh she toed off her kid slippers and wiggled her toes. "What made you come today, Gideon? I know how you hate calls."

"I suspected that Eustace would be here. I am not about to let you face him alone, Amy."

She smiled. "I am not afraid of him, you know."

Gideon frowned. "Perhaps you should be. He is a very angry man, and angry men can do unexpected things."

"I was happy to see you. It is always good to have you here. How long do you stay at Horse Guards, do you think?" Amelia wanted to be distracted from the unsettled state of her life. She knew she should be thinking of the future, of what she would do, where she would go, but somehow no answers occurred to her. She wanted only to live from day to day without troubling herself about the large, unanswered questions of her life.

But Gideon, who knew her better than anybody except her father, of course, was not to be distracted. "I can have a carter here tomorrow. He can put everything in storage until you decide where you are going to live."

She frowned, forced by his words to concentrate on a future she couldn't see clearly. "I don't know, Gideon. Somehow it seems wrong to take everything. After all, Eustace is the duke, the head of the family—such as it is. I'm not sure—"

"We'll go through the house, and you can decide what should be left for the duke and what you want." He held out his hand and pulled her to her feet. "Mrs. MacAdams and Somers can help you with the practicalities like linens and pots." His hands slid down her arms to clasp her hands lightly in his large, warm ones. "Shall we begin?"

Amelia sighed. She wanted only to rest by the fire and let the slight melancholy that had afflicted her since her father's death wash over her. But she knew Gideon. Once he had decided that you ought to do something for your own good, he would not rest until he had helped you do it. As a child, he had seen to it that Amelia's sums were done correctly, and there was no deflecting him with ponies or picnics until they were. Now he was making sure that through fatigue and inattention she did not leave her father's things for Eustace and his mother to use.

"Do not leave him anything that he might pawn," Gideon said. "You don't want your father's belongings in some cents-per-center's window."

Amelia nodded, and Gideon led the way to the duke's library. "I will make the list," he said, "while you look about you and tell me what you want taken."

Amelia awaited her cousins two days later with carefully concealed anger. She had sent word to Eustace, naming the hour that she would welcome him and his mother. The note she had received in reply had been very ungracious.

Amelia had been angry. She prided herself on her even temper and quiet disposition, but Eustace and his mother managed to rouse the devil in her soul. She admitted to herself that there was something so repellent as to be almost frightening about Eustace and Hortense. They were always smiling, and yet she had the unmistakable feeling that they could smile and smile and still be villains. She could have used a staunch cavalry officer at her back as she tried to buy time to pack up her belongings and leave. *Nonsense!* She needed no help from Gideon—or any man.

When they finally arrived, she greeted the new duke and his mother, offered them coffee and, after they had drunk it, amid exclamations of its excellence and her goodness in serving it to them, she showed them around the house. As they made their way from room to room, Amelia felt a lump lodge itself in her throat. Everything, every piece of furniture, picture, and ornament reminded her of her father and of happier times. The mahogany desk that he had used every day. The brilliantly colored Sienese landscape painting he had told her made him smile every time he saw it. The silver sugar shaker with the dent where it had hit the floor when she had tried to use it all by herself at age four. Everything. She was suddenly overwhelmed with gratitude toward Gideon, who had known she would feel this way and had insisted she keep what she most treasured. When they descended once more to the book room, Amelia forced herself to smile, though the vulpine expression on Cousin Hortense's face repulsed her.

"My dear, I know it must pain you to leave this behind," Hortense said, all but rubbing her hands in anticipation.

Amelia paused, wondering if Hortense had forgotten that the contents of the house had not been left to her son. Before she could think of what to say, Somers entered to announce Captain Falconer, and Gideon strode into the room on his heels.

"Amelia, Mrs. Mannering, Eustace," he said, completely ignoring the titles to which the Mannerings were now entitled. "I thought I might find you here. I came to tell Amy that I have found a carter who can come to take what you want and keep it in storage until you can decide on another dwelling."

Amelia noticed in passing that Cousin Hortense's face had turned a shade of red that reminded her of her father's best claret—crimson with just a hint of purple.

"What do you mean, barging in here? You have intruded on a family conference." Hortense's eyes narrowed. "I know you have been permitted to run tame in this house for years, but my son and I do not subscribe to the strange social ideas of the late duke. We do not entertain mongrels, nor do we allow them access to the young, unmarried girls of the family." Hortense drew herself up and puffed her substantial bosom out like a pouter pigeon. "I would ask you to leave, sir."

Gideon stood motionless and silent for a moment, then he gave Hortense a look that would have frozen the marrow of a far braver soul than she was. She gave a start and took an involuntary step backward.

Amelia's cool voice took command before Gideon could speak. "Captain Falconer is a guest in my home, Cousin Hortense. I will be leaving here just as soon as possible. After that, it will be your home, and you may bar the door to anyone you see fit. Until that time, Gideon will be welcome here whenever he chooses to come."

Utter silence followed. Hortense's mouth hung open at an unbecoming angle, and Gideon's eyes danced. He and Amelia shared a tiny smile. Neither of them saw the fury that swept over Eustace's face, only to be quickly wiped away.

"I must say, I find all this family brangling to be most fatiguing," he said, his voice almost a parody of the die-away dandy. "Do let us go, Mama. I am sure Cousin Amelia has much to discuss with the gallant captain." Eustace's malicious smile warned Gideon that he had made an enemy.

Much he cared for that! If only he could find a way to keep Amelia safe and happy as she had been while her father lived, Gideon would consider any enmity well worthwhile.

"Mannering." Gideon managed a bow. "Amelia will inform me when you and your mother may take up residence here. I will avoid the street entirely after that date."

"Doncaster," Eustace said through clenched teeth. "Really, that is an excess of caution. I do assure you, I have no desire to deny you the use of the public streets." Eustace tittered, but his eyes remained cold as agates.

"Heavens, no," Hortense interjected. She placed a restraining hand on her son's arm.

"You misunderstand me." Gideon's voice was even. "It is the pervading stench of your scent I wish to avoid." Another bow, and he walked away toward the other end of the room before Eustace, his face growing paler by the moment, could respond.

Amelia looked at her cousin and his mother, apprehension tingeing her practiced smile. "Cousin Hortense, I hope you will feel free to come at any time to measure the rooms and consider whatever changes you may wish to make."

"Thank you, my dear, but I must reiterate our invitation not just for the holidays but for the future as well." Hortense's hand tightened on her son's sleeve. "My son wishes it as well, do you not, Eustace?" Her voice held a warning. "Captain Falconer does not enter into the matter at all." Amelia could see a thin line of perspiration break out on Cousin Hortense's upper lip. "All that matters is you, Amelia. Is that not so, Eustace?"

But Eustace was still staring after Gideon. He either had not heard his mother or chose to ignore her words. "You can take a gypsy lad out of the caravans and camps, but apparently even your sainted father could not remove the stink of them from the boy, no matter how dashing his uniform." He turned his unwinking gaze on Amelia, and a shiver ran up her spine at the malevolence she saw burning there with a cold flame. "Your servant, cousin." Eustace shook off his mother's restraining grip, bowed, and left the room, his step jerky with what Amelia was sure was suppressed rage.

"Well! Oh, my." Hortense cleared her throat and essayed a tentative smile. "I am afraid that Eustace sometimes allows his feelings to overcome his manners. It is the result of an excess of sensibility." Her smile widened as she warmed to her subject. "You must know the tender feelings Eustace cherishes for you, my dear Amelia. It causes him to behave rather badly when he feels another man might have dreams above his station."

Amelia had heard all she could bear from her Mannering cousins. There was not a syllable of truth in anything they had said. That Eustace cared for her was absurd! He wished only to find a way to ensure that the Bradshaw money would follow the Bradshaw title into his hands! As for Hortense, she wanted whatever Eustace wanted.

"I do not wish to discuss Captain Falconer," Amelia said, her tone as cold as she could make it. "He was my father's ward and is my friend. *He* has no interest in my fortune, but only in my welfare."

If Hortense heard the slight emphasis Amelia placed on the pronoun, she gave no sign. "Of course, my dear. I am sure Eustace will apologize when next he sees you." She extended her hand. "If you do not mind, I will take my leave of you now. Please do not on any account make any plans for the future before we have a chance to discuss them." Another meaningless smile and a pat on the cheek. Amelia had difficulty not flinching away from the unwelcome touch. "I stand as your only female relative now, Amelia. As a young, unmarried girl, you must allow yourself to be guided by me in matters of ton."

Out of the corner of her eye, Amelia could see Gideon approaching, his frown still in place. She decided to let the idea of being guided by Hortense go unchallenged for the moment. To avoid another set-to, she smiled and bowed her cousin out of the room before Gideon arrived at her side.

"Interfering busybody," she muttered as the door closed behind Hortense. "How dare Eustace talk about you that way!"

"As if I were some gypsy brat?" Gideon shrugged. "It's most likely exactly what I am, Amy. They aren't the only ones who look at me askance, and wonder what you and your father were thinking of to take me in as you did."

"Father was prouder of you than anything else in his life, Gideon." Amelia reached out to touch his arm. "And you are the best friend I have ever had. Nothing anyone else says will ever alter that!"

His hand came out to cover hers. "I hope you are right, Amy. But Society can be cruel, particularly now that the duke is no longer here to protect you. I will never tarnish your reputation by my presence. Promise me that if I ever become a detriment to your standing in the ton, or threaten to ruin your chances, you will tell me."

"My chances for what, Gideon?" Amelia's hand tingled under the warm clasp of his. "An advantageous marriage? How many times must I tell you that I have no desire for any such thing?"

"You may well change your mind now that your father is gone. There is nothing wrong with wanting a man by your side, to help you over the rough spots."

"Now you sound just like Cousin Hortense," Amelia said, more annoyed by Gideon's masculine incomprehension than she cared to admit to him. How could he fail to see how much more his friendship meant to her than some hypothetical marriage?

Stung, Gideon bowed stiffly. "Perhaps I had best take my leave in that case."

Amelia reached out her hand. Under the fine broadcloth, Gideon's arm was hard as steel. She sighed. Sometimes his head seemed almost that hard.

"Gideon, do try to remember that this is Amelia, not some little Society miss who has not the least idea how to go on without darling Papa or brother dear to guide her." Exasperation mounted as she saw the stubborn, wooden look on his face.

When Gideon assumed that mask, nothing short of a direct command from a superior officer would change his course of action.

"I never thought that of you," he said stiffly. "I have every respect for your abilities, Amy, you know that."

"Well, I thought I did." Amelia removed her hand from his arm and moved away to stand before the window looking out over the back gardens. "But all this sudden talk of husbands as necessary appendages sounds as if you have begun to doubt me." The trees were bare, and the flower beds raked and mulched for the winter. Amelia shivered a little as a sudden feeling of cold and emptiness swept over her.

She could feel Gideon behind her. "It isn't that," he said, his voice filled with concern. "I worry, I suppose, because of Eustace—and all the other Eustaces out there waiting for a chance at a beautiful, unprotected girl."

"I am quite capable of discerning who is interested in me and who cares only for my fortune." Was she a victim? Was that how Gideon saw her? Amelia's sense of wintry desolation grew.

"I know that." His short, crisp words told her Gideon was annoyed. "But persuasion is not the only tool of a man desperate for money."

Amelia turned away from the dead landscape to look at her friend, smiling at his worried expression. "Gideon, you have a very melodramatic mind. I know one hears of young girls seduced into marriage, but—"

"Seduction?" Gideon's expression changed. His eyes, as he looked down at her, held an arrested look, as if he were grappling with a new idea.

Amelia felt her face heat. This was not a subject she and Gideon had ever even flirted with before. She was not sure how to answer him. "Well," she temporized, "one does hear of such things. But I am not a foolish girl, someone who could be swept away by sweet words and—and—" *Do not be missish!* she told herself firmly. "And passion." She took a deep breath. "I am never less than sensible, Gideon, you know that," she said firmly, hoping it was true.

He smiled down at her. Gideon's smile, so different from the purely social smiles he had perfected over the years, was rarely given, but when it was directed at her it never failed to lift Amelia's heart. It transformed his face, giving it an easy charm he otherwise never displayed. It always made Amelia long to give him whatever he needed to make that confidence and happy ease permanent.

Helplessly she smiled back at him. "Please tell me you know I am a sensible female long past the age of foolish indiscretions."

"Of course you are sensible. And you are your father's daughter, so you would never care for someone . . . unworthy." Gideon's smile faded as he took her hand in his large, calloused one. "But you are also intrepid, and so I worry about your safety. Perhaps I have no reason to feel as I do, but nevertheless please humor me. I will remain as close to you as my duties, and Society, will permit. I am at your command, Amelia. For anything, at any time."

Her heart lifted. Gideon was not angry. "Thank you," she said. "I don't know what I would do if you were not my friend."

The word hung between them. Always before it had warmed her heart to be Gideon's friend. It had felt like an accolade, a prize won by very few. Now, somehow, something seemed to be missing, but as she held out her hand and watched him smile again, she became even more mystified as to what it could be. She scolded herself. She had Gideon's regard. He was her friend and always would be. Surely that was all she needed or wanted.

"Amy, you know that you are all the world to me." His voice was deep and rough as if he struggled with some strong emotion. Amelia's heart beat faster. "You are all that is left of your father, and as his only child, you are my special care and concern."

Amelia felt her smile freeze and every warm thought congeal in her breast. She was to be taken to the opera and called upon, rescued from obnoxious relatives and kept safe from fortune hunters. His benefactor's daughter. Her heart shriveled.

"I appreciate your kindness, Gideon." She extended her hand with a formal smile. "But I hope that I will not have to presume upon your good nature too much. I am sure that I can find a few friends who will not find it onerous to escort me here and there. I would not have it said that I hung upon your sleeve." She managed to meet his eyes, hoping that her anger and hurt did not show. "I will release you from your promise to escort me to Lady Maltby's soiree this evening. Jane and I will do very well by ourselves."

He looked down at her gravely. "I would take it very much amiss if you were to break our engagement for this evening. Sir Richard has assured me that he plans to come and engage you and Miss Forrester in conversation, thus avoiding the marriageable young ladies Lady Maltby plans to parade in front of him. You must not disappoint us."

Amelia nodded briefly. "I thank you for your concern, Gideon. I will be ready when you return." *But I will find companions of my own when we arrive. I am not so old-cattish that I cannot find a few gentlemen who wish to know me, not my fortune!*

Gideon left, wondering why Amelia had withdrawn from him. He always knew when she was angry with him. She would pull away from him, and he swore he could feel cold air when she became formal and chilly with him. Without the warmth of Amy's special care, he felt bereft and alone as he had when he had lived on the streets all those years ago. He resolved to be as amiable as his presence at an evening party would allow him to be.

Chapter Four

Gideon sighed as he arranged his cravat that same evening. He had attended two musicales and an opera during the past week, and tonight was going to appear at a rout given by one of the ton's aspiring hostesses. Gideon loved music. Musicales, where both professionals and amateurs appeared were torture to him. The professional artists were drowned out by the chatter of the audience, and the young ladies who tried to perform on harp or pianoforte were usually without a grain of talent.

The opera was a slight improvement. He had escorted Amelia and Miss Forrester, and they had been blessedly silent. Amy played no instrument. She often laughingly explained that her music instructor had told her father he would not take money under false pretenses, no one could teach her to play. But he had taught her to appreciate music. It was clear that the opera was a rare treat for Miss Forrester.

He surveyed himself in the small shaving mirror, which was all his rooms provided. His dark hair was tidy, the natural wave ruthlessly subdued. His cravat was crisp and still reasonably comfortable. He glanced down at the rest of his sober evening dress and turned away, ready to suffer yet another evening attempting to keep Amy safe.

Gideon knew he was accepted only to a certain point in the world of the ton. He was invited to the larger parties, those where there would be no dancing. Mothers and fathers of marriageable young girls did not want their darlings losing their hearts to ineligible young men of unknown birth, no matter how handsome or dashing they might be.

Ordinarily, he avoided the entertainments offered by Society's hostesses, but Amelia was rich and beautiful and Eustace was not the only fortune hunter who would seek her hand and estate. Thus Gideon must be her protector, because he alone would guard her with his life. It almost seemed to him that the duke, who had left him in his will a sum sufficient to provide him with a tidy competence, had done so in order to insure that the heretofore ineligible Captain Falconer would have entrée into at least the outer courts of Society's temple.

Since the places where fortune hunters could meet beautiful young heiresses were the haunts of the Haut Ton, Gideon realized he would have to put in an appearance at as many of these functions as he could arrange invitations to.

So he prepared for another evening of being ogled by matrons seeking excitement outside their marriage vows, giggled at by chits who thought he must be exciting because he was ineligible, and greeted as if he were contagious by matrons with daughters to marry off. In short, an evening as stifling and dull as could be envisioned. For no one but Amy would he have endured it.

Fortunately, he had enlisted the aid of Sir Richard in his duties; otherwise, he would have been helpless to know who was genuinely captivated by Amelia's charm and goodness and who was in need of her fortune. Sir Richard's knowledge of the ton was immense. He viewed everyone through a lens of cynicism, but his judgment was infallible. He knew who was solvent and who needed an infusion of gold, who was a true gentleman and who required marriage as a disguise for other less reputable activities. Gideon told him, with the humor that was a recent part of their relationship, that had he not been in the military he would have undoubtedly been an arbiter of the ton.

"The Beau Nash of the London Season," he had said, naming the dandy who had virtually dictated the social life of Bath for many years.

Sir Richard had winced. "I hope I'm not so frivolous. But if you mean that I no longer have any illusions about Society and am experienced enough to know how right I am in that view, then you are correct."

Gideon sighed. He had never harbored any such illusions. The ton was the froth on the surface of life. Underneath, where most of the world dwelled, where he had once lived, life was not composed of parties and routs and gossip. He despised the ton. He could not help it. He hated wasting one single evening doing the pretty and being regarded as an exhibit from a raree-show—the duke's gypsy ward.

Squaring his shoulders, he went off to repay in some small measure the debt he could never hope to repay to the late Duke of Doncaster by safeguarding his daughter.

Jane Forrester looked around the crowded, overheated rooms of the Countess of Bedlington's rout. It was a sad crush and even Jane realized that meant the occasion was a success. She glanced down at her simple, dark blue silk dress and hated the fact that she was aware for one single moment of how frumpish and out of place she looked. Her life was concerned with more important issues. She did not care how she looked at a ton party. Her fists clenched. Of course she did not.

"Why did you insist that I come tonight, Amy?" she whispered sharply in her companion's ear. "I am as out of place as a pig in a palace."

"Nonsense." Amelia looked at her friend. "You of all people know how little appearances matter. But if you feel that way, you should have let me transform you into a stylish beauty. It would have been fun and would have been far easier than you think with your height and presence and gorgeous hair. You must let yourself unbend and enjoy a few frivolities, my dear. It is sometimes the only way to bear the misery we see around us."

Gideon approached them, a small smile touching his lips at the sight of them. He reached them as Amelia said, "Sir Richard Sinclair is also being pressed into service this evening. I sometimes think Gideon believes Sir Richard would be a good husband for me."

Gideon stood as if turned to stone. Angrily he told himself not to be stupid, that he should welcome Amy's thought of Sir Richard as a possible suitor. She had done nothing but protest that she had absolutely no need for a husband. Why, when she had finally shown some slight interest in marriage, did he grow angry at the very thought? Amy should marry. It would keep her safe, give her a family to care for.

He knew better than anyone how important a family could be. He had felt its absence for as long as he could remember. At one time he had pretended that the duke and Amelia were his family, but he had known it was only a boy's fantasy. Lady Amelia Bradshaw was not for him. From the moment when, as a ragged, starving gutter rat, he had first beheld that golden, angelic dream of a girl he had known just how far above him she was. The world did not regard him as half as ineligible as he himself did.

But that some other man, even one as fine as Sir Richard, should take that place in her life was like a knife in his heart. He had her devotion, he knew. He would have it forever—as she would have his. Yet her marriage would make that close bond inappropriate. Even the thought of that loss hurt amazingly. Fortunately, military training gave one a fixed and immobile expression that hid anger in a ballroom as effectively as it did fear on a battlefield. He went toward Amelia with a glance as calm and apparently disinterested as any he had cast toward the French cavalry.

"Lady Amelia," he said, bowing slightly, "I fear that I return with my mission aborted. The waiter assured me that more champagne will be available soon, but for now there is none."

"Thank you, Gideon." She smiled happily, looking glad to be in his company. How would she look at Sir Richard when he came?

Her smile softened, seemed intended for Gideon alone. It held a hint of mischief, almost of flirtation. "You have suffered so much boredom in the past few days and weeks at Horse Guards and then doing the pretty with me. I wonder how you have borne it. Has anything amused you?"

"I have enjoyed the music. And I wished to see how those who enjoy the society of the upper ten thousand actually conduct themselves." He looked at her with disfavor. When had she begun to flirt? When had she developed the habit of fashionable clothing? The pale green dress she was wearing hugged her slender body much too closely. He could see the way it positively caressed her breasts—

"You are looking very lovely this evening, Lady Amelia." Sir Richard's voice broke into Gideon's entirely inappropriate thoughts. The older man bowed over Amelia's hand, and Gideon found himself feeling alone and frozen out. Was Sir Richard the man who would win Amelia's hand? Surely, as his friend, Gideon should wish him nothing but success. Two friends marrying should bring him nothing but joy. But he did not feel joy. Instead he recognized anger. Jealousy. Unreasonable emotions. The kind he did not allow himself.

He turned to Miss Forrester with a sense of relief. Here was a woman he could talk to—one who dressed appropriately in something dark with a high neckline. No frills or flirting for Miss Forrester. He could depend on her for rational conversation. Maybe she could bring his mind back to calm and reason.

"Miss Forrester," he began with a smile, only to be interrupted once again by Sir Richard.

"I hope I see you well, madam." Sir Richard's voice had changed. It held a chill as he addressed Jane Forrester. "I had not thought to see you at so frivolous an event."

To Gideon's surprise, Miss Forrester flushed a painful red. "Good evening," she said with an evident effort. "Sir Richard, Captain Falconer."

A silence slightly too long for good manners ensued. It was Amelia who broke it. She turned and took Jane's arm, presenting a united front. "I prevailed upon Jane to waste a perfectly good evening coming here with me so that I might more easily hunt for open purses." She glanced around the crowded room, as if looking for wealthy acquaintances.

Sir Richard's eyebrows rose. "Miss Forrester is practicing her skills as a cutpurse, perhaps?"

Amelia laughed, a silvery sound Gideon had long thought identical to the chiming of bells. She had laughed with him a thousand times, but tonight he wondered if she were deliberately enticing Sir Richard with that happy, glinting sound. He found he disliked that thought amazingly.

"Lady Amelia is convinced that if she can but talk to every member of the ton and explain the virtues of charitable giving, every one of them will become the kind of person her father was." Gideon gave her a wry smile. Amelia's belief in the perfectibility of mankind was one of the things he liked best about her. Not because he agreed with her—he knew from personal experience how wrong she was—but because it was part of the optimism and largeheartedness that was so much a part of her character, of what gave Amelia her special quality.

She looked at him gravely for a moment, then turned to Sir Richard with a smile. "I am naturally on the hunt for a husband, and I find that a pretense of interest in the less fortunate has gentlemen crowding around me," she said with heavy irony. She looked around the crowded room, realizing that she risked seeming rude if she stayed at Sir Richard's side. He was regarded as a catch—good-looking and in line for a marquessate.

Sir Richard laughed. "I can see, Lady Amelia, that you have adopted the views of your friend." He turned to Jane with an entirely false smile that looked more like a shark baring his teeth, Amelia thought. "It is Miss Forrester who carries the banner of the downtrodden. Do you not, Miss Forrester? I believe you were telling me between the acts at the opera the other night that men who spent their lives killing others ought to make up for their bloodthirsty profession by giving at least a tenth of their wealth to hospitals and missions." He looked down at Jane's averted face. "I am correct, am I not, Miss Forrester? A tenth was the sum you suggested?"

Goaded, Jane raised her eyes to his. "You found me officiously meddlesome, Sir Richard. I plead guilty. It would have been sufficient simply to tell me so, however." She looked away, surveying the room as if looking for escape.

Amelia stared at her friend. She had never seen Jane put out of countenance, yet she was now flushed with anger, her hands clenched at her sides and her eyes hot with misery. Angrily Amelia turned to Sir Richard. "And you, sir, do you believe that killing is sufficient public service, that charity would be superfluous?"

He smiled at her, a smile at once charming and cynical.

"Why, Lady Amelia, I do believe you are as much of a reformer as Miss Forrester."

Amelia inclined her head. "I have that honor, sir."

Gideon looked at the threesome and frowned. It was really quite simple, he thought. One did what one was capable of doing to alleviate suffering, especially of children, and one did it in secret, with as little fuss as possible. He had happened upon a church once when he was a child on the streets and had heard the gospel story of Jesus recommending that one do good by stealth. The minister in that nonconformist church had given Gideon a crust of bread and told him to stay and wait for the parish council to take him to the workhouse. Gideon had run away, of course, but he had taken the bread and the story with him. He had been sorry but not surprised that the minister had not acted like a saint.

Now Gideon interrupted his friends with barely concealed annoyance. "Even I know that such intense conversation has no place at a social function. We must laugh and wait to drink the champagne that should be forthcoming soon, and act as if we have not a care in the world. I am the one noted for displaying an unbecoming seriousness at a party. Anyone watching you would think you had learned your manners from me instead of the other way around." His faint smile almost took the sting from his words.

Amelia tucked her hand into his arm and said, "Let us simply leave these two to argue to their hearts' content." She led Gideon away from the small alcove where they had been standing. "In order to pry money out of these people, I must talk to them. So we will stroll about the edges of the room and see if I can ensnare any unsuspecting peers in my net."

Gideon looked down at her. She was only joking, of course, but somehow hearing Amy talk of ensnaring gentlemen made the muscles between his shoulders bunch and clench beneath his sober evening coat.

"Why are you frowning, Gideon? You knew this was my reason for coming this evening." Amy's eyes challenged his.

Gideon couldn't lie to her. "I do not like to hear you talk thus. It—it makes you sound as if you are trying to trap—as if you are, in fact, looking for the husband you insist you do not want." He knew his face was stern, his brows drawn together in the look he sometimes gave to a recalcitrant subaltern. "Your father would not—"

"Gideon, I wish you would strive to remember that I am four and twenty and perfectly capable of leading my own life. I do not need—" She stared daggers at him.

As angry as she was, Amelia looked beautiful at that moment with her cheeks stained with rose and an angry glitter in her enormous blue eyes. Her bosom rose and fell rapidly as she struggled to keep her emotions under control. A lady did not engage in angry exchanges in the middle of a rout, and Gideon knew that she was embarrassed by her loss of poise. A strange warm clutching feeling in the vicinity of his heart warned him that strong emotion—something he banished routinely from his life—was about to cause him some difficulty.

It often happened that way when he was with Amelia, or sometimes when he even thought of her. He straightened his spine and drew in his breath. The battle against strong feeling was one he had fought all his life. The rage he had felt as a child would have gotten him killed had he given full rein to it. A few bad beatings had taught him the price of emotion, and it was a lesson he had learned well. Only in battle could he afford to give full rein to his anger and his love of combat. Control, complete icy command of himself under all other circumstances, had saved his life and kept him sane throughout his military career as well as in his early days.

"I am simply trying to help Jane raise money for her school. She refuses to let me underwrite it completely." Her voice trembled but he could see angry sparks still gleam in her eyes. The combination of vulnerability and bravery made the warm tide of emotion threaten him again and once more he beat it down.

"Really?" Gideon crossed his arms on his chest and fixed her with a dark gaze. "What Miss Jane Forrester has to do and what Lady Amelia Bradshaw ought to do are two very different things, and you know it."

They might have stood toe-to-toe and argued all night if a

handsome young man in an elaborately embroidered satin waistcoat had not stopped and smiled at Amelia. She greeted him as if he were her dearest friend, laughed and chatted and introduced him as Percival Sturdevant, and then, under Gideon's glowering eye, she calmly walked off with him.

"You really must try to hide your emotions if you plan to go about in Society, Captain." Sir Richard's voice, light and humorous, reached him from someplace far away, although the colonel stood only a few feet away. All of Gideon's concentration had been focused on Amelia and her escort, as if by keeping them in view as they walked away he could somehow stay linked to her.

"What emotions?"

Sir Richard's knowing smile made Gideon's anger flare. It grew even hotter when Sir Richard replied, "Those emotions you seem to reserve for Lady Amelia alone. The ones that are causing you to glare at poor Sturdevant's back as if you would like to plant a knife there."

"Is he a fortune hunter?" Gideon asked abruptly.

"No. He's not outrageously rich, mind you, but he's certainly plump enough in the pocket to afford a wife." Sir Richard raised an eyebrow. "You look disappointed."

Gideon gestured impatiently. "Is that Miss Forrester talking so earnestly with Lady Maltby over there?"

"Yes, indeed. She, too, is spending the evening trying to talk to people about giving money to her school for superannuated virgins, or whoever they may be." Sir Richard spoke with his usual acidity but with somewhat less of his usual detachment.

Gideon looked about the crowded room and felt more stifled and breathless than he had in the heat of an Iberian summer. Suddenly it all rushed in upon him—the heat and overpowering scent of fresh flowers and stale perfume, the high-pitched sound of a hundred voices raised in gossip and laughter. He turned toward the tall windows that lined one wall of the long reception room, hoping to find a breath of cold air if he could get near.

"How do you people stand it? The noise is like peacocks screeching, and there is no air in this room."

"Lady Amelia is over by the long windows." Sir Richard

interrupted him. "Still talking to Sturdevant. Shouldn't think he'd want to spare much for the widows and orphans."

Gideon glared at him, resenting both the fact that Amy seemed to be so fascinated by that fribble in the waistcoat and the slighting way Sir Richard spoke of the orphans Gideon held secretly so dear. His friends were behaving with uncharacteristic bad manners—Amelia flirting, Sir Richard mocking the poor, and Miss Forrester monopolizing Lady Maltby, who was clearly trying to escape.

Without replying to Sir Richard, Gideon made his way toward Amelia, who was smiling up at Percival Sturdevant. She spoke but Gideon was still too far away to hear what was said. Sturdevant seemed to find whatever it was delightful, for he bent his head nearer to hers and laughed. Gideon clenched his fists. He started forward when Sturdevant quickly unlatched one of the long windows. Amelia smiled and laid her hand on his arm. Together they stepped out onto the moonlit terrace.

"Careful, old man," Sir Richard, who had kept pace with him, said. "You look ready to do murder. It won't do, you know. If you storm out there, you will cause very unpleasant gossip. She is perfectly safe. There are at least ten other couples taking the air as well as several chaperons."

Gideon scarcely heard him. He could see Sturdevant take Amelia's hand and raise it to his lips. A roaring filled Gideon's ears, and he covered the few feet of parquet floor between him and the door in one long stride.

"Gideon!" Amelia said happily, with a sweet smile. "I am so glad you are here. Mr. Sturdevant has agreed to give fifty pounds to Jane's school. Is that not wonderful?"

"Wonderful, indeed," Gideon responded dryly. "I assume that such munificence is the result of a great desire to talk with you at length about the education of the poor."

Amelia smiled, but Mr. Sturdevant flushed to the roots of his hair. It was obvious that Gideon's sarcasm regarding the young man's motives had found its mark.

"I think it is wonderful of Lady Amelia to try to do good," he said earnestly. "She is an angel."

The look of adoration he turned on Amelia caused Gideon to

clench his fists. The silly young clunch! Of course, Amelia was an angel. She was *his* angel, his personal savior. That she worked for others was part of what made her Amelia, but that work was done in conjunction with Gideon. Together they endowed schools to educate poor children in the worst sections of London.

"Oh, really, Mr. Sturdevant," Amelia began.

"Nonsense, Sturdevant. It will hardly do Lady Amelia's campaign any good at all for her to be known as some sort of heavenly being. No one thinks an angel needs help." Gideon spoke in the unnatural tone of an elderly family friend. The tone Amelia had objected to before. She was clearly no happier about it now.

"Gideon, if Mr. Sturdevant thinks I am angelic, I wish you would refrain from disillusioning him." She smiled at him, but Gideon could see the hint of steel behind the pleasantry.

"Oh, he couldn't," Percival Sturdevant said. "No one could disillusion me about you, Lady Amelia." He took her hand. "I should very much like to call on you and to see Miss Forrester's school as well. Would tomorrow be acceptable?"

He was as eager and enthusiastic as a puppy, Gideon thought. How young he seemed. Almost as young as Gideon himself had seemed when he had first appeared at Horse Guards with his brand-new commission.

"Tomorrow will be splendid, Mr. Sturdevant." Amelia turned her back on Gideon. "Until then." She gave Mr. Sturdevant her hand. When he had bowed and left, she wheeled again to face Gideon. "What in the world has gotten into you, Gideon?" She had begun to walk away, when Jane appeared.

But this was a Jane Amelia scarcely recognized. Her tall, commanding presence had somehow shrunk, and her face was pasty. "I am feeling very ill," she said abruptly. "I fear I will have to go home now. Please do not think you need to accompany me. I will have a servant call a hackney." The words seemed somehow to have been jerked out of her.

"Nonsense, we will go together. I have obtained a pledge of fifty pounds. That is victory enough for one night." Amelia took her friend's arm. "Would you see us home, Gideon?" She gave him a look that told him she was sure he would always come to her aid.

"Of course I will see you home." Gideon's heart lifted. When she needed help, Amelia turned to her oldest, truest friend.

He knew he had annoyed her by acting as if he were her guardian, but he also knew he would risk her further wrath by continuing to do so when he deemed it necessary. It wasn't only Eustace. Percival Sturdevant was not to be trusted, he was sure, and even Sir Robert was unworthy of Amelia.

Someone had to look after her.

He hurried after the slender figure descending the stairs like a green-clad woodland sprite, floating ahead of him, and as always, just out of reach.

Chapter Five

Eustace Mannering's creditors were not of a mind to leave him alone to grow accustomed to his new position or to use it to persuade others to lend him even more blunt. They aimed to collect what was due them immediately.

Eustace had been subject to an ever increasing series of threats, leavened by the occasional promise of new loans once the old ones were repaid. He had thought hazily that all his troubles would be over once he succeeded to the title. It had never occurred to him that the old duke would not leave him the fortune to go with the title. But now he found himself with houses and lands representing hundreds of thousands of pounds, but without any means of reducing any of those assets to cold, hard cash.

In desperation, he had told the leader of the informal syndicate of moneylenders whom he owed that he had every expectation of marrying the duke's daughter in the new year. Yes, January, February at the latest, should see him solvent and happily legshackled, he told his chief tormentor with what he hoped was a confident smile.

It was a promise he had repeated several times, in attempting to explain why there had been no announcement of the upcoming nuptials in the *Gazette*. Neither the smile nor the promise carried any conviction.

"Marry her you must," said the tall, cadaverous man known as Josiah Blakeley, who spoke for all those who had lent Eustace money. "But you cannot wait until January to do so. You can raise money on her fortune as soon as you're riveted, but it must be now, Yer Grace," he added sardonically.

"She is a gently bred female who has just lost her father," Eustace complained. "I cannot rush her into matrimony."

Blakeley's thin lips turned down, and he glared at Eustace. "We don't care nothin' about that, Yer Grace. We want our money. Throw her over your saddle and ride to Scotland if you must, but make the lady yer duchess or there'll be trouble. For you and yer ma," he added.

The look in the man's eye told Eustace that he had better do something toward advancing his case with Amelia or face some form of physical coercion. With that threat in mind, he appeared at Jane Forrester's on a morning a week after he and his mother had moved into Doncaster House.

It was just like Amelia to remove to a house in Hans Town, far from the fashionable part of the city, to live with a renowned crank like Jane Forrester, whose views on the education of women and the likeness of marriage to slavery were well-known. He was shown into a tidy reception room that, though light and airy, had not the least claim to elegance. The maid had a most unfortunate country accent and actually looked him in the eye instead of keeping hers discreetly lowered.

Amelia entered the room like a sunbeam, dressed in a yellow wool morning dress with a demure lace fichu.

"My dear cousin." Eustace bowed over Amelia's hand and mentally rehearsed what he had to say.

She withdrew her hand. "Eustace. I trust you and Cousin Hortense are comfortable at Doncaster House." Her smile was pleasant, but her eyes did not reflect it. There was something cool and appraising in that candid blue gaze that threw Eustace out of countenance.

"My dear cousin," he began again, then paused. His speech pledging undying love and asking her to be his bride had flown quite out of his head.

"Yes, Eustace?"

Was there a little genuine amusement in her smile now? "I-I . . . There is something important I wish to discuss with you. To ask you actually," he said.

"Yes, Eustace?" She gestured for him to take a seat, then

seated herself opposite him in a most uncomfortable-looking wooden chair.

"You must know I have always held you in the highest regard, my dear—"

"Miss 'Melia, I finished my sampler. Look, Miss 'Melia!" A tiny urchin in a calico dress came dancing into the room, waving a grubby piece of canvas.

Amelia smiled at her, but Eustace was revolted. "Really! This is Lady Amelia Bradshaw, you wretched little brat! See that you address her proper—"

"Eustace!" Amelia's tone brought him up short.

Damn! He should have remembered that Amelia adored these snot-nosed little thieves.

"We are all merely Miss and Mister here. It is one of Jane's rules."

"Pardon, my dear. It is just that I hate to see anyone treat you less than respectfully." Eustace stretched his lips into what he hoped was an ingratiating smile.

"Ise 'spectful," the child said, stamping her foot and glaring at him.

"Of course you are, Molly," Amelia said. "And your sampler is beautiful. You run along, now. I have to talk to the gentleman."

"I stay."

Eustace stared at the wretched child, who proceeded to sit down on the floor and fix her dark, shoe-button eyes unwinkingly on him.

"No, Molly." Amelia picked her up and set her on her feet. "You go back to the schoolroom. You still have lessons to learn."

Molly frowned, which made her little monkey's face look even less attractive. "I stay. Until Mr. Gideon comes, I stay. I guard."

What nonsense was the brat babbling now? He saw Amelia smile at the child, lean close, and whisper something. Molly looked at him again, frowned again, and then with dragging steps and many a backward glance, she slowly left the room.

"Now, Eustace." Amelia sat down in the same wooden chair,

and looked up at him. "You had something you wished to speak to me about?"

"Yes." The damned little guttersnipe had thrown him completely off his stride. He needed time to recover. "I wonder if Miss Forrester's household might have an extra cup of tea to spare for a visitor." He tried to sound humorous.

"I *am* sorry, but I am afraid that tea is served only at teatime," Amelia said. She was clearly not the least bit sorry. "Another of Jane's rules. It is also a necessary economy measure. If you would care to contribute to the school, you could specify that your gift be used to furnish tea for guests."

Eustace felt a giggle tickle the back of his throat. Contribute to Jane Forrester's school? He was fully prepared to shut the place and padlock it once he had Amelia and Amelia's money safely under his control! It galled him past bearing that Jane Forrester should be receiving money that was by rights his. He could feel impatience tug at him, fraying his already uncertain temper.

"Amelia." He began to pace the room, although he had planned to fall to one knee in order to demonstrate his passionate devotion. "You must know that I hold you in the highest esteem. Never would I want to be the means, however unwitting, of ruining your life. So, my dear, dear Amelia—" he broke off. Mama had stressed the importance of emotion in his proposal, and he tried to look overcome with love and any other positive feeling he could think of. "Please, please do me the inestimable honor—make me the happiest of men—say you will be mine!" He played his final trump. "Let me make you the Duchess of Doncaster."

Amelia did not look happy or surprised or show any of the other emotions young ladies who had just been asked to marry a duke were popularly supposed to feel. Instead she looked cool and faintly pleasant, as if she were listening to a shopkeeper extol wares she did not want. She was polite, but she did not appear ready to purchase.

"Oh, Eustace, I think not," she said. "I do not want to marry anyone, and even if I did, truly we should not suit. Thank you for your offer, which I am sure was prompted by kindness and concern for my welfare." She rose to her feet, held out both her hands to him, and smiled. It was not, he noted, as warm a smile as she had given to the ugly little urchin. "But truly you need not worry. I am more than contented with my life as it is. Thank you, Eustace. But no."

He could feel a tide of anger and despair sweep through him. She had to marry him. She had to! "You do not perfectly understand." He clenched his hands at his sides to keep from clenching them around her neck. "It is important." No, that would not do. "It would make my mother very happy." He saw Amelia's eyebrows go up. That would not do, either. "It would make me very, very happy."

The desperation he felt must have sounded in his voice, for Amelia looked at him with an arrested expression in her eyes. Eustace decided to continue to speak the truth. "I will be so unhappy, so *desperately* unhappy if you do not become my wife. I need you, Amelia. Truly I do." His voice shook with emotion. He meant every word.

Amelia looked uncomfortable, even a little sad. "I am so sorry, Eustace. But I simply cannot marry you."

Rage and fear commanded him now. He stepped forward and grabbed her arm. He shook her a little. "You don't understand! You must marry me! You must!"

Amelia tried to pull away, but Eustace was past reason. He could see his future slipping away from him. Instead of life as the Duke of Doncaster, he was going to have to flee England for France or one of the colonies. If he could not pay his creditors, they had made it very clear they would see him in debtors prison. There was no choice but flight if Amelia failed him.

And here she was, the simple little fool, looking like a marzipan angel in a Christmas centerpiece, shaking her head and opening her mouth to cry out—

"No!" he cried. "No, you shall not summon that Miss Forrester. I am fighting for my life and for our good name. You owe me that, Amelia. You must help me salvage the family name!"

"What have you done, Eustace?" she whispered, her eyes, huge and shadowed. "Why is the family at risk?"

He pulled her toward him. "Never mind. Don't ask so many

questions. Just say you will marry me, and all our troubles will be over."

"Your troubles might be over, Mannering, but Amy's would be just beginning." Gideon's cool voice came from the doorway, where he stood with Molly jumping on one foot by his side. He strode rapidly to where Eustace and Amelia stood, locked in a parody of an embrace.

"See, Mr. Gideon. See!" Molly was triumphant. "I did just what you said. I guardeded."

"Gideon!" Amelia's voice rang with relief, and her face reflected the release of the fear she had felt.

"Falconer!" Eustace spat the word. It might as well have been *nemesis*. "Damn you, do you follow her around like a puppy, hoping for a pat on the head? That's all you'll ever get, you pathetic nobod—"

But Gideon had seen the duke's hands tighten on Amelia's arms and had watched as she tried anew to pull away. In the grip of a fury he had not felt since he last faced the French, he wrenched Eustace away with one hand and sent him spinning across the room, to land sprawled on the floor.

"Amy!" Gideon took her in his arms and ran his hands gently up and down her arms. She seemed unhurt, and the look she gave him made him feel like a hero. "Are you hurt? Did he harm you in any way?" His voice was low and hoarse. He looked deep into her eyes, and for once he did not try to guard his feelings, but let them blaze out toward her without constraint or disguise. He didn't think of what was appropriate, or what the late duke would have thought, but only of what he felt—an emotion so strong and deep that he could not have found words for it if he had tried. He merely looked at Amelia and saw that she was not hurt and that her smile was wholehearted and wholly for him.

For a long moment they stood staring into each other's eyes, oblivious to Eustace and everyone else in the world. Then Eustace scrambled to his feet and turned a face distorted with rage and frustration to her.

"Amelia!" His cry was heartfelt. "Amelia, don't look at him

like that. He is nobody. Nobody! Please, Amelia, look at me, pay attention to me."

"Get out." Gideon's voice was flat, uninflected. It never occurred to him that Eustace would not obey. "And do not ever lay a hand on her again."

"For God's sake, Falconer! I have done nothing wrong. I want to marry her! You have no right to interfere!" The duke flung out his hands—half in supplication, half in threat.

Amelia took a step away from Gideon. Eustace had finally penetrated the haze she had been wrapped in since Gideon had taken her in his arms. "Eustace, we have nothing more to say. Gideon has nothing to do with my decision. I reached it entirely on my own."

"Do not send me away, Amelia. You must marry me!" Eustace took a step closer to her.

Gideon simply turned and looked down at him. "I would very much like to break you in half, Mannering."

"Gideon!" Amelia put her hand on his arm, restraining him.

"But I will refrain because it would distress Amy." He reached down and hauled Eustace to his feet without apparent effort. "If you ever lay a finger on her again, or threaten her or cut up her peace in any way, I will kill you." His voice was calm and almost pleasant, but he knew his face bore the expression it did when facing an enemy—implacable resolve. He waited silently for perhaps ten seconds before Eustace gave up and stumbled out of the room, his steps jerky with rage and defeat.

"Come and sit down, Amy, and I will get Molly to fetch you a cup of tea." Gideon gently led her over to the one comfortable chair in the room, a large wing chair, and seated her as if she were made of blown glass.

"We only have tea at teatime," Amelia explained for the second time that afternoon. "Jane does not make exceptions."

"She will for me," Gideon said simply. "Molly, run and fetch Miss Amelia a cup of tea, please."

The little girl nodded once and sped off to the kitchen. While they waited, Gideon squatted by Amelia's side and asked her very quietly to tell him exactly what Eustace had said. She complied, speaking in a low but perfectly controlled voice.

"I am not overset, Gideon," she said, smiling a little tremulously down into his eyes. "I knew that Eustace would propose sometime. I had not expected it so soon. I thought he would leave me at least six months of mourning before he pressed me, but I knew it would come. He is more desperate than I thought. I fear for him."

"Your kind heart does you credit." Gideon spoke almost at random. The pure blue of her gaze as it met his dazzled him, and her smile struck at his heart. He had betrayed himself, and now he found it all but impossible to draw back into the fortress he had made of his emotions. He could no longer deny what he felt for this glorious golden girl who looked at him now with such warmth and love—

Love? Impossible! He surged to his feet in one strong, lithe move and stepped away from her just as Jane entered the room, a cup of tea in her hand.

"Amelia, are you all right? Are you hurt?" Jane stopped in front of the wing chair and gave her friend a searching look. "Eustace did not physically harm you, then?" She turned to Gideon. "You sent him packing, I am informed." A small smile played around her wide mouth, and she glanced back at the door where Molly stood, her shoe-button eyes taking in everything.

"I am not sure he will stay routed, Jane." Gideon frowned down at Amelia. "You must be vigilant. Promise to inform me if you see him anywhere near here. Send Molly or one of the boys from the orphan school to find me."

Amelia got to her feet. "Really, you two. I am perfectly fine. Eustace did try to restrain me, but I was never in any jeopardy, I assure you."

"You forget, Amy, I saw him. Eustace was ready to do more than hold you. You might have been in real danger." Gideon could see from the stubborn set of her mouth that she was not convinced. The very fact that she despised the man made her underestimate him.

"I will not argue with you," he said calmly. "I will simply ask Jane to watch over you."

"Of course," Jane replied. "I have never trusted that little weasel, Amelia, and I am very sure that he will make trouble for you if he can." Jane believed she had a plain woman's ability to judge men accurately. They did not try to charm her, and so she saw them as they were, without any illusions.

Amelia nodded in acquiescence. "Very well. I can see that you two will do whatever you choose regardless of anything I say. So I might as well save my breath to cool my porridge."

"Good girl." Gideon's tone was the same one he had used when at twelve Amelia had followed instructions in some elaborate game they'd been playing.

Amelia felt a spurt of anger along her veins. After what she had seen in his eyes and felt in his arms, she was unwilling to be treated like a younger playmate. "Good lad," she responded in exactly the tone he had used, and rose to her feet. "Thank you, Gideon. I believe that I am due in the schoolroom to help the younger children with their sums. Good day." As cool and gracious as any of Almack's patronesses, she smiled and inclined her head in dismissal. "Jane, I will see you at luncheon." And she was gone.

To Gideon, the sunlight abruptly went out of the day with Amy's departure. He turned despairing eyes after her, but it was clear that she already had her mind on pedagogy. He had misread her. Those few moments when he had held her in his arms clearly had left her completely unimpressed. Uninterested. He squared his shoulders. Hussars did not admit defeat.

But with Amy what exactly did victory consist of?

Chapter Six

What had he done? Gideon asked himself that evening as he looked around yet another room filled with overdressed people at some ton function. He couldn't remember just what it was or who was hosting it.

All he could think of was Amy. Had he risked a lifetime of friendship for a moment of passion and protectiveness, holding her in his arms? Could he have been that stupid?

A rapid review of the morning's actions told Gideon he had indeed done just that. In disgust, he looked around the room, hoping for a glimpse of Amy or Jane. If he could talk to her, surely he could convince Amy that it was possible to return to the easy camaraderie they had enjoyed all those years, before he stupidly allowed them both a glimpse of how he really felt.

Since this morning, he had been forced to admit to himself that what he felt for her wasn't friendship or the pure love of a knight for a royal lady who stood far above him yet gave him her favor to carry in the tournament. What he had called chivalry had been instead the same kind of hot, possessive passion that any man felt for the woman he wanted for his own.

Though he had never realized consciously how he felt, the idea did not shock Gideon. At some level he had always known. But if he was not surprised, he nevertheless knew how hopeless his love was. His position in Amy's life was and had to remain one of friend and protector. If he had ever aspired to be more and win her love, her father had made it clear that he would jeopardize Lady Amelia Bradshaw's high standing in the ton. The duke had trusted the boy he had befriended not to attempt to do so. Gideon could not betray that trust. Besides, he knew the duke had been right.

What he had read in Amelia's eyes that morning told him she had feelings for him that were more than friendship. Knowing Amelia, he was sure she would not be content to be only his friend just to protect her reputation. Amelia did not care the snap of her fingers for reputation. If she did, she would not be sponsoring Jane Forrester at every event Jane could be persuaded to attend.

It was, therefore, up to Gideon to protect her from herself and her own kind, loving heart. She might well believe that she could marry Gideon and risk nothing more than a little gossip and possibly having a few doors closed to her. Nothing, Amelia would think, that she cared about in the least.

But she would care. When her children were not certain whether they would be welcomed as the grandchildren of a duke or scorned as the children of an unknown guttersnipe. When her daughters were not sought after by the most eligible men and her sons not invited to join the most exclusive clubs, then she would feel the weight of her folly. Gideon had observed Society from its far boundries for a long time, and he had seen the lengths to which people would go to remain in the Haut Ton. Look at Eustace, who would stop at nothing to get Amelia to marry him!

Gideon, outcast gypsy that he was, could afford not to care about the opinions of the upper ten thousand. But Amelia, much as she thought herself equally free from such concerns, was not an outcast but a leading member of that august group. Since she was unwilling to protect herself from the penalties of social ostracism, Gideon would do it for her. Exactly as the duke had known that he would. Automatically his hand reached for the small iron ball he always carried, but of course in his tightly fitted evening clothes, there were no convenient pockets into which he could fit his talisman. Damn!

If only he could find her in this miserable crowd, he could commence his efforts immediately.

As he gazed around, he became aware that people were

staring back at him. He stood alone as he had since he had entered the room, and when he thought about it, he realized he was frowning into every face he saw. No wonder everyone was giving him a wide berth, he thought with sardonic amusement.

"No, do not begin to smile now," Sir Richard remarked as he came up to Gideon. "It will unnerve people far more than the frown is doing."

"I am hardly formidable enough to render these hardened party goers fearful. After all," Gideon said with a wry half smile, "they brave Almack's, something I am not likely ever to have to do."

"I will not argue with you about the courage necessary to speak to Lady Jersey as opposed to that required to charge the French cavalry." Sir Richard smiled at someone over Gideon's shoulder. "Ah, here are your wards now." His smile suddenly disappeared. "What in the world has Miss Forrester done to herself?"

The tone of disapproval in Sir Richard's voice made it difficult for Gideon to refrain from turning around to stare. He wanted to turn and look at Amelia, but now he also wondered what costume the eccentric Jane had donned for the evening. Jane was becoming noted for the Quakerish simplicity of her dress. She would have to go far to exceed her already plain gowns unless she affected something truly outlandish like calico or linsey-woolsey.

"Captain Falconer." Jane's voice was tentative, not her usual self-assured tone. "Sir Richard."

Gideon turned and tried hard not to stare. Always noticeable because of her height, tonight Jane was the cynosure of all eyes because she was dressed in a fashionable gown of shimmering gold satin, with her chestnut hair falling in shining curls from a Psyche knot on the top of her head.

"Why, Jane," said Gideon, smiling at her obvious nervousness, "you look beautiful."

"It was Amelia's idea," Jane said uncomfortably. "I feel a perfect fool." She gave Gideon a tentative smile and turned to greet Sir Richard. He looked at her with grave displeasure written all over his face, and Gideon could see Jane's self-confidence begin to melt away.

"Miss Forrester," Gideon said, "would you care to take a turn around the room so everyone can see you?"

She stared at him, obviously uncertain of just what he meant. "I—I don't think. I mean, I—"

"Jane is afraid that she has let me talk her into more fashion than she is ready for." Amelia spoke at last, a rueful smile on her lips. "It is because she is so beautiful. It has taken her by surprise."

Sir Richard's smile was forced and perfunctory. "It has taken us all by surprise. It is hard to think of Miss Forrester the schoolmistress as this—fashion plate." His voice held a faint chill.

"Thank you, Gideon, I would like a turn about the room," Jane said, taking his arm with what felt like a steel claw.

Looking after them as they strolled away, Amelia said, "I cannot believe that one dress and a few curls could make such a difference. Jane is beautiful. Is she not, Sir Richard?" Amelia was hoping that someone would admire her efforts on Jane's behalf. So far, stunned silence seemed to be the only reaction, although Gideon appeared to be approving. Sir Richard, however, looked positively grim.

"Of course she is beautiful. But you have made her look like every other woman here." He sounded angry.

"Exactly my idea," Amelia explained patiently. Really, men could be so obtuse. "Jane felt that she stood out in company, that she did not fit in. Now she does. She can be comfortable at parties like this one." Amelia looked around the room. Though taller than most of the women in the room, Jane no longer looked as if she did not belong.

"Why should she look like everyone else when she is not in the slightest degree like anyone else?" Sir Richard demanded, his eyes boring into Amelia's. "She looked like what she was—an Original, a—" He broke off, and when he spoke again it was in his usual humorously ironic tone. "Oh, well, I cannot expect you to understand, Lady Amelia. It is merely a fancy of my own and of no importance."

"You understand her." Amelia was surprised at his perspicacity. "You value her for herself, as I do. As all her true friends do." When she looked up at him, she smiled.

Gideon saw that smile as he and Jane returned from their promenade, and it made his heart ache. Perhaps he needn't warn Amy off after all. Perhaps she had decided for herself that he was not for her and turned to his friend instead. The sharp arrow of jealousy that stung his heart merely served to remind him that while he would remain devoted to Amy and none other all his life, it was only appropriate that she find another man to love and marry. The arrow twisted and gouged.

"Several people did not seem to recognize me," Jane said. "Until I spoke."

"You might have fooled them a little longer if you had managed to refrain from bringing up the corn tariffs," Gideon said with a laugh. "You should have seen the looks we got when Jane insisted on discussing the evils of a conservative trade policy. All the gentlemen wanted to do was look at her figure, and the ladies were determined to discover the name of her dressmaker." He was happy that Jane had been a success. Amy must be very proud of her protégée. But when he looked at her, Amy wasn't smiling, she was gazing thoughtfully at Jane and then at Gideon.

He knew instantly what she was thinking. It was exactly what he had thought when he saw Amy with Sir Richard: *Here is someone who belongs in the life of the one I love, who would fit into it in a way I myself never will.* He smiled wryly and tucked Jane's hand in the crook of his arm.

"I believe you have the outward look perfected, but some work on frivolous conversation would not be amiss," he said.

"I do not believe that women should talk of nothing but hairstyles and babies," Amelia said, her eyes flashing. "And neither does Jane."

"Bravo." The deep, bored voice of Sir Richard sent color to Jane's cheeks. "I, too, believe that women as well as men can stupefy their listeners into sleep by prosing on about politics."

Jane stood stock-still and then removed her hand from Gideon's arm and rounded on Sir Richard. Standing squarely in front of him, she faced him with undaunted courage. "I cannot believe that anyone who has fought for England can be so light-minded as not to care at all about the future of his country!"

"Then, believe, at any rate, that he does not care to discuss that future with a collection of brainless fribbles at a rout!" Sir Richard's frown was thunderous.

"I am not a brainless fribble!" Jane clenched her fists and glared at him.

"Jane, dear," Amelia murmured, "people are beginning to stare."

Jane and Sir Richard both ignored her. "Not you," he said impatiently, as if she should have known better. "All those fools you were trying to talk sense to."

Gideon realized that he was fast losing control of the situation. If he did not act quickly, Jane and Sir Richard would leave Amy and him alone to all intents and purposes. This was not the pairing that Gideon had in mind. Spending more time with Amy would test his resolve beyond his capacity. Horses and men could break when strained physically beyond what they could bear, and he had to acknowledge that he might reach his breaking point emotionally as well.

"Jane," he said. But Jane and Sir Richard were passionately discussing the proper way to tax agriculture and were paying no attention.

"Gideon," Amelia said, and for the first time he looked directly at her. She was dressed in deep rose silk with an overdress of spangled silver gauze, and as usual she was lovely enough to stop the breath in his chest. When he saw her eyes, though, he could tell that something was wrong. Her usually candid gaze was clouded and uncertain as her eyes met his. "Gideon, I—" She stopped short.

Oh, God, he thought, she couldn't even talk to him. He had ruined everything by his precipitous actions. She might forgive him, overlook his presumption in thinking he could hold her in his arms even for a moment, but she could no longer be easy in his company.

Gideon felt as if he had been kicked in the stomach. He had lost the most precious thing in his life, Amy's friendship and trust, and he had no idea of how to go about winning it back. He did not believe he could lie to her successfully or he might have told her that he had merely been acting as her friend, that his embrace had been brotherly.

But it wasn't true, and she would not believe him. Amy had always had an uncanny ability to read his thoughts. Anytime he had lied, she had known. She had never told the duke, she was too good a friend to betray his childish misbehavior. But she had known. And she would know now. He was sure of it.

"Amy, please don't worry. There is no reason why we cannot still be friends, good friends. I should not have—I will never again—I know how you must feel—" Gideon had never felt so stupid and inadequate, not even when he had first joined the army, as green a Johnny Raw as had ever ridden in formation. If only he knew how to tell her that she needn't worry, that he would never do anything to remind her of his feelings. No matter how he felt, he would always be her faithful knight.

"You can always depend on me, Amy. I will always be your friend."

For some reason, this did not seem to reassure her. Her full lower lip trembled, and her large blue eyes seemed to be even more troubled.

"I know you will, and I am grateful for that." Her voice sounded dejected, but she smiled bravely up at him.

"We can forget all about this morning and be comfortable with each other." Gideon's voice sounded false to his own ears, and he knew Amy could hear it as well. "As the old friends we are."

"Yes. Of course." Amy seemed to withdraw into herself for a moment. Then she squared her shoulders, gave Gideon a dazzling smile, which somehow did not reach her eyes, and turned away from him.

As if conjured up by some evil fairy, Percival Sturdevant appeared in front of her, smiling like the village half-wit. Gideon could feel his eyebrows draw together in a frown. Sturdevant greeted him with a certain wary cordiality, as if Gideon were Amelia's elderly guardian who needed to be placated before Sturdevant could carry the lady off to eat an ice and flirt with him.

Gideon felt at least a thousand years old as he nodded grimly at Sturdevant and watched him offer Amy his arm and stroll away with her. Gideon looked after them with a hopeless ache in his heart. This was only the beginning of his suffering, he knew. Despite the fact that he had been wounded in battle, this pain was far more difficult to bear because he knew it would continue unabated for years.

"She does not really care for him, you know." Jane spoke from just behind him, and Gideon turned to look into her sympathetic face. "Or indeed for any of them."

"Perhaps there is no one yet," he responded, "but there will be. Despite what she thinks now, Amelia will marry."

"Yes, I agree with you. She needs love, children, a family."

"Then, why do you encourage her to think that foundling homes and female emancipation will take their place?" Gideon wasn't angry. He genuinely wanted to know.

"I do not encourage her" was Jane's surprising reply. "She came to me after having read one of my articles. It is her decision entirely, and I am not sure why she feels so strongly about it. Though one could hazard a guess, of course."

"Of course." Gideon had scarcely looked at Jane. His attention was focused on Amy—a slender figure in silver-spangled silk whose progress through the crowded room had been slowed by all the people—all the young men—who wanted to talk to her. "I imagine it is because she believes the duke would want her to follow in his footsteps. Though I know he wanted her to marry."

"He told you so?" Jane sounded surprised, and Gideon spared a look for her.

"Yes. He told me that he trusted that he could depend on me to make sure that she did not fall prey to some fortune hunter, but that she nevertheless must marry." Gideon bit off the rest of that memory.

"I think she must," Jane said.

"I thought you did not approve of marriage." Sir Richard, who had listened in uncharacteristic silence thus far, at last joined the conversation. His voice was sharp, and he fixed Jane with a keen gaze.

Startled, she looked at him through narrowed eyes, as if trying to divine his thoughts. "I do not disapprove of marriage. For some women it is an ideal life, a noble calling. I simply do not regard it as universally so."

"And for Amy it would be a noble calling?" He moved closer, his dark blond head bent toward her chestnut one.

Jane held her ground. "I believe so. She is clearly cut out to be a mother. The young ones adore her." She smiled a little.

"But for you, it would be slavery?" The hazel eyes stared unsmilingly down into hers.

Gideon decided Jane deserved rescue. "You are beginning to sound like a barrister in full cry, sir. This is supposed to be a social occasion, after all." He tried a slight social smile to soften his words. Clearly, it did not have the desired effect.

Sir Richard turned to him, his eyes glacial. "So it is. I suppose we have been standing here conversing among ourselves so long we must be perceived as unsociable if not downright rude. Very well." He extended his arm to Jane. "Miss Forrester, will you take a turn about the room?" He looked around at the crowd, which had grown even more dense since they had been talking. "If we can make our way through this throng. So long as we do not attempt to approach any food or drink, I think we will return unscathed."

"Very well." Jane laid her hand on Sir Richard's arm with a wary look and, Gideon thought, very much the air of one who is about to walk unarmed through countryside that looked peaceful but was known to be infested with snipers.

"Good. We can continue to discuss your reasons for believing that Lady Amelia may safely risk what would be your undoing." With that opening gambit he led her away, leaving Gideon alone once again.

Not for long, however. Apparently what had to be avoided in a ballroom, where an ineligible man might cozen his way to a waltz, was regarded as unexceptionable at a rout. Several giggling young ladies managed to engage him in desultory conversation for a few minutes—until a watchful mama came up and swept them out of harm's way.

Circulating throughout a room that was growing progressively hotter and more crowded held little charm for Gideon, but he felt he had to find Amelia. He recognized that his reason for seeking her was not altruistic. Now that he had admitted his feelings for her to himself, it was obvious that his solicitude had masked a fierce, possessive love. Letting go of the mask, if only in his thoughts, was liberating. He breathed a little easier, knowing why he sought her out.

At last he located her, talking with several gentlemen. Her expression was earnest, and she was clearly trying to interest them in some serious topic. They, on the other hand, were vying with each other to entertain her in the only way Society understood—complimenting her on her beauty, her exquisite taste, her charm. Gideon couldn't hear a word of their conversation of course, but he knew. He could tell by the fatuous smiles and subtle jockeying for position next to her. He shook his head. Did they know nothing of Lady Amelia Bradshaw? They must have failed to study their quarry—a fatal mistake as any military man could tell them. Anyone who thought she would rather discuss the size and clarity of her eyes than the size and direction of her charitable activities clearly did not know her. Fools!

He quickened his step and ended standing before her at a parade-rest stance, his hands behind his back and his brows drawn together in a frown. Several of her attendant lords backed away, loath to engage this farouche-looking gentleman in any kind of discussion whatsoever.

"Are you ready to leave, Amelia?" he said, his voice harsh and his use of her Christian name deliberately provocative.

"No, I shall wait until Jane is bored." Amelia's eyes were stormy. She knew what he was doing, but misunderstood completely his reasons, Gideon realized suddenly. "I do not wish to leave now." The words were deliberately dismissive. "Thank you, Captain," she added carelessly.

Jane and Sir Richard appeared at that moment. They did not appear to be any happier than Amy and Gideon. Jane looked as if a quarrel was well underway, and Sir Richard's bland smile did not quite disguise his anger. Amy quickly made her smiling excuses to the group and departed with Jane, leaving two angry and frustrated men behind them.

Chapter Seven

Eustace appeared at Jane's house again the next morning. This time he tried to buy Molly's absence with a penny for a sweet, but that young lady was staunch in her chosen job and scornfully refused the coin. He seemed to Amelia to be even more frantic than before. He threw himself on his knees in front of her and grasped her hands in his feverish ones.

"You must marry me, Amelia," he gasped. "You must!"

"I am sorry, Eustace," she said, her patience strained to the utmost. "You know my answer. I cannot marry you."

"You *can*, you know you can. There is no impediment. We are only second cousins. And since you can, you must help me, for you are the only one who can," he added with the supreme self-concern that was typical of him.

Angrily Amelia pulled her hands away and tried to distance herself. But Eustace refused to let her go. He clutched at her skirt and repeated that she had to marry him. In another minute Amelia might well have struck him. She was a duke's daughter, and she was not used to anyone's laying importunate hands upon her. Even her father had never done so. That Eustace should dare—

She opened her mouth to deliver a blistering set-down when Jane swept into the room. Taking in the scene at a glance, she advised Eustace to get to his feet and stop making a cake of himself. Faced with such cool common sense, Eustace did so, but he looked as though he longed to take her neck between his hands.

"Do not refuse me, Amelia," he said, his eyes showing white

all around like those of a frightened horse. "You will be sorry if you do."

Is he threatening me? she wondered. She looked at his weak face and dandified clothes, and dismissed the idea.

"I try and try to tell you that I have no desire to be a duchess, Eustace. I know firsthand what such a role demands, and I have no desire for it."

Eustace gave Amelia a look of such loathing that she instinctively recoiled. Then without another word, he turned on his heel and left the house. Amelia crossed her arms protectively and asked herself if that had been a serious threat. He had looked angry enough to do murder.

"He frightens me," she said to Jane. "His insistence that only I will do as his bride—it's not quite normal, Jane."

"Nonsense. Like every other male he does not want to take no as his answer," her friend replied. "You must simply treat him as the child he is and continue to say no quietly and firmly. He will understand eventually."

"I wish I could be as sure as you are that is all it is." Amelia shook her head. "No matter. He is gone, and there is very little he can do in the face of my refusal. I have control of my money, so he cannot persuade a trustee or a father to marry me off."

She frowned. Something about that idea gave her pause, and she began to turn it over in her mind, searching for the elusive thought. Before she could get far, however, Molly came in to tell her that she was needed in the schoolroom. Amelia dismissed everything but teaching from her mind, and left the room.

Later that day Sir Richard was ushered into the parlor, where he stood, impatiently tapping his foot, as he waited for Lady Amelia to come down. He had promised Gideon that he would try to talk her into leaving town for the holidays. Why in the world he had taken it upon himself to give advice to the self-assured duke's daughter he could not say.

Jane Forrester entered, and Sir Richard suddenly had a very clear idea of why he had come. This afternoon she was wearing a simple gray dress with a white collar and cuffs, her bright chestnut hair braided and coiled into a chignon pinned at the back of her neck. The contrast with her appearance at the rout made him all too aware of how inappropriate she was as an object of his interest.

"Miss Forrester." He bowed, unsmiling over her hand. "I had hoped to see Lady Amelia."

"She has taken some of the children out for a walk. If you care to wait, they should be back in a short while." Jane's face never lost its expression of polite interest. Yesterday evening, with its sharp exchanges and undercurrents of attraction and admiration, might never have happened. Here was the old, guarded, no-nonsense Jane, who never trusted any man, certainly not one who set off fine tremors in her arm when he touched it.

Sir Richard was an old enough hand at the game of dalliance to know when he affected a woman the way he had Jane Forrester. The way she affected him. He stared at her, this totally inappropriate woman, and resolved to put distance between them, starting now.

"I have come at Captain Falconer's request. He is most desirous that Lady Amelia quit the city and go to stay with one of her friends. Apparently she refuses to consider it." He could feel his face assume its habitual expression of bored hauteur. "Perhaps you, as her closest friend, may persuade her to change her mind."

"Why should I?" Jane spoke carelessly and shrugged her shoulders. "She is doing important work here with the children. I see no reason why Eustace and his strange fits and starts should govern Amelia's movements."

"Because Gideon Falconer, an experienced soldier, believes that the Duke of Doncaster is a danger to Lady Amelia. Surely that should take precedence over the temporary needs of a pack of urchins."

Jane drew her shoulders back and pulled herself up to her full height. Sir Richard could feel his breath catch in his throat. The woman's figure was nothing short of incredible! He had to pull his eyes away from her bosom or be frozen forever. The only way was to leave before he either shook Jane Forrester until her teeth rattled or kissed her senseless.

"Tell Lady Amelia what I said, and that it is Gideon's advice as well as mine." He looked at Jane soberly for a moment. "There are threats to the rich and wellborn, you know, not just to the poor. Amelia may be in danger."

"Do you think she is?" Jane asked bluntly.

"Gideon does, and I have learned to trust his instincts over the years."

"She saved his life. If the sun were too strong on her face, Gideon would shoot it out of the sky if he could." How absurd all that emotion was! her smile said.

"Just deliver the message if you would. Knowing the lady, I am sure she will ignore it and continue to conduct her life exactly as she chooses, but I am duty bound to convey it."

They stood slightly closer together than propriety decreed, neither of them aware of anything but the tension between them. He had better leave. This was no place, and she was no woman, for the heir to a marquessate, no matter how reluctant the heir might be. Sir Richard took her hand. "Good afternoon, Miss Forrester."

"Sir Richard." With queenly disdain she inclined her head. "I will tell Amelia when she returns."

Eustace was still certain that if he could just play long enough, he would come about. He had secretly pawned two elaborate silver candlesticks, Doncaster family heirlooms, for enough guineas to stake him to a game at one of the lesser hells where he was not known.

Like all confirmed gamblers, Eustace was sure he couldn't lose. But the cards continued to favor other players. He looked around at the others in the room. A young man who announced he had been sent down from Oxford, a sleek-looking article Eustace knew for a Captain Sharp, and an older gentleman in outdated clothes whom Eustace instantly decided was a lamb for the fleecing.

He introduced himself as "Mr. Mannering," and asked the

gentleman, whose name was Undershaw, if he would care to play piquet.

"Why, yes, indeed I would sir," the gray-haired Undershaw replied with a frank smile. "'Tis my favorite game. I am accounted quite a dab hand at home in West Runton."

Eustace gave his rustic friend his very best smile and sat down, ready to win enough to keep the wolf from the door for a few more weeks at least.

An hour later when he arose, his money was gone. To add insult to injury, Mr. Undershaw refused to accept his vowels, saying that such things were not done among friends in West Runton.

"Damn West Runton!" Eustace burst out. "Are you telling me you will not accept my promise to pay a debt of honor? You insult me, sir!"

Suddenly Mr. Undershaw's eyes did not seem quite so guileless. "I shan't be here in two days' time, Your Grace. Can you pay up by then?"

Eustace stared at him. This was no country flat. Undershaw knew his title—and his reputation. "Never mind," Eustace said abruptly. "I have played enough." As he shrugged into his greatcoat, ready to brave the December cold, he chanced to look back into the room. He saw Captain Sharp and Mr. Undershaw grinning at each other as they stood in close companionship in front of the fire. Fellow sharps! He had been taken by the oldest trick of all. Seeking to avoid one professional gambler, he had fallen victim to his partner.

Eustace slammed the door as he left. As he stalked down the street, he angrily thought that losing tonight was another misfortune to be laid at his damned cousin's door. The time to act had arrived.

But what to do and how to do it? Never known for his intelligence, Eustace found himself without a plan. His steps slowed as he cudgeled his brains. When he chanced to look around, he could see someone behind him, a man who was hurrying toward him. Damn! He had no money, but he might have a very bad time before he could convince this thief of the truth of that.

" 'Old 'ard, Yer Grace!"

"Blakeley!"

"None other. 'Ow about 'avin' a glass wiv me?"

The man's smile was sharklike rather than friendly, but Eustace badly wanted a drink. Ungraciously he accepted the invitation.

Once seated at a nearby tavern where Blakeley appeared to be well-known, Eustace decided to lay his problem on his companion's shoulders. After all, he was the one who wanted to be paid. Let him work for his money!

Before he could speak, Blakeley said, "When are you fixin' to get riveted to yer pretty cousin?"

"She won't have me," Eustace said, and swallowed his brandy in one swallow. "Damned awful stuff, Blakeley! Can't your friend get any better drink than this?"

"Not for them as aren't payin'. Now, let's talk of 'ow yer goin' to get the lady to see it yer way. A 'op to Gretna mayhap?"

"I am not going to spend days shut up in a carriage with Amelia." Eustace shuddered. "She was a dreadful hoyden as a child. She would spend the entire time telling me of my sins. She might actually fight to escape."

He sighed. Marrying Amelia was going to cause him a great deal of trouble, and trouble was something Eustace tried to avoid at all costs. Hortense dealt with the realities of life for him, and he took the easy way out of every situation. Now he was faced with an impasse—if he didn't act, terrible things would happen; if he did, he would have to deal with Amelia forever.

"Yer 'ouse in the country," Blakeley said. " 'Ow far away is it?"

"Not far. Several hours' drive only." Eustace brightened. "Do you think we could take her there?"

"Not 'we.' Me. You stay in London until she's safely 'id. Then you tell every bleedin' person you know that you and 'er ladyship is spending the 'oliday season together."

Eustace looked at the tall, cadaverous man with admiration. "All right. But what about my mother?"

Blakeley looked at him with what might have been scorn—but was not of course. Moneylenders did not scorn peers of the realm. "Tell 'er to stay 'ere and go to parties. Or tell 'er the truth. Just be sure the world knows you and yer lady cousin are there and yer ma's 'ere."

For a moment Eustace toyed with the idea of emigrating and leaving the title and his debts behind. One look at Blakeley's eyes changed his mind. He had a feeling that he would not be safe from the man no matter where he went.

"Very well. Better do it soon. We've only two weeks before Christmas." He had already turned the problem over to Blakeley.

"Once yer there, it's up to you, Yer Grace." There was a threat in every word. "We 'ad better see a marriage announcement by Boxing Day."

"Yes, yes, you will." Eustace tried to back away from the cold light in those dead-looking eyes.

"Acos if we don't . . ."

Eustace waited, but Blakeley said nothing more. Eustace could feel himself begin to shake. He would persuade Amelia. He had to.

Amelia went to take tea at Lady Maltby's with several old cronies of her father's, hoping as always to detach them from some of their fortunes to aid her charities.

As she left, she looked around for a hackney. When she saw the familiar carriage with the Doncaster crest on the door panel begin to slow to a stop beside her, she smiled. What good fortune that Cousin Hortense should happen along at this moment.

She was taken completely unawares when a strange groom hopped down and opened the door for her. Some sense of danger made her hesitate, and the man lifted her by her elbows and flung her into the coach. She landed on her hands and knees on the floor as the vehicle took off at a spanking pace.

" 'Ello, yer ladyship." An unfamiliar voice. Before she could respond, someone held her nose and a sharp tasting drink was poured down her throat. Sputtering and coughing, she struck out blindly. She knew a brief moment of satisfaction when her foot made sharp contact with some part of someone's body and she heard a grunt of pain. Then darkness descended, and she lost consciousness.

She knew immediately she was no longer in the carriage when she awoke. Her head ached abominably, and she had a raging thirst. Her mouth was so dry she could hardly swallow. She shivered and became aware that her dress had been removed and she was wearing her petticoats and camisole and stockings. Her shoes were gone. The room in which she found herself was dark. Still, her body was free, though she was in a prison of some sort.

Dizziness overcame her, and abruptly she slid down to the floor. Drawing her knees up, she rested her head on them and tried not to let terror swamp her. She bit her lip hard and clenched her fists until she could feel the sharp sting of her fingernails in the skin of her palms. The tiny pains seemed to help clear her head, but fear still beat like a wild thing at her mind. She refused to let it in. Gideon never said that he was afraid when he'd run away from the fighting man and lived on the streets or when he'd gone into battle, but she'd always known he had felt it. Yet he had never given in to it. He had conquered it, and she could, too. He would expect it of her.

She took a deep breath and tried to slow her heartbeat.

In, out, deeply and slowly. Thinking of Gideon, she could feel some of his courage flowing into her. It was almost as if she could hear his voice. Whether it was the thought of Gideon or the act of breathing itself, Amelia found her panic ebbing.

She tried to think. Eustace was the only person she could think of with reason to kidnap her, but the voice she'd heard in the carriage sounded rough and slum-bred. Where would Eustace go to find someone like that? He would take no chances himself—he was much too great a coward. The only reason for him to take such desperate action was to force her to marry him. If they were on their way to Scotland, she could not understand why they had stopped. Surely it would be hard to force an unwilling woman in and out of a carriage even on the road to Scotland. So if not a kidnapping disguised as an elopement, what was it? Why was she traveling with an unknown ruffian instead of her despicable cousin?

She tried but could think no further. Her head was pounding, and her thoughts seemed to be coming from inside a reverberating drum. She closed her eyes and rested her cheek on her knee. For a few minutes, she dozed sitting upright on the floor. Even that short nap did her good, reducing her headache and the lassitude in her limbs.

Yawning and stretching, she stood and looked around. Slowly her eyes became more accustomed to the dark. She could make out the outline of windows, high above her. They were a lighter gray, and she harbored a hope that they would let in a bit of light when day came again. She began to move through the slowly clearing room, hands in front of her, scraping her feet forward, feeling even flooring, not dirt or stones. Her fingers scraped a wall, and she ran her hand down it, over material that was smooth and cool, like marble or finished stone. She moved around the room, feeling the walls and the floor until her knee struck what seemed to be an iron bedstead.

She touched the thin, lumpy mattress. She patted the bed and discovered a rough blanket at one end. She was as excited as if she had found an open door. Fearing that she would lose her courage if she sat down and thought about what had happened, she wrapped the blanket around her and kept moving, hoping to discover something else, something that might help her escape. After a thorough search, she realized that the room contained nothing except the bed. If there was a door or a window she could reach, she had failed to find it. Disheartened, her head still aching abominably, she groped her way back to the iron cot and lay down.

Now she could not control her thoughts or her fears. Was it Eustace who had seized her? What did whoever it was intend to do with her? What arguments, what strategy could she use to defeat him? And behind these thoughts, one plea dominated her mind.

Gideon, where are you? When will you come for me?

Chapter Eight

Gideon called on Sir Richard, only to hear that Amelia had been out when the colonel had visited and instead Sir Richard had seen only "that termagant" Miss Forrester. Gideon paced a little, fingering the small iron ball in his pocket, growing more and more uneasy about Amelia's safety.

If he and Sir Richard had not had business at the Horse Guards that afternoon, he might have called at Miss Forrester's and seen Amelia before she left to visit Lady Maltby. But they did, and it had taken the entire afternoon, and they had accomplished absolutely nothing. What Wellington needed in the Peninsula was not more military second-guessing but more supplies and firmer support from London.

Gideon arrived back at his rooms in a foul temper. Relieved that he had no engagement—Amelia had told him she was going to spend a pleasant evening reading—he threw himself on the bed and wished himself back with the duke in Portugal. At least then he knew himself to be useful. Although his unusual sponsorship in his regiment had caused talk, his superb horsemanship and sangfroid in battle had provided the only credentials necessary with his fellow officers.

He loved the cavalry. All his anger and fear, his burning sense of injustice could be channeled into action. When faced with the enemy, Gideon had fought as if the chimney sweep, the fighting man, and the gypsies had all been facing him instead of merely French soldiers. He fought with a sort of joyous rage that made him legendary.

Now he was faced with another kind of enemy entirely, one he felt peculiarly unfit to deal with. He couldn't charge at

Eustace Mannering or outflank Percival Sturdevant. All he could do was stand guard and glower at any threats to Amy—threats he sometimes thought he alone perceived. He felt like an aging, useless bulldog, unable to protect his beloved mistress from harm.

He grinned at his own fancies and prepared to spend a solitary night dining at a tavern and reading in his room. It was after nine when he returned from the tavern to find a message waiting for him from Jane and Sir Richard. He hastened to the house in Hans Crescent.

Amelia had not returned from her afternoon visit, and Jane had begun to worry. She sent a note to Lady Maltby. When the reply came that Amelia had left hours before, Jane immediately contacted Sir Richard. She had not asked herself why she turned to him instead of Gideon, but when he joined them at Jane's house, disheveled and glaring, Gideon asked her.

"I—I don't know. I thought all three of us would do better thinking—I mean—"

Sir Richard smiled at this garbled response, but Gideon was far beyond caring for anything but news of Amy. "It doesn't matter." He paced around Jane's sparsely furnished but cheerful sitting room like a caged animal, the iron ball twisting in his fingers. "What has happened? She never came home?" he rapped the question at Jane.

"No. The message came back directly. Amelia left at half past five." Jane sank into a straight chair near the small fireplace. "Sit down, Captain, you are making me dizzy pacing like that."

Gideon ignored her. He could not sit still when every instinct cried out for action. Something was wrong, he could feel it.

"What do you think has happened, Falconer?" Sir Richard asked.

Gideon turned, his face grave. "I think Amy hasn't returned, because she cannot do so."

Jane gaped at him. "You think Amy's been injured?"

He shook his head, his straight dark hair gleaming in the lamplight. How could he justify this feeling he had that something was terribly wrong? All that the others seemed to see was that Amy had apparently gone elsewhere and had as yet failed to return, though it was now ten o'clock. Hardly grounds for alarm. Lady Amelia Bradshaw moved in circles where the evening's entertainment had scarcely begun at that hour. But he knew.

"Not injured. She would have been carried here, or Jane would have been notified. She was not going anywhere that was not nearby and heavily trafficked by the ton."

"Then, you think she has been kidnapped?" Sir Richard said. "Why?"

"Call it gypsy intuition," Gideon said, trying for lightness, though his heart twisted within him. "But let us act on it."

"If you are right, it must be the duke who is behind it," Sir Richard said. "We can call in the Runners if you think it advisable."

Gideon smiled a little crookedly. "Thank you for your willingness to humor a junior officer, but I doubt the Runners will be able to do much. We need to find out where Eustace has gone."

"No difficulty there," Jane said briskly. "I can send Molly's brothers and several others out to inquire. They are old enough to have connections with servants of the families of the ton, and we should have some word within a few hours."

Sir Richard looked at her with admiration. "Splendid idea, Miss Forrester."

"Yes, thank you," Gideon said. "I should have thought of it myself. It is amazing how much street children see and understand, particularly since most of the time no one even knows they exist." There was silence in the room for a moment. Gideon seldom mentioned his childhood even obliquely, and as a result his friends tended to forget how dangerous and difficult it had been.

He turned away, ignoring them. He seemed to pull thought and solitude around him again like a cloak. After a moment he turned back to the two worried faces and said, "We are assuming it is Mannering—Doncaster. Yet the city is full of men who are thinking to marry to their financial advantage. Mr. Sturdevant, for example. I think we should check the northern roads to see if any coach traveling fast and containing a man and a beautiful blond young lady has passed. Everyone on the damned road must know what eloping couples are like, especially if no maid is there to lend a veneer of propriety!"

He ran an angry hand through his hair and clenched his jaw. "Go, Jane, and see if one of your famous young sleuths can lay a hand on Eustace while we check the road to Gretna. Whoever it is, I'll kill him."

Sir Richard stared with a keen eye at his friend. "Where else besides Gretna might the duke have taken her, if it is he and she is in fact missing? Have you an idea? Either of you?" He looked also at Jane, who was giving a note and a few whispered instructions to a poorly dressed but sharp-eyed lad who looked to be about twelve.

"He might have taken her to the Abbey," Jane ventured.

"Why would he go there?" Gideon demanded. "He is almost completely unknown to the servants there. Their loyalty lies with Amy, not with Eustace. Once they know she is there—"

Jane had returned from her whispered colloquy. She looked thoughtful as she replied, "But they might not know. And I'm not sure Eustace would see things that way. To him, once you are the duke, everything you do is forgiven. He could well believe that the servants' loyalty will have been transferred to him and not remained with Amelia because that is what his mother told him in his youth."

Gideon's lips set stubbornly. "I still say we look for some other hiding place. Has he any friends who might lend him a hunting box, or some other out-of-the-way place?"

"Eustace has never had any friends that I know of," Jane said. "Amelia swears he was an odious little boy, and he certainly hasn't improved over the years."

Sir Richard put his arm around Gideon's shoulders for a moment. "We will find her. Remember, the duke has no resources, so he can't have planned anything very elaborate."

Gideon tried to smile. He could see that both Sir Richard and Jane were worried about him. They did not share his apprehension. How could they? They did not know Amy as he did, did not share the bond that had kept him close to her through all the years he had spent fighting abroad. They thought he was behaving strangely.

Let them! What mattered was finding her. If, please God, they found her at some Society function she had forgotten to tell Jane about, he would be the first to laugh at his fears. But he knew they were not going to be that fortunate.

He had to do something to find her. Inactivity was driving him mad. It was almost as if he could hear her calling to him.

Gideon, where are you? When will you come for me?

"I am going to ride north. If I can't find a trace of them by dawn, I will return in time to get your news about Eustace." Without waiting for a reply, he swung out of the room almost at a run, relieved to be finally taking some action.

Eustace had been attempting all evening to establish his presence in London, but with little success. He needed to secure his alibi not so much with the law as with public opinion, and he did not have access to the haunts of the Haut Ton. Lack of money, lack of prospects, and a shabby reputation kept many doors still closed to him.

He attempted to find someone to take him to White's or Watier's as a guest, but to no avail—who wanted to sponsor a man who could not pay his debts? Finally he decided to go to the opera and later attend a dinner at the home of a cit who welcomed anyone with a title.

Relieved, he circulated around the opera house greeting as many people as he could, telling them that Amelia and he were engaged and were going to spend Christmas together at Doncaster Abbey. He never noticed the sharp-eyed lad who darted away once he had taken a close look from behind a pillar. So far Blakeley had taken all the risks. Eustace would go down to the Abbey in the morning in order to establish that he and Amelia were there alone together. She would have to marry him, the world would give her no choice. It was a simple plan, but one that had worked more times than anyone could count. His mouth curved in a smug smile.

* * *

A door slid open, and a shadowy figure stood looking at Amelia. A man, but one she did not recognize. Amelia shivered, remembering that she had no dress on. Someone—this man?—had removed it. Clutching the thin blanket around her and hunching her knees to her chest, she stared at him.

"So, yer ladyship, we're awake are we?" His voice was harsh, his accent proclaimed his birth within sound of Bow bells.

"Who are you?" Why had she asked that? What difference did it make?

"Call me Mr. B. At yer service, ma'am." Josiah Blakeley sketched an awkward bow.

"Eustace hired you?" Her voice was steady she noted with pride, although she was beginning to know real fear. This man might act like a stage buffoon, but she could hear the hard note in his voice.

He laughed. " 'Im 'ire me? Not bleedin' likely. No, no yer ladyship, the duke, 'e's in no position to be 'irin' nobody. You might say I agreed to do 'im a small favor. A business proposition, more like."

Slowly the man advanced into the room through a doorway Amelia had not been able to find. The light coming from behind him was suddenly augmented by that of a candle he drew from around the side of his body. In its flickering light Amelia could see the hard planes of his face, the lank greasy hair, and most of all the cold, cold eyes that took in her figure hunched under the thin blanket.

"So, yer ladyship, you about ready to give in and marry the duke? Or will it take more persuasion?" He closed the distance between them and stood looking down at her. Amelia felt like a small animal cornered by the hunter.

She threw up her head. Nonsense! She was no one's victim, least of all Eustace's. "No, I am not ready to wed anyone, least of all my odious cousin! You can give up that idea right now."

Quick as lightning, Mr. B. reached over and grabbed her hair with one bony hand. He dragged her head back until her face was directly under his. "Oh, I would not be too sure of that, my fine lady. Get too 'igh-and-mighty wif me and some very bad things might 'appen to you. Very bad." With his other hand, he stroked her cheek. Amelia felt as if her very flesh shrank from his touch, but she could not move her head.

She could, however, still move her legs, and with a mighty heave she brought both of them up and jackknifed them into Blakeley's stomach. With a cry, he let go of her and stumbled backward. Amelia jumped to her feet and ran headlong toward the door. She had just reached it when he grabbed her arm and almost wrenched it from its socket. He whirled her around and hurled her into a corner of the room.

She lay helpless, the breath knocked from her body, as Mr. B. walked slowly to her and stood over her, still breathing with difficulty. "I should kick yer bleedin' ribs into yer bleedin' backbone!"

Horrified but unable to move, Amelia stared at his thick boots only inches away from her eyes.

"But I ain't goin' to do it. 'And why is that, Mr. B.?' you may ask." She could hear his snigger, and it sent a chill down her spine. She should never have tried to escape without a plan. Gideon would deplore her lack of tactical skill. How many times had he told her to think before she acted?

"Acos I got bigger plans fer you, Lady Amelia Bleedin' Bradshaw, that's why."

The boots turned away, and she could hear the man retreat. The door slid shut, and Amelia let out the breath she wasn't aware she'd been holding in a long sigh. Slowly she got to her feet, her body aching from the manhandling she had received. She made her way back to the iron cot. Her eyes once again growing used to the semidarkness, she moved with greater assurance around her prison this time.

Her body aching, her head still a little muddled from the drink Mr. B. had given her, Amelia curled into a ball on her hard bed. Often Gideon had had to go days without sleep. He had told her that a soldier learned to sleep as much as he could as often as he could so as to be ready for action when it came. She would be ready. She closed her eyes and slept.

* * *

It was after seven in the morning when Gideon returned to the house in Hans Crescent. Sir Richard was there looking remarkably fresh. He and Jane hurried out to the hall to greet Gideon with the news brought to them by Jane's young friends. They told him Eustace had remained in London and that Lady Amelia had gotten into a large black carriage with a crest on the door just outside the house she had visited.

Gideon, mud spattered and grim, slumped on a chair and gulped down the cup of coffee Jane handed him before reporting the results of his efforts. "Nothing," he said. "Not a trace. Unfortunately, there was a couple who had taken the road north yesterday afternoon, so I chased them down. By the time I found them at some little cottage not that far out of London, it was almost dawn."

He shook his tangled dark hair off his forehead with an impatient movement. "A waste of almost ten hours! And still no word. I cannot believe that we have been able to do nothing." He clenched his fists and shut his mouth in a grim line. There was no point in blaming either Sir Richard or Jane.

Jane removed the cup from Gideon's slack hand. "Is it possible that she never left London? That Eustace has kept her at Doncaster House?"

"It seems unlikely," Sir Richard said. "There is no impropriety if his mother is there, and we have had no word from Miss Forrester's legions that either of them has left town." He went over to Gideon, still slumped in the chair, and put a bracing hand on his shoulder. "I am afraid that all we can do for the moment is await events."

Gideon's tired eyes blazed, and he rose to his feet. "I cannot. I will not! Amy is out there somewhere at the mercy of God knows who! I know that Eustace is involved somehow, some way. I am going to Doncaster Abbey. It is only a short ride, and if she is there I know I can find her. There are a hundred ways to get onto the property and stay hidden and I know them all."

His fatigue seemed to fall away from him like a heavy, wet cloak, and he felt a surge of energy and hope. He grinned at Jane. "The cavalry cannot abide awaiting events. Sir Richard has spent far too much time at Horse Guards—he has lost his dash and daring!" With a grin and a handshake for Sir Richard, Gideon left the room. He was on his way to a fresh mount and a bruising ride to Doncaster Abbey, where he had a sudden heart-lifting conviction that he would find Amy.

Gideon, where are you?

"I'm coming, Amy," he whispered. "Hang on, my angel, for just a little while longer."

Chapter Nine

Something jolted Amelia awake. The door slid open, and she saw the man who called himself Mr. B. silhouetted in the opening. She sat up, trembling, every sense alert. He stood looking at her for a moment, then dragged a large bundle onto the middle of the floor, stepped back, and closed the door. She heard the clank of a bolt, the rasp of a key.

No sound came from the heap on the floor. As her eyes became adjusted once again to the lack of light, she could distinguish the deeper, more solid blackness of that menacing pile.

It moved. She took a deep breath and tried to still the terror that clamored within her. What had he imprisoned with her? A wild animal? A snake? Something threatening. It had to be that.

"Amy?" The whisper was so quiet, it hardly seemed to disturb the air that carried it. Yet Amelia knew immediately who was there.

"Gideon!" She leapt to her feet. "Oh, Gideon, thank God you have come!" She crossed the room in two bounds and knelt at his side.

"Hush!" Again, it was but a breath of sound. "We must whisper. I think there is a guard outside the house, probably immediately under the window."

"How did you find me? Are you hurt? Do you have a plan to escape?"

"I must teach you how to whisper sometime, Amy. You never did know how. You always got us caught." Impossibly there was laughter in his voice, the sound of Gideon having a wonderful time in the midst of a scrape that threatened to land them both in the briars. She hadn't heard that precise sound for a good many years.

"Never mind whispering," she said. "Just be glad I've learned not to squeal!" She hoped she sounded brave, because she could feel herself shaking with a mixture of emotion and cold.

A low groan was her only response. Terrified, she reached out to him. "Oh, God, you are hurt. Where, Gideon?"

She touched him and sighed. He was warm and breathing regularly, thank heaven. Her fingers began a frantic search to see if she could detect where he had been wounded. Another groan. She felt her heart lurch into her throat. She could see his face, but not clearly. She ran her fingers over his beloved features, tears overflowing her eyes when she realized that there was no wound there. She smoothed his hair, murmuring his name, and felt a warm stickiness when she took her hand away. "Oh, no. Gideon. A head wound." Without stopping to think about it, she tore the ruffle from her petticoat and wiped his head. "They bleed a great deal, but I seem to remember your telling me that they weren't necessarily serious. Please, Gideon, don't be hurt badly. Please don't."

She hardly knew what she was saying. He was here because of her, and he was wounded. They were alone in the dark, facing God alone knew what and he was hurt.

"I'll try not to be, my lady. I would not want to inconvenience you." There was still a note of humor in his voice.

Hope sprang alive again at the sound. "You cannot be badly hurt if you can still joke."

"The merest scratch. Once again, I have to give thanks for a hard head. I'll hold that scrap of cloth here while you tear more of it for a bandage. What are you tearing up?"

"My petticoat, of course." Amy bit off the end of her ruffle. She was trying hard not to cry. She handed him the ruffle and sat back on the floor. "How do you feel, Gideon?"

"Angry at being caught flat-footed by that rat from Seven Dials." He wound the second ruffle around his head to keep the pad in place. "A hit on the head with something like a cudgel, I imagine. No worse than taking a fall from a horse, and I've done that a hundred times." He took her hands. "We'll come about, Amy. We are going to get ourselves out of this fix."

We. She liked the sound of that.

"I came as soon as we made sure that Eustace was still in London and had not taken you to Scotland. If I had not been so eager to find you, I would have scouted around here more carefully and not let myself be taken. But at least now I am here, and together we'll find a way out."

Now he was here. Amelia yearned to put her arms around him and hold him, simply hold him. As if by placing her body next to his, she could absorb some of his courage and give him some of her strength. Together they would escape, she was sure of it. As long as he was with her, Amelia felt warm and safe and indomitable. She laced her fingers with his as they had done when they were children and sat down next to him on the cold stone floor.

"Gideon." *My friend, my love, my life.*

"Did they send the Doncaster carriage? How did they get you here?" His words pulled her back to the practical, and she took a deep breath.

"The carriage must have been waiting for me. The man—he calls himself Mr. B.—forced me into the carriage and poured something down my throat. It may have been laudanum. When I woke up, I was here."

"He did not—you were not—" The grip on her hands suddenly became so hard it was painful.

"No, Gideon." She knew what he meant. "He must have been the one who removed my dress and my shoes, but I think it was just to keep me prisoner more easily."

He ran his hands up her arms. "My God, he took your clothes and you are freezing. And I hadn't noticed. What a dolt you must think me."

He chafed her skin, and his palms reminded her of how chilly she was. He released her for a moment, and then she felt the heavenly warmth of his coat as he placed it around her shoulders. She was enveloped in the smell of him and the heat his body had generated. For a moment she felt safe and almost happy.

"Thank you," she said.

"Oh, Amy, I have done nothing thus far but get hit on the head and make you tear up your petticoat. As a rescuer, I leave much to be desired."

Not as far as Amelia was concerned. "You are here, and I am safer than I was when I faced that man alone."

He pulled her into his arms. "You are sure that nothing happened when you were drugged?"

"Yes, Gideon. I am sure."

She heard his sigh and felt his grip on her waist loosen, though he still held her firmly within the circle of his arms.

"Then, perhaps I will let him live." To her shock, he sounded perfectly serious. For a moment he leaned toward her and rested his forehead against hers. She could sense the way he allowed the tension to seep slowly out of his body. He released her, and Amelia felt bereft until he spoke again.

"If anything had happened to you—" She heard a long, shuddering breath.

"Where are we, Gideon, do you know? It is so dark I can hardly see you, much less anything else. I couldn't feel anything I recognized when I walked about the room."

"We're in the old dower house. In the pantry, I think."

Amy thought for a moment. "Of course. That's why the windows are so high in the wall. It is downstairs by the kitchen. What have they done? Boarded them over? Then, they must have planned to bring me here. But why? Surely they cannot think that I would marry Eustace after they did this!"

"They hoped that you would be so thoroughly compromised that you would have to marry him." Gideon's anger was clear in his words.

But Amy only laughed. "They'll catch cold at that now, will they not? It is you who have spent the day with me alone in a dark room. And me scarcely half dressed. I am very much afraid you will have to marry me, Captain Falconer, when we free ourselves from this coil."

"That is not something to joke about, Amy." His voice had returned to the serious, commanding note that she had so disliked in his recent conversations with her. It was the sound of the stiff martinet who always played by Society's rules. That was not Gideon. In the past few minutes she had rediscovered her old friend, but now he had vanished again. The minute marriage came into the discussion, Gideon became as starchy as Mrs. Drummond Burrell.

Amy was not going to put up with it. "Very well. Allow me to be forced to marry Eustace if you feel so strongly that only a title will do for my husband, no matter who carries it." She strove not to cry. It was anger that made the tears spring to her eyes, she told herself. Rage at his perfect masculine incomprehension.

"I do not think now is the time to discuss your matrimonial prospects, Amy."

"Oh, go to the devil! I don't have any matrimonial prospects. The only prospect I want is too thickheaded and stupid to understand the first thing about—matrimony!" Horrified, she heard her voice crack. They stood in potentially deadly peril, and she was picking a quarrel over her hypothetical marriage! Jane would apostrophize her as a weak-minded woman.

"Enough, brat."

And Gideon thought her a child. She drew away from him and felt him struggle to rise to his feet.

He managed to do so, but Amelia could feel him stagger. She rose quickly. Enough of this foolishness. She meant every word, but there would be time to deal with Gideon's feelings and her own after they had escaped. She reached out for him, seeking to reassure him with a helping hand. When her hand touched his warm solid back, she patted him gently, then put her arm around him and said, "Let us find the windows. You are tall enough to feel them."

"Yes. Right. Excellent idea." He sounded relieved by her retreat from emotion. She knew he could deal with action, which was the essence of his profession.

Holding hands, they made their way carefully across the room until his knee struck the iron cot and he staggered. She took his weight for a moment, then staggered herself and landed on the thin mattress with Gideon falling on top of her.

The breath had been knocked out of her, and for a moment

Amelia thought she might faint. Then the feel of Gideon's body stretched out fully on top of hers began to seep into her very marrow, and she reacted by clasping him in her arms and pressing him close to her.

His breath was warm on her cheek. Instinctively Amelia turned into that warmth, and her lips met his in a kiss that at first was as light and innocent as a butterfly's wing. Then she angled her mouth against his as if she had been doing it for years. No, she had only *wanted* to do it for years. Their mouths fit perfectly together. Gideon's arms went around her like steel bands, and his mouth opened over hers in a kiss so deep and demanding that Amelia could feel herself spinning out of control. But it didn't matter. She was with Gideon. Gideon, who had come to save her.

At that moment the door opened, letting in a shaft of light that seemed so bright as to be blinding, though it was actually only the pale reflection of mid-afternoon winter's light. Amelia froze.

"Well, well, wot 'ave we 'ere?" The false joviality of Mr. B.'s voice raised goose bumps on Amelia's flesh. "A little slap and tickle, is it, guv? Not a nice way to treat 'er ladyship wot's engaged to another bloke."

In a flash of movement, Gideon rolled off her and stood. "And who might you be?" he asked. He sounded as haughty as any nobleman in the kingdom.

Amelia sat up slowly, still dazed but trying to think of some way to turn this to their advantage. She could see the large pistol in the blackguard's hand. She looked at Gideon. "It is the man who kidnapped me," she said.

"Ah, yes, Eustace's mysterious friend." Gideon sounded positively happy to face the enemy. "And he has a very large pistol, which he no doubt used to knock me out before he dragged me here."

Amelia got to her feet and moved toward Gideon, but he waved her away. "Did you ever see anyone else with him, Amelia, or was he always alone?" His eyes still held the light of battle and triumph.

"Alone," Amelia said, her voice amazingly calm. "I have never seen anyone else with him."

" 'Ere, 'ere," the man said, clearly angry at being ignored. " 'Oo's the one wit' the gun, I ask you? It ain't Mr. Bleedin' 'Ussar 'ere. It's Josiah Bleedin' Blakeley wot 'as the gun!"

Before Amelia could do more than gasp at the man's lapse in admitting his identity, Gideon was shoving her down to the floor. He whirled around and dove toward Blakeley. There was a roar like a thousand Guy Fawkes fireworks in her ear, the thud of something heavy falling, and then silence.

"I told yer," Blakeley's voice said, "it was me wot 'ad the gun."

"You—you devil!" Amelia raced across the room and threw herself on Blakeley. "You've killed him!" She raked her fingernails across the astonished Blakeley's face. Before she could do more damage, he flung her off him and retreated out the door, which he slid shut and locked.

"You little 'ellcat, we'll see wot 'appens to you when 'Is bleedin' Grace gets 'ere!" Blakeley yelled from the other side.

"Coward!" Amelia raised herself to her knees and yelled back, her heart pounding in a mixture of fury and terror. What had happened to Gideon? Her heart hammered, and she screamed through the door, "If you have killed him, I will kill you!"

Arms reached around her, and she fell back against his chest. "Oh, my God, Gideon, are you all right? Did he hit you?"

"No, he is almost as bad a shot as you are." His arms tightened around her, and his breath tickled her ear as he whispered, "My fierce warrior comrade. Did you ever think in the old days that we might face an enemy as dangerous as old Josiah? When we pretended to be Cavaliers and Roundheads?" His chuckle warmed her almost as much as the pressure of his arms and the warm strength of his body against hers.

"You are sure you are all right?" She turned in his arms and ran her hands down his arms and chest. "I was so afraid he'd killed you."

"Gypsies have more lives than cats, Amy, you know that."

He stroked her hair, and she closed her eyes, basking in the sheer pleasure of his touch for a brief, fugitive moment.

"I only wish you wouldn't risk as many of yours as you seem determined to do." She breathed deeply of his scent: soap and leather and, now, clean masculine sweat. It was intoxicating.

She felt a touch, light as thistledown, on her hair and knew that it was Gideon's kiss, secret and unacknowledged.

She could only breathe his name, before he resolutely took her arms and set her at a safe distance from him. "We had better start looking for those windows," he said.

"Right-o, Captain." Absurdly she was still happy. More than anything else he had ever done, that quiet kiss told her that Gideon loved her. No matter how stiff and formal he acted, no matter how much he might deny it or try to marry her off to someone else, he loved her. With that knowledge she could face anything, because she would never give him up now. Whether he knew it or not and no matter how he might fight against it, Gideon Falconer was going to be hers.

"Do not be cheeky to your superior officer." Gideon grinned at her. "A little respect, if you please, Corporal."

She raised her eyebrows. "Corporal? I thought I was promoted to sergeant when I was twelve."

"Right you are, Sergeant, I forgot. Let's see about the windows."

They rose and made their way to the wall, where the lighter gray of the windows gleamed. Gideon raised himself to his full six feet and stretched his hand.

"Here we are." His fingers barely grazed the lower end of the frame. "Damn. I think we will have to drag the bed over here so I can stand on it and get a good look. Can you help?"

"Of course I can!" Amelia was insulted. "I have never yet cried craven, have I?"

It took some minutes to push the bed across the floor to the wall. But when Gideon finally stood on it, he could reach the window.

"Damn! They've boarded it over on the outside." He tugged at the frame, but it was solid. "We could break the glass, but broken glass would be dangerous in the dark and we still would have no tool to pry the boards off."

He sat down on the cot, and Amelia joined him. For a moment they thought in silence. Then Gideon snapped his fingers and turned to Amelia with a grin.

"Of course! It is an iron bed, is it not?"

"Yes." Amelia looked at him doubtfully.

"And thus these long bars that form the rectangle from which the bed frame is woven are made of iron."

He looked at her as if he expected an intelligent answer, but all Amelia could think of to say was "Yes."

"So if we took the bed apart, we would have several long pieces of iron, pieces that could be used to—"

"Pry the wooden shutters off the windows!" Amelia finished triumphantly. "Gideon, you are a genius!"

"Not really a *genius*," he said with mock humility. "Just very, very intelligent." He gave her another of those joyous grins, his teeth gleaming white in the gloom.

Amelia found herself grinning back, as if she were simply sharing another adventure with her best friend. "Well, Captain Intelligent, sir, we had better see if we can take this contraption apart in the dark before Mr. Blakeley returns."

She rolled back the sleeves of Gideon's coat while he stripped the cot of its mattress and turned it on its side. "The legs are bolted in. I don't see how we can take them off without tools. But the bottom webbing is simply tied on. And"—he shook the long side of the bed and bent close to it—"I think this side is in two parts and may come apart if we pull it. Shall we try?"

"Of course. Wait until I take off my stockings so that my feet will not slip." It was the work of a moment to remove the stockings. She looked over at Gideon as he stood opposite her at the foot of the bedstead. He flashed an appreciative grin at her. He might not admit it in well-lit parlors or crowded ballrooms, but here alone in the dark and in peril, Gideon revealed his feelings for her and Amelia rejoiced. With a deep breath she braced her back against the wall, set her feet as well as she could on the smooth floor, and prepared to pull with all her strength.

"Now," Gideon ordered, and Amelia pulled.

She felt herself being slowly dragged away from the wall by the force of his muscles. Just as she was about to begin to slide, she heard Gideon grunt and the bed went slack in her hands.

"We did it, angel, we did it!" In his excitement she was sure he did not realize what he had called her.

She was wrong. He knew perfectly well, he just could not prevent the name from coming out of his mouth. Somehow in the dark and danger, his carefully controlled feelings for Amy had burst their bounds, and he couldn't round them up and put them back in their stable. He was not even sure if he wanted to.

Angel. He had called her that in his thoughts ever since the day he had first seen her, leaning over him as he lay half unconscious with cold and hunger. Her blond curls had been a sunlit halo about her face, but it was the compassion in those deep blue eyes that had made him think of a heavenly being. But only occasionally had he slipped and allowed himself to give voice to that name.

These past few hours—with their frantic combination of danger, passion, and laughter—had stripped him of his drawing room manners and turned his head into a volatile mixture of love, courage, and recklessness. He shook his head as if to clear it.

To business. He waved the long iron slat with the bedstead still attached in triumph. "With this we should be able to pry those shutters off once we break the window," he said.

Ordering Amy to stand out of the way, he broke the window with one sharp blow and then began to pry open the wooden shutters. The length of the slat gave him purchase, and his own muscles supplied the rest of the strength needed. With a creak and a loud groan, the first slat of the shutter splintered and gave way, letting in a thin stream of light. With the added leverage the opening gave him, Gideon made short work of two more of the shutters.

Excited by this partial victory, he used the iron bed slat to feel around the ground outside the window. Suddenly he felt the end of his pole being grasped and held. He jerked on it to free it, but whoever had the other end held on.

"Master Gideon," a familiar voice said. "Is Lady Amelia there with you?"

"Sidley?" Gideon responded. "Is that you?"

Hugh Sidley, the longtime bailiff of the Abbey and a friend to both Amelia and Gideon, stuck his face in at the newly freed window.

"Aye, 'tis me, Master Gideon. We've been that worried about the two of ye. Give me half a tick, and we'll have you free of those devils!"

At that moment Gideon heard the rattle of keys from just outside the door to the pantry. Damn! That cockroach Blakeley was going to discover them before he had a chance to work out any plan at all with Sidley.

"Shove those slats back in place, and then get away from the window, Sidley. If they catch you, they may do you harm. You and the others just keep watch to see where we are. Blakeley will probably move us if he sees what we've done, but if not, he may let us remain. We will work out a plan of escape later."

"Aye, Master Gideon." And Sidley was gone.

Gideon grabbed Amelia's hand, and together they stood facing the door, waiting for what would come.

Chapter Ten

In London, Jane spent an anxious day trying to keep busy while awaiting some news of Eustace. A number of her former students and their male relatives fanned out across the city as others, now employed in households of the ton, listened for news of the Duke of Doncaster's movements.

Unfortunately, Eustace had few friends and went nowhere that day. There was nothing to report to Sir Richard. Which, Jane thought angrily, was just as well because she had heard nothing from him all day.

Jane was happy to have classes to teach and household duties to see to during the interminable afternoon. At last, as she was sitting down for a cup of tea, Molly came into the parlor, her small face alive with excitement. "Miss Jane, ma'am, Tim's here and he seen something. Come on, Tim, tell 'er what you told me!" She pulled a tall, scrawny youth with the same bright black eyes as his sister into the room.

"Tell 'er," Molly said again, pushing him forward.

Tim twisted his cap in an agony of self-consciousness. He bobbed his head at Jane.

"Yes, Tim, tell me," Jane said with a kind smile that reduced the young man to even more speechless agony. "I need to have your information in order to help Miss Amelia."

At that, Tim managed to speak. "He left. The duke. He took a curricle, and he left the house in a pelter."

"When?"

"Pr'aps an hour ago. I came as soon as he left, but I had to walk. He left in a tearing hurry. Sprung the horses, he did. He had a bag with him, but he didn't take no groom."

"Did you see anything else, Tim? Did anyone bid him good-bye?"

"Yes'm. The old lady, she came out and hung on him. She were trying to stop him, it looked like. Might've been crying."

Jane thought for a few moments. She glanced at the clock over the mantel and frowned. There was no help for it. She could not do the job by herself. She would have to seek our Sir Richard. For a moment she contemplated sending Tim, but soon realized that the boy would have no idea where to go or how to gain entrance to any of the many haunts where Sir Richard might be found.

She smiled at her two allies. "You've both done very well, and I am proud of you. Molly, why don't you take Tim to the pantry and see if you can find some of the gingersnaps we made this morning? You both deserve a treat for a job well-done." Jane picked up the tea tray and handed it to the little girl. "And you may take this out as well."

With visible reluctance, Molly and Tim left the room. Once the door was shut behind them, Jane hurriedly left instructions with one of her student assistants and set out to find her quarry. She decided to try the Horse Guards first. By the time she had been leered at by at least a dozen half-pay officers and told to go elsewhere by another dozen busy officials who did not have time to keep track of Colonel Sinclair, she had wasted almost an hour.

Realizing that by now he would probably be at home preparing to go out for the evening, she decided to seek him at his lodgings. Of course, she knew he would regard her doing so as scandalous, but if she was lucky, no one would see her. Besides, she had a feeling that he would hear a great deal about the Amazon who had been searching army headquarters for him.

Gideon had once mentioned the colonel's address, and Jane obtained a hackney and gave him the location with what she thought was great aplomb. Any possible damage to her reputation did not greatly concern her, but what Sir Richard himself might say to her invasion was another matter. She was rather dreading that.

As it happened, he surprised her. He was at home and alone

when she arrived. His manservant announced her with raised eyebrows and a frosty glare, which made her dread his master's reaction.

But it was very different.

"Miss Forrester, what have you heard? Has Eustace left for the Abbey or have Falconer and Lady Amelia returned?" He strode over to her and took her cloak, then led her to the armchair by the fire and seated her, taking the chair opposite hers.

Jane was thrown off balance. She had expected a fight and instead had met with chivalry and complete unconcern for the conventions. Exasperated, she lashed out.

"I have been chasing you all over London for this past hour and more," she complained. "Meanwhile, Eustace is probably almost to the Abbey. Why weren't you where you were supposed to be?"

Although his eyebrows had arched when she began her speech, by the time she finished, his habitual sardonic smile was in place. "And where was that, Miss Forrester?"

"The Horse Guards, of course."

"Of course. You sought me there?" His lips twitched, but though Jane looked at him suspiciously, he did not smile.

"Yes. I got word that Eustace had left London, and I sought you to see if we could go after them. I do not have a carriage, but I am sure that you do and—"

"I will go." He rose and bowed over her hand. "I will bring them back. Unless Gideon has managed to rescue Amelia, and they are already on their way home."

He smiled encouragingly, but Jane did not return it. She rose to face him and frowned. "You will never learn, will you? If any rescuing has been done, I am sure Amelia participated in it fully. And if you think you are going to leave me here while you have all the fun, you may think again."

She held up a hand to forestall the discussion she knew was coming. "Do not bother to argue with me. Amelia will need the support of a female friend, if anything—untoward—has happened."

She saw refusal writ large on Sir Richard's face, but she knew she had tenacity equal to his. She felt her eyebrows draw together and her mouth turn down. It was the look she wore when someone tried to gainsay her. She regretted that she had to use it with Sir Richard. For a while she had sensed that he liked her and did not regard her unconventional life and outspoken opinions as a bar to friendship. Jane had never had a male friend, and she regretted that the promise of this one was being cut short by her insistence on having her own way.

But she had to help Amelia. Jane had seen women who had been raped and beaten. She could not bear the thought of Amelia in that horrible situation left to the care of servants and men.

Sir Richard surprised her again. "You are right. She might be—hurt. Gideon will do everything in his power, but she ought to have a woman with her. If we drive around to your house, can you be ready to go in half an hour?"

Jane smiled at him with relief and something warmer that he must have seen, because he smiled back at her. "I will pack a small case, pick up my basket of remedies, and then I am ready."

"Admirable woman," he said. "I myself am ready. My saddlebags are always packed. We have only to stop at the stables and get my curricle, and we can be off." Some wayward imp made him add, "It is an open carriage, so no harm should come to your reputation even though we will be traveling alone together and at night."

As he expected, Jane's eyes flashed. "As if I cared for Society's strictures on my conduct!" She turned away in what in a lesser woman would have been a huff. "We could travel all night in a closed carriage for all the difference it would make to me." She did not linger to see the appreciative grin that greeted her outburst.

They were on their way out of town in less than half an hour. The night was cold, but Sir Richard had wrapped her in a fur cloak and tucked a thick carriage robe around her before they left. For the first hour Jane hardly felt the December weather.

They spoke little at first. There seemed to be nothing to say. Speed was of the essence, and Sir Richard's every thought had to be for his team and the condition of the road. Jane allowed herself the luxury of simply sitting. The night was quiet, the stars overhead were brilliant, and the man at her side was skillful and single-minded. Sir Richard's face had the look of frowning concentration that she knew her own often wore.

After the first miles, Sir Richard turned to her, a smile of apology in his eyes. "I am sorry to have been so uncivil, Miss Forrester, but my team was fresh and I am not familiar with this road."

"Pray continue to concentrate on what is important," she replied. "I do not need to be entertained."

"Entertained? My dear Miss Forrester, how can you—"

"Do you know," Jane interrupted, "whenever you call me your dear Miss Forrester, I know you are about to say something truly insipid."

"Insipid!" He was clearly incensed. No one had ever dared to call the dashing Colonel Sir Richard Sinclair insipid. It was a word reserved for particularly boring milk-and-water debutantes whose conversation was limited to monosyllables.

"I meant that you always have some idiotish social stricture to give me on my conduct. And now I collect you are going to tell me that the art of conversation is one that gently bred females must cultivate above all others. Particularly gently bred females with no pretense to beauty or wealth." She had not meant the last words to sound bitter, but he turned to her and she awaited some set-down for her rudeness.

"Who told you that you were not beautiful?"

Jane gave him a sardonic smile. "My mirror."

"No, it is an idea someone put into your head. No one who saw the way gentlemen looked at you the other night when Lady Amelia had you dressed like Christmas beef could possibly think such a thing." His eyes never left the road, and his hands were steady on the ribbons as his two matched bays trotted briskly through the evening. But his attention was on her. "Who told you that?" he repeated.

Jane sat stunned into silence. It had never occurred to her that the dress and the coiffure Amelia had insisted on had done anything more than make her appearance acceptable to Society.

"You refuse to answer, Miss Forrester?"

"You are being willfully obtuse, Sir Richard. Your question does not require an answer." Jane sat up straighter and stared into the night.

"Yet I want one." His voice had deepened, softened yet he still did not look at her.

She took a deep breath, somehow compelled to respond. She almost believed it was a genuine question. "I have always known what my gifts were and what they were not. I manage well. I have managed people and money since I was thirteen years old. When my parents no longer needed me, I decided to teach, to use those talents for good."

"I would never argue that you are not a manager and teacher par excellence," he said. "But that wasn't my question. I want to know why you seem not to know how—well, for lack of a better word, let us say how striking you are."

"My parents were both artists, Sir Richard. I grew up from my earliest years knowing what beauty was. I saw it all around me. I knew I had none."

He shook his head. "I can see that nothing I say will disabuse you of that notion. Have you never felt a desire to have a life that had more warmth, more personal affection in it?"

"Have you?" she challenged, goaded beyond endurance. Who was this odious aristocrat to tell her she was not as plain as she thought and then criticize her choices in life? "Aside from your regiment and your army friends and colleagues, who is there in your life to provide you with—how did you characterize it?—warmth and personal affection?"

"You are angry with me." He did not sound particularly perturbed. "I will tell you. I, too, have no one. It is a trait I share with Gideon Falconer. Oh, I have a family, but it is a singularly unhappy one. And the reason they are unhappy is that I have survived my betters. So I stay away from my home and have done my best for almost twenty years to get myself killed as expeditiously as possible. But fate has decreed that while I have survived an enemy who bent every effort to cut me to ribbons, my older brother and my brother's child have met with untimely deaths in the peaceful English countryside."

As he spoke, the pain and bitterness in his voice grew, and

Jane could see a muscle in his jaw work spasmodically. She reached out and laid her hand on his arm.

"I am sorry. I did not mean to bring up a subject so painful to you."

His smile was more of a grimace. "Nor I you. I did not mean to offend you, Miss Forrester. It surprises me that one with your obvious intelligence and beauty has never even thought of marriage." For a moment he took his eyes off the road and smiled into her eyes.

Again, he had shocked her into truthfulness. "Oh, I spent a good part of my girlhood thinking of very little else. But it was borne in upon me that girls with no fortune other than what their brains could earn for them would do much better to aim at a life of useful service."

"As it was borne in upon me that the less my family saw of me, the happier they would all be."

"Why? What makes an officer in His Majesty's forces such an unworthy heir?" She removed her hand and folded it decorously in her lap.

"I wish you would not take your hand away," he said. To her surprise, Jane found she missed touching him, and she put it back.

"Thank you." His voice warmed for a moment. "To answer your question, it is not that I am unworthy of being the heir of the Marquess of Southbridge. It is that the others were supremely worthy—charming, warm, handsome, able to summon all the qualities necessary for the task of running enormous estates and keeping a large staff and fractious family in line. I have been told that I am conspicuously lacking in all of them. I do not even resemble them. They were dark and handsome, while I am the sandy one without conspicuous qualities of any sort."

Jane smiled. "You could hardly lead men into battle if you were not gifted with qualities of leadership and courage. But I thought you said your brother's little boy died. How could anyone tell if a child was able to command the respect and affection required?"

Sir Richard was silent for so long that Jane thought he was not going to answer her question. Then, at last, he said, "Francis was the apple of everyone's eye. After his death a number of legends grew up around him."

"Legends?" Jane had no idea what he was talking about. "That sounds most unusual."

"He was an unusual child, very bright and courageous and charming. But I think that if he had died of an illness or an accident that people had seen occur, he would not have been so idolized. But he disappeared, you see, and no trace of him was ever found."

"How could that be? He must have had nurses, governesses, a whole host of people to look after him. And he just vanished?"

"So it would seem. It was twenty years ago. I was up at Oxford, so I do not know exactly what occurred. No one saw, it appeared. Francis was outside playing with a group of children, and he went down near the river that runs through our property to chase a ball or some such."

"And?" Jane was growing impatient. He had started telling her this tale. The least he could do was finish it without her having to drag every detail out of his mouth.

"And he vanished. They searched high and low for him, of course, but no trace of him was found. I think everyone assumed he drowned, although the river was not abnormally swift at the time and his body was never found."

"How dreadful. Nothing could be worse than that. The uncertainty must be unbearable." Jane's ready sympathy for those in pain or difficulty of any kind went out to little Francis's mother.

"His mother still refuses to believe he is dead. She is certain that one day he will be returned to her."

Once again, Sir Richard turned to look at Jane, and the bleak expression in his eyes touched her.

"How unbearably sad. You said your brother is dead, too. She must be very unhappy. And you as well. Were you and your brother close, Sir Richard?"

"Do you think it would be possible for you to call me Richard? I have told you more about my life and my family than I have said to anyone for years. I would feel much less foolish about having done so if we were truly friends." Gathering the reins in one hand, he laid the other over hers. "Please, Jane? As a friend?"

"Very well . . . Richard." The word rolled off her tongue as if she had been using it forever.

That Rubicon having been crossed, Jane felt suddenly shy. She had a large number of male acquaintances, men she knew from her work. But she realized suddenly that she had no real men friends. Yet somehow this trip through the frozen night toward some unknown danger had made this difficult, sardonic man her friend.

To Jane friendship was a sacred thing, and she intended to be Richard Sinclair's friend in word and deed. But she knew she did not belong to his world and indeed understood very little about it. She numbered several titled gentlemen among her acquaintance, but she did not know them well. However, what she had seen of them made her certain that friendship with one of them would have been impossible.

She was not certain what set Richard Sinclair apart, but she felt that their view of the world was not so different. They had both seen a great deal of the sordidness of life. And she felt that, like her, he nevertheless did not despair. They shared the fundamentals, and though all the accidents of life—gender, wealth, circumstances—separated them, those fundamentals allowed them to be friends.

"I would be proud to be considered your friend," she said, formally setting the seal on their new relationship.

"Thank you. I share the sentiment." Silence grew between them until at last Richard said, "I think we are within a few miles of Doncaster Abbey. What do you say we spring 'em. I think they still have plenty of heart."

"Whatever you say," Jane agreed, and felt a twinge of regret when he released her hand so that he could take a firm grip on the reins.

Chapter Eleven

Blakeley was not as unobservant as Gideon and Amelia hoped. This time he brought a covered lantern with him. When he entered, he looked at the pair of prisoners standing in the middle of the room and narrowed his eyes.

"Oh, my, wot 'ave our little mice been doin' while the cat's been away?" That awful note of false jocularity scraped at Amelia's nerves, but with Gideon's warm hand in hers, she plucked up her courage and looked their captor in the eye.

"Come on, now, tell old Uncle Jos all about our little plan, wotever it was." He crept closer, careful to keep his back to the wall. The lantern light wavered in the darkness, but Blakeley could see the ruin of the cot.

"Ah, 'ere we are. Your secret's out, my pretties. Better tell me wot you 'ave done with this. Got too excited, did you, Captain? Wore the young lady out, did you?"

Amelia could feel Gideon's hand clench in hers, but he said nothing. Blakeley crept closer to the window. Another step or two, and his boots would crunch on the broken glass.

"He and I are going to be married. We can do whatever we wish," Amelia said, trying to get Blakeley's attention.

"You ain't marryin' with nobody but 'Is Grace." Blakeley had stopped at her words and turned to face her.

"It is a little late to try to save me for my cousin," Amelia said with as much insouciance as she could muster. "I am betrothed to Captain Falconer."

"Now, now. No argufyin'. You're marryin' the duke and turnin' over all that lovely brass from your dear departed papa to 'im. And then 'e's turnin' it over to me." Blakeley grinned and stepped away from the wall, moving toward Gideon and Amelia in the middle of the room. She breathed a sigh. So far they were safe. If she could only keep the odious man talking, maybe Gideon could think of something they could do to escape.

"You cannot force me to marry him. Especially not now that I am—unchaste." Amelia lowered her eyes, trying to look as if she were crying.

"My darling," Gideon said, squeezing her hand tightly, "you cannot convince this ruffian of anything. But I am sure that the duke will understand that our love cannot be denied. He will let you go."

Blakeley stared at the two of them, then slowly began to applaud. "Better than a play, you two are. But you can forget all about it 'acos I don't care nothin' about true love. And neither does 'Is Grace."

He moved a little toward the cot and stared down at it. Seizing the moment, Gideon dropped Amelia's hand and moved like lightning toward Blakeley. He had almost reached the other man when Blakeley's head and hand came up in the same instant.

"Step back, Captain Bleedin' Falconer." The gun gleamed in the flickering lamplight.

Gideon looked at it, at Blakeley, calculated his chances, and retreated to where Amelia stood, silent and fearful.

"Good," said Blakeley. "Now what 'ave you two been up to? This 'ere cot don't look like it's been used for sport—"

Before he could finish the thought, his foot crunched on the broken glass from the window above the cot. "Ah," he said, looking up for a brief moment before he turned once again to Gideon. "So we've broken the window, 'ave we?" Again, that jocular tone. Amelia shivered, and Gideon drew her to his side for a moment before letting her go. She felt bereft of warmth and comfort, but knew that he needed to keep his hands free should the chance come to take Blakeley.

"Well, well," Blakeley went on, "I am afraid that we're goin' to have to tie you up so's you don't go getting into any more mischief before 'Is Grace arrives."

He gave a sharp whistle, and after a moment Sidley shuffled in the door. It was a very different Sidley from the one Amelia once knew. This Sidley hung his head and refused to look either Gideon or her in the eye. He nodded to Blakeley when told to fetch rope and tie the two prisoners up. Then he sidled out the door again.

Amelia was too shocked to speak. What had happened to the bluff, hearty man who had given her pony rides and shown her where the new litters of barn cats were to be found? This sneaky, hangdog man was not Sidley. She glanced at Gideon, but his face evidenced none of the shock she felt. For some reason, that made her feel better. Whatever was wrong, Gideon thought he could handle it.

She tried to think of some way to ask Gideon what they could do without being overheard by Blakeley, but she could think of nothing. Sidley returned and managed to tie her up without once looking at her. He finished with Gideon, and then as he turned to leave, he gave them both one long look and Amelia's heart raced with sudden hope.

The Hugh Sidley who had looked into her eyes was her old friend, not the cringing lackey who had entered the room. If he could help them he would, she was sure. Flexing her wrists, Amelia found that though the bonds looked tight, they gave her room to move her hands and arms. Perhaps enough room to escape.

She didn't dare look at Gideon, but she knew he had seen what she had and probably understood it even better than she did. If the ropes binding him were loose as well, perhaps it would be a simple matter to free themselves.

It was not simple. Sidley tried to make the job look good, but Blakeley came to inspect it and tightened the ropes around Gideon's wrists. The minute Blakeley and Sidley left the room, they began to work to free themselves. It seemed to Amelia that she had a little room to move within the bonds.

"Move around until we're sitting back-to-back," Gideon instructed her. "Then we can try to untie each other."

Amelia complied, and for a time neither spoke as they tried

and failed, then tried again to get a fingertip around one of the rope strands. Finally she could stand the silent effort no longer.

"Talk to me, Gideon," she demanded. "I cannot bear this silence any longer. Just talk to me."

"What would you like me to talk about, Amy?" he said, a smile in his voice.

"Tell me . . . tell me . . ." She thought for a while. "Tell me what you remember about your childhood."

"I do not want to think about that. I have told you as much as I want to remember about that time." He was angry. He hated to talk about the past.

Amelia was well aware of his aversion, but this time she didn't care. She wanted to know. "Not about the sweep and the fighting," she agreed. "Tell me what you can remember about the time before."

"Before?" His voice was tentative, quiet.

"Yes. Before. Tell me about your life before."

He was quiet for a long time, though his fingers kept busy trying to pick her bonds loose. Then at last he said, "I can't remember much. And what I do recall seems like a dream, something I made up to try to forget about the cold and the rats."

Amelia's hands clenched instinctively. She hated his life on the streets and as a climbing boy. She had always hated it, but she had made Gideon tell her about it years ago. She had to know because, loving him as she did, it was essential that she understand him. His life on the streets was a large part of what had made him the person she loved. Even as a child, she had known that.

"Some of it must be real, otherwise how could you have known to dream it?"

He gave a short, dry chuckle. "I suppose that makes sense, in an upside-down sort of way."

Amelia flexed her wrists. Were her bonds beginning to loosen or was that her imagination? "Of course it makes sense. I always make sense."

"Well, then, I will try." He sighed. "I remember being warm, first of all, and full of food. I've always thought I made that up, just so I could think about it and pretend it was true. And laughter and a pony—that part may be true. Gypsy children often have ponies, and there is laughter at a gypsy camp.

"And I remember a house. At least, I think it was a house, not a caravan or a camp."

Amelia could feel her wrists, raw and painful. "What kind of a house?" she asked to distract herself and Gideon.

"Big. Huge, in fact. With a double staircase in the hall that seemed to go up and up forever. But I was just a child. Anything would look huge to me. And to a gypsy, any house would be impressive." He dismissed his memories as unimportant. "How are your wrists? Can you move them? Slip them free?"

"Not yet, but they are looser. Just a bit more, I am sure." Amelia could feel the cold through her bare feet and legs. She tried to keep her hands from shaking so she could continue to work to free Gideon. "I want to hear more about what you remember. Do you have any images of people at all?"

"A woman," he replied, his voice sounding strained. "She has dark hair, and she—sings to me." He cleared his throat. "In my dreams I can sometimes remember the song. It was a lullaby, I think." After a pause he added, "It makes me very sad to think of her. I don't know who she was. My mother, perhaps. After all, she had dark hair, and I remember a feeling of something like safety."

"I wonder what the song was," Amelia mused, trying to think of all the lullabies she knew. There weren't many. Her mother had died at her birth. Amelia herself taught the older children and had never had much occasion to sing children to sleep. That brought an unexpected pang to her heart as she realized that she wanted very much to sing her own children to sleep. Hers and Gideon's.

That thought made her heart ache with a vengeance. Gideon refused to see what to her was so simple. They belonged together, were meant to be together forever. And his stubborn insistence on some incredibly stupid idea of class differences was going to keep them apart forever instead.

To her surprise, he went on with his memories without her prompting. "The clearest thing I remember is water, running water. Some sort of stream, only larger. A river, perhaps. The sound and the feel of cool water. And then it changed, and it was no longer cheerful. It was frightening, and I felt as if I were drowning."

He shrugged. "It was only a dream. It used to come often in the gypsy camp, but once I was in London, I started to dream of the woman and warmth and food."

"I wonder if it means more than that. Perhaps these are memories of people you knew, things that happened. Perhaps you lived in that house with the double staircase."

"I cannot imagine what difference it makes, Amy. We are here. There is no water, no warmth, no food. Whether my dreams were true or not really does not make the slightest difference in my life. It never has. Now, try to get a bit closer to me. It will make it easier to untie the rope."

She did as he asked, but suddenly as she sat in the dark, at the mercy of a man with a gun and her unspeakable cousin, Amelia felt as overwhelmed with hopelessness as Gideon said he had felt swamped by water in his dream.

"We could die here, Gideon," she said, her fingers falling still. "We could die with you still insisting that we can't be together."

"Amy, don't—" His voice was anguished and tired.

"I can't help it, Gideon. I love you, and I know you love me."

"Of course I love you, Amy. I always have. You saved my life and have always treated me like a broth—"

She could not bear to listen to him try to turn the conversation. "I do not love you like that." Her voice was high and quivered with strain. "I never needed a brother, and I never wanted one. I have treated you like a friend, because you are and always have been my best friend. And I want to treat you like a lover, because I have desired you that way as well." Amelia tried to stop her voice from shaking. This kind of honesty was hard even at a moment like this. She began picking at the knots around Gideon's hands once again, trying to keep her mind off the terrifying fact of her love and the nearness of death.

"Amy, Amy." She felt Gideon's fingers at her wrists. "You are hurt. The rope has rubbed you raw." He worked on the bonds a few more moments, and then the rope fell away.

Amelia felt the unutterable relief of being able to move her arms and hands. They had almost gone to sleep, kept alive only by her own activity on his behalf. She turned around and quickly untied the knots holding Gideon captive.

"Gideon, Sidley may have turned against us. We cannot count on Sir Richard coming after us in time. After all, he does not know who our captor is. He may think we can easily escape from Eustace and anyone he might use." She swallowed hard and moved closer to him so she could look into his dark, stormy eyes. "I love you." A sob tore at her throat. "I wanted you to know that. Just in case. You are the only man I will ever love, whether Blakeley kills us today or I live a hundred years."

Gideon remained silent, though his throat worked as he swallowed hard. He reached out and took hold of her shoulders. Then, never letting her gaze escape his, he pulled her closer. "And I love you. That has never been in question. I have always loved you and always will."

"If you tell me you care for me as a sister—" Amy's voice broke.

"No, angel, not as a sister." He bent and kissed her forehead, and Amy could feel the smile on his lips. "I love you as the sun in my sky, the smile in my heart, the other half of myself."

Amy sighed and put her arms around Gideon's waist. He felt warm and solid and indestructible. But no one was that, not even Gideon. She decided to take one further chance.

"Gideon, will you marry me?"

"Amy, any man in the world would be lucky to be your husband. I am only—"

"Gideon, we may die soon. I do not know what Eustace will do when I refuse to marry him. He may kill either of us. Both of us. Just tell me that if we get out of here with a whole skin, you will admit you love me before God and man and—"

"Of course I love you." He buried his face in her hair. "I'd walk through fire for you. And I will marry you. I want nothing more, if only I thought—" His voice broke, but he cleared his throat and added, "I will not hold you to it if you change your mind when we are out of here. And we are going to get out of here, never doubt it."

He sounded so positive, she had to believe him. "I will never change my mind. Remember your promise."

He grinned at her. "We are wasting time, angel. Help me take the shutters off that window again. If Sidley does not come, you may be able to crawl through and go for help."

They moved over to the wall a little faster this time. The bulk of the ruined cot stood out and marked the way. It was the work of a few minutes for Gideon to break the shutters free again and let in the pale late afternoon light. He swept the iron side of the cot around the window to clear it of glass, and stood on the end of the cot to look out.

"There is nobody here. The yard is deserted. I think you are going to have to go for help, Amy. I'll boost you through the window."

"But—I don't have my dress!" Amelia said, then could have bitten her tongue. At a time like this, how could she sound so missish?

"True. Though I think the loss of your shoes is going to cause you more difficulty." He grinned at her. "You look very fetching. In fact, I begin to think that the less you are wearing, the more fetching you look." He sobered and stroked her cheek. "You have my jacket, and my overcoat is in my saddlebag. Once you are on Jupiter, you can ride to the village and get help." He held her close, and once again, Amelia felt for a magic moment that she could do anything.

"If you see Sidley," Gideon added, "and he seems disposed to help, send him to me here. We'll find a way to at least provide a diversion if we can't overcome Blakeley by ourselves."

"Very well. I am ready. The sooner I go, the sooner I'll be back," she said resolutely. "Tell me where you left Jupiter. I don't want to have to go all the way to the stables if I don't have to."

"Right. I hid him in the copse, by the old smith's forge."

Amelia knew the exact spot. It was very near but out of the way, so few people thought of it. She and Gideon had played around the deserted forge often as children.

"If Blakeley hasn't found him, I should be out of here in

a few minutes." She hoped she sounded more certain than she felt.

"Up you go, then." Gideon lifted her as easily as if she had been made of thistledown.

She began to wiggle out of the window when she heard the door below her open and Eustace shout, "She's getting away, Blakeley, you fool. Stop her!" Amelia paused, but Gideon gave her a violent shove that sent her skidding headfirst on the ground just under the window. There had been no drop and Amelia wasn't hurt, just momentarily winded. She paused to listen for a moment to what was happening to Gideon in the pantry with Eustace.

"Come back here, Amelia, you little bitch!" she heard Eustace shout from just below. Shocked back to reality, Amelia took off as fast as she could run toward the aspen copse and the old forge, praying that Jupiter was still waiting patiently there for Gideon.

Chapter Twelve

"Heroic to the last, eh, Captain?" Eustace spoke in the same high-pitched, affected voice he always used. But Gideon could see that his eyes were all but rolling in his head, like those of a frightened horse, and a tiny trickle of spittle clung to the corner of his mouth.

Eustace Mannering, Duke of Doncaster, was very near the breaking point. For the first time since he had known him, Gideon felt a jolt of alarm. There was nothing more frightening to a military man than a loose cannon, and that was what Eustace resembled at the moment.

Gideon glanced at the doorway behind the duke. Blakeley lounged there, his gun silhouetted against the bright lantern light. Blakeley might be dangerous, but he wasn't mad. The more he looked at Eustace, the more Gideon thought the duke might well be close to losing his reason.

"Mannering." Gideon stood his ground as Eustace approached. "What brings you here? You're a bit early for Christmas. But greetings of the season in any case." He grinned at his adversary. "Your guest accommodations leave something to be desired, but I am sure that you'll see to that before your next house party."

"Pity you will not be on my guest list," Eustace purred as he advanced on Gideon. "Blakeley, you had better go after my cousin, had you not?"

"The old man, Sidley is it? 'E's gone after 'er." Blakeley didn't move an inch.

Pray God he had read the look Sidley gave him rightly and Sidley had not turned against them, Gideon thought. *Keep*

Amelia safe, he prayed, a little surprised that he still could. There were no atheists in battle, he had heard said many times. And this was a battle. One he had to win. *Please keep her safe,* he amended. *Please.*

"I may have to marry the little bitch, but I see no reason to keep you alive," Eustace said, his drawl more pronounced than ever and the faint tremor that had been only in his hands now affecting his entire body. "Do you, Blakeley?"

The moneylender looked at his debtor as if he, too, could see the signs of imminent moral and physical collapse. " 'Ere now," he said, "let's not be talkin' of killin' till we got to." He spoke in the calm and reasonable tone one might use to address a child.

"But we do got to," Eustace said, wiping his forehead. "Have to, I mean. We do have to. I cannot let the good captain live after this."

"And why might that be?" Blakeley's voice was as pleasant as ever.

"Because he will tell everyone. And then I will not be accepted. He can do that." Eustace spoke earnestly, genuinely trying to make Blakeley understand. Gideon felt his blood congeal.

"He truly can," Eustace continued. "Even though he is only a bastard gypsy brat, he can break me. He has a reputation, you see, for truthfulness and honor."

"You exaggerate, Doncaster," Gideon said, carefully giving Eustace his title. "You are a duke. You can go wherever you want. I have no influence with the ton."

Stubbornly Eustace shook his head. "Yes, you do. So I will have to shoot you." He raised his pistol. It shook violently, but Gideon knew that did not necessarily mean it would not do a perfectly adequate job of killing him.

"Now, now, Yer Grace." Blakeley straightened and went to stand directly behind Eustace. "We'll 'ave none o' that." As calmly as a mother taking a dangerous toy from a child, he plucked the gun from the duke's shaking hand.

Gideon found himself letting out a breath he didn't know he had been holding. Quietly he began to ease himself farther back into the room, where the shadows might hide him should either

Blakeley or Eustace decide that killing him would be a good idea after all.

"Stand where you are, Cap'n," Blakeley said, his voice not at all soothing.

Gideon froze. He wanted to keep these men talking as long as he could to give Amelia the greatest chance to escape. Pray God she had found Jupiter and was on her way to the village for help. She should have no difficulty there. Everyone had known her from babyhood. Now all he had to do was stay alive himself. The odds seemed a little better now that Eustace was unarmed but—

"What would 'appen if the lady were to die sudden like?" Blakeley asked, breaking the silence

"What?" Eustace looked around him blindly, as if he had just been awakened. "What do you mean?"

" 'Oo would get 'er money, that's wot I mean, Yer Grace." Blakeley all but called him stupid.

"I don't know," Eustace said. "What difference does it make? As soon as she marries me, it is mine. That is the law," he added with great satisfaction.

"But if she was to die now, afore she marries, 'oo gets the blunt?"

Eustace might not see the point, but Gideon knew instantly what Blakeley was driving at. And he was right! Amelia had not made a will. Everything would pass by operation of law to her nearest relative: Eustace Mannering, the Duke of Doncaster.

"She has left it to her friend, Miss Forrester, for her school," Gideon said quickly.

Not quite quickly enough. " 'As she now?" Blakeley studied his captive pensively. " 'As she indeed? It seems like the sort o' thing a young lady might not think of—makin' a will. Could be she left off doing it until some later time. Could be our friend the duke 'ere will take it all without 'aving to marry her. 'Im bein' 'er cousin and all."

"Miss Forrester's school is very important to Amelia. She made the will shortly after her father's death." Gideon tried to sound convincing. "Amelia is not the sort of girl to forget a thing like a will. Why, she used to do her lessons every day even when her governess was sick. Her father said she was the most responsible girl in the world."

He was talking too much. He was so afraid that this casually evil man would kill Amelia that he could not stop talking, trying to prevent it. He was acting as he had seen men do before a battle they were anticipating with too much desire to win. He was afraid that Amelia would die because he would be unable to protect her. This was what he had always dreaded, that his chance to repay Amelia for saving his life would finally come and for some reason he would fail her.

Blakeley's eyes were flat as stones as they studied him. "I think you're lyin'."

"Are you willing to chance it?" Gideon said. "Once she is dead, there is no going back. Married, the money is her husband's. Dead before that, it may all go to Miss Forrester's school."

"He's right, damn him," Eustace said. "I will have to marry the boring little prig." He sighed, and for an instant Gideon welcomed the idea of Eustace's marrying Amelia. Anything to keep Blakeley from trying to murder her.

But Blakeley had suddenly changed the subject. "Where is Sidley? 'E should 'ave 'ad 'er back 'ere by now. If we're going to marry, we'd best be smart about it." He glared at Eustace. "The man works for you. Go find 'im and find 'er, too, while yer at it."

Eustace opened his mouth to protest, but one look from Blakeley and he shut it again and went out.

Amelia's feet and legs were numb with cold. She ran as far as she could, hoping to find the horse before the frozen ground gave her frostbite and she fell. It took longer than she planned, but she had no mishaps and encountered no one.

Jupiter was right where Gideon had said he would be, waiting patiently in the copse where Gideon and Amelia had played as children. She knew Jupiter, and he greeted her with a soft whinny.

She mounted him and immediately felt safer, if no warmer. Gideon's horse could outrun any nag Blakeley might have.

Then she thought of Sidley. He might be her enemy, and he had access to the Doncaster stables. She decided to go through the fields to the main road rather than take the estate drive. It might be treacherous, but she knew the way and Jupiter was a trained cavalry mount. She decided to risk it.

Halfway across the five-acre field where the stubble showed wheat had grown, she heard a man's voice call her name. She looked back to see a large figure coming after her, mounted on a bay she recognized as being from the estate's stables. Terrified of what recapture could mean, she kicked Jupiter into a canter and bent low over his neck.

"Come on, boy. For Gideon. For the captain."

She might have imagined it, but she felt a surge of power from the animal under her and they easily outdistanced whoever was following them.

As she and Jupiter swung out onto the main road, Amelia spared a thought to her appearance. Barefoot, clad only in a man's jacket and a torn petticoat, her hair tumbled about her dirty face, she scarcely resembled the Lady Amelia the villagers knew. It did not matter. They would recognize her and her plight, and would help her, she was sure. It remained only to get there, tell her story, organize a rescue, and return to the Abbey.

Too late. The words beat in her head. By the time all that was done, Gideon would be dead—and she might as well be. Desperately she urged Jupiter on when before her on the road, she saw a smart curricle and pair being driven at a spanking pace and heading right toward her. As the equipage drew near, she thought she recognized Sir Richard driving. And was that Jane seated next to him?

Relief made her weak. No need to go to the village or to explain anything. She hailed them, just as the man from the Abbey, whose existence she had forgotten in her anxiety to reach the village, came up behind her.

"Sir Richard!" she called.

"Lady Amelia," she heard Hugh Sidley say behind her.

"Amelia!" Jane's voice betrayed her shock and her relief. "Are you all right?"

"Frozen and hungry and angry enough to kill," Amelia

said. "Thank God you came. Gideon is still a prisoner back at the Abbey. Blakeley and Eustace are both holding him at gunpoint."

"Blakeley?" Jane said blankly.

"The moneylender Eustace owes his soul to. Never mind that now. We have to get back." She turned to Sidley, who sat on his huge bay gelding saying nothing. "Are you with us or against us, Hugh? Speak now. We have no time for games. If you betray me—" She couldn't think of anything dire enough to threaten him with. If harm came to Gideon through this man, she would find some way to make him pay.

Something of what she felt must have shown in her face, dirty and strained as it was. "I am with you," Sidley replied simply. "We'd best be quick about it. The new duke is fair crazed, and I do not know if the London man can keep him bridled."

"Let's go." Sir Richard did not wait to hear more. He urged his team to a canter and headed down the road. Amelia dug her bare heels into Jupiter's side and took the lead to show him the way to the dower house.

It took only a few minutes, but disaster had taken even less time.

"They've both gone," Eustace said when he returned, out of breath, from his search for Amelia and Sidley.

"Gone?" Blakeley's eyes flashed fury for a moment before his habitual pretense of humor was in place again. "Gone, gone, all gone. Well, Cap'n Falconer, sir, now that I think on it, we 'ave very little use for you without the lady. Perhaps 'Is Grace should shoot you after all, just to keep you from making trouble about the nuptials."

He grinned at Eustace. "You'd like that, now, wouldn't you, Yer Grace?"

But Eustace's temper had cooled. He backed away from Blakeley. Gideon took the opportunity to move unobserved toward the broken window. If he had to, he could pull himself up and try to slide through the opening. He was not at all sure it was possible for him to get his shoulders through, but it was that or try to go through both Blakeley and Eustace and make for the door. The window, however difficult, seemed a better bet than facing the two men.

"I see no reason to kill him. There would be no end of trouble. The man's a captain in the hussars, for God's sake. They can't turn up dead without raising all kinds of questions." Eustace tugged at his wilted cravat.

"Footpads," Blakeley said, shaking his head. "It 'appens to the best of us, Yer Grace. We leave 'im out on the road, and 'oo's to say when or 'ow 'e died? A tragedy, but the roads is so unsafe and these things 'appen."

"No," Eustace said. "Not here. Not near my home. It would cause gossip."

"Gossip!" Blakeley all but spat the word. "And 'oo cares about gossip? You won't swing for gossip. That's all that matters, Yer bloody sniveling Grace."

Gideon had almost reached the window. The ruined cot still stood under it. He figured he had at most five seconds from the moment he began his attempt to make his escape. Not a lot of time but enough, he thought. He'd better try it while they argued about killing him. It wouldn't be long before Eustace changed his mind again. He tightened his muscles and prepared to leap.

"Now, Yer Grace, look what we've done. We've bored the good cap'n so much 'e's thinkin' of leavin' us." Blakeley's mocking tones reached Gideon just as he jumped for the cot and then in one bound for the window frame.

Just a half a second more, Gideon thought, before a crack-like thunder resounded in the room and fiery pain stabbed his side.

"Oh, damn, not again," he said as he fell back into the room and everything went dark.

"A shot!" Amelia threw herself off Jupiter and ran toward the back door to the dower house. Sidley followed behind her as fast as he could. She could hear the clatter of the curricle's wheels on the stones of the courtyard as she ran. "Gideon!" she called. "We are here!"

The sound of boots running directly behind her caused her to speed up. Just as she reached the door, she was swept aside and Sir Richard entered the room, his pistols at the ready.

"Stand right where you are," he ordered. His voice carried the ring of command, and both Eustace and Blakeley remained unmoving, their pistols still aimed at the spot Gideon had occupied.

Amelia pushed past and ran to the wall where Gideon lay crumpled, blood slowly oozing from the wound in his side.

Chapter Thirteen

The swirl of activity that followed left Amelia untouched. She was focused on nothing but Gideon. Staunching the wound, making sure his earlier head wound had not been reopened, conferring with Jane about treatment for possible fever and weakness—that was all that concerned her.

While she cared for Gideon, Sir Richard took charge. He held Blakeley and Eustace at gunpoint while Hugh Sidley rode to the village for the doctor. He called Jane over and had her guard the prisoners while he conferred with Amelia over what to do with the duke.

But Amelia was not interested. Instead, in a pain-racked whisper, Gideon insisted the doctor not see Eustace held at gunpoint as Blakeley's confederate. He also told Amelia to go to the house and change, or she would cause gossip. Reluctantly she agreed and slipped out to go to the Abbey.

Sir Richard waited until he heard Sidley return with the doctor before hitting Eustace smartly over the head. When the round, fussy little man Sidley introduced as Dr. Leverett came into the dower house, his eyes went wide at the signs of mayhem before he pulled himself together and became the complete professional.

Sir Richard explained that Eustace had been injured while trying to protect Gideon. Then Sidley and another worker carried Eustace to the Abbey proper before he awakened. Sir Richard had bound and gagged Blakeley and had him taken to the library in the Abbey.

Amelia dressed in some clothes she had left behind on her last stay at the Abbey. She found the doctor in the drawing room, binding up Gideon's ribs and giving Jane instructions. Amelia felt much more the thing now that she was warm and dry. She still carried Gideon's coat and could not be parted from it until she could place it tenderly over him as the doctor supervised his removal to the duke's bedchamber. Dr. Leverett asked to see Eustace, but Jane insisted that he had gone to rest and that she would see he was taken care of.

Later, as Gideon slept, Amelia sat by the vast, ducal bed staring at him. His face was flushed, and his body was restless. She had been in this chamber when her father had lain on the bed at the beginning of the illness that would take him from her a few months later. She would not lose Gideon as she had lost the duke. She would keep watch and make sure that death did not steal a second loved one away from her. Impatiently she waved away offers of food and drink until Jane came in to see her, ready to do battle.

"Amelia, you must come downstairs and deal with this imbroglio," Jane told her without roundaboutation. "Your cousin has attempted to murder Captain Falconer. Do you want him bound over to the magistrate? Would the trial be in the House of Lords? You cannot ask Sir Richard to make decisions like this, and nothing can be done about that moneylender until the question of Eustace—"

Roused from her intense concentration on Gideon, Amelia felt the world rush back in with the strength of a spring flood. Of course she had duties to fulfill, decisions to make. She took a deep breath, then got slowly to her feet and shook the wrinkles out of her simple blue day dress.

"You are right, of course, Jane. I'll go down now. Sir Richard must wonder where my wits have gone to leave him alone like this." She gave Jane a perfunctory smile that did not banish the shadows from her eyes and hurried down to the library, where Sir Richard had established his command post.

"Lady Amelia," the colonel said as he rose to his feet to greet her. "I hope you do not mind that I have usurped your room and even your desk."

Amelia went over to him and took his hands. "I cannot thank you enough for what you have done today, Sir Richard.

For coming to the rescue and taking charge while I was—preoccupied." She smiled slightly.

He returned her smile with an ironic one of his own. "Escaping from murderous kidnappers does tend to drive other concerns from one's mind. Captain Falconer and I had a similar situation in Portugal." He led her carefully around the desk and seated her in the armchair that flanked it. "How is he? Jane—that is, Miss Forrester, said that he was doing well."

"Fever has set in." Amelia's hands twisted together in her lap.

"That is to be expected. Miss Forrester has some herbal concoction that she says will help." He frowned at her, but she did not see.

Amelia could not look up from her hands until she was sure that her eyes were not going to overflow. Tears were not going to help. She had decisions to make, so she firmed her voice and said, "You wanted to see me about Eustace?"

"Yes. You have some difficult decisions to make. Do you wish to lay charges against him?"

Amelia looked at him at last. Thinking about something other than the chance that Gideon might die gave her something to hang on to. "What would that entail? A trial? Jane said something about the House of Lords. And then what? Prison?"

Sir Richard shook his head. "You will have to consult a lawyer to get all those answers. There will be a trial, certainly."

"The trial of a peer for attempted murder and kidnapping—there are bound to be articles in the papers, are there not? Caricatures in the shops? Gossip." She knew her voice was calm, almost disinterested. In truth, she was not very concerned about Eustace. Whatever happened to him he had earned.

"Almost certainly."

"Gideon would have to testify? And I as well?"

"Falconer almost certainly. You might be spared by the court, Lady Amelia. Gently bred females often are."

She thought for a moment. It was not a difficult decision. She had only to do what her father would have wanted. "No trial. Perhaps he can go abroad. I know he does not have any money." She tapped a fingernail against her teeth for a moment while she weighed her options. "I am willing to give him a small allowance and to assume all responsibility for maintaining the property if he will agree never to return to England. Do you think that will answer?"

Sir Richard looked at her with undisguised admiration. He had wondered if Lady Amelia could possibly be intelligent and strong enough to take charge of the late duke's many properties and businesses. Now he knew. After all she had been through, she could still think, and think clearly.

"I believe that I can convince him to leave." Actually, he had no doubt about it whatsoever. And if convincing the sniveling little coward took physical force, so much the better. "But what about Blakeley? He was the mastermind of the scheme, I assume. He could be brought to book. And he should be. By God, kidnapping you and shooting Falconer—"

"No, Sir Richard." Amelia knew Blakeley far better than Sir Richard could. She knew what he would do if he were faced with the certainty of prison. "He is a truly evil man, I believe." The thought of that false humor and those dead eyes made her shudder. "But if there is a trial, he will lay the blame, very convincingly, on Eustace. Then my family's name will be muddied as certainly as it would if Eustace himself were to be tried and convicted. My father detested Eustace—that may have been partly because he was such a beastly little boy. Papa had very little patience with cowardice and less with whining—but he would not want our name dragged through that kind of a trial."

"Yet we cannot allow the man to simply go free," Sir Richard argued.

"Perhaps losing the money Eustace owes him, and if we could also somehow end his moneylending—" Amelia found herself without another idea in her head. Like a horse who has run as far as he can, she could do no more. Her body ached from all its unfamiliar exertions. She was tired and hungry and most of all worried about Gideon.

"I have exhausted you," Sir Richard said with remorse. She was so intelligent and had such iron control over herself that he had forgotten this was a slip of a girl, not a hardened soldier. She had been through an ordeal that would make many a Peninsular veteran give out. "Why do you not get some rest. I will watch Falconer for you, and promise to wake you should there be any change in his condition."

Amelia felt herself sinking into a kind of mindless lethargy. She could do no more. "Thank you," she murmured. "I am tired, I think. I will look in on Gideon, and then perhaps I will nap for an hour. You have been so kind, Sir Richard, to shoulder my responsibilities. I cannot tell you how much I—"

He waved away her thanks. "Please go up and sleep before you drop and I have to get one of the footmen to carry you." He gave her his sardonic half smile again as she rose and left the room.

The housekeeper sent up a tray of tea and buttered toast. Amelia finished it quickly, then slipped off her shoes and pulled the quilt over herself. She was asleep almost before she closed her eyes.

When she awoke, the moon was riding low in the sky, shining directly through her uncurtained window. With a low cry of distress at having slept so long, she quickly sat up and reached her toes around to find her shoes. Within minutes she had straightened her crumpled dress, dragged a comb through her hair, and splashed cold water on her face from the ewer a maid must have brought while she was asleep.

Gideon, she thought as she moved swiftly down the hall to the duke's bedroom, *how is Gideon?* As soon as she entered the room, she knew he was worse. Jane was leaning over the restless figure in the bed, a cloth in her hand. Sir Richard was bending over the bed, trying to still the thrashing limbs.

Amelia said nothing, simply hurried over to stand with her friends, trying to draw strength from their concern. She looked down. Gideon's eyes were open and staring, bright with fever. She reached over to take one of his hands in hers, but with the strength of delirium he pulled her down on top of him.

"So, Blakeley, you think to kill me yet?" he growled as his hands reached around her throat.

"Gideon, no! It's—" She tried to tell him who she was, but he shook her as if she were a rat in a terrier's jaws.

"Damn you! Kill Amy will you? I'll see you in hell!"

Amelia felt darkness grow at the edge of her vision. "Gideon!"

He stilled suddenly, looking around with unseeing eyes. His hands, so painfully strong, gentled and began to stroke her face. "Amy?" he said, his cracked voice a caress. "Is it you? Are you all right?"

"Yes, it is I, and I am—"

"You should have seen your father! He was mad as fire that we took the curricle out. He knows it was me." A youthful grin spread over his face. "You should have heard him! Called me a hell-born babe! But he is going to send me to school, Amy, not back to the street."

She knew instantly where he thought he was, or rather when he thought he was. "Yes, Gideon, of course you'll be going to school. He would never send you back. And that's fine for you, but what about me?"

His expression sobered. "I'm sorry you can't come. You're cleverer than any of them. It is stupid that girls cannot go to Eton. I told your father so." His eyes still focused on some faraway scene, he grimaced.

Amy's heart melted. It was one of her fondest memories—Gideon standing up for her right to learn. Her father had listened, too. As a result, she had continued her studies with the vicar for another five years. "I am sure Father will let me study with Mr. Collins, Gideon. And I will have you to thank for my fine education."

But Gideon no longer heard her. His eyes had closed, and his hands fell to his sides. He gave a low groan, and his breathing grew labored. Jane thrust Amelia aside and placed her hand on his forehead.

"The fever is higher," Jane said. "Help me raise him, Richard, please." As Sir Richard lifted his inert body, Gideon stiffened and began to speak once again. This time his voice was higher, lighter, the voice of a young child.

"Mama? Mama! Where are you? Where have you gone? Why won't you sing to me, Mama?" His head thrashed about, and he all but dashed the cup of medicinal tea from Jane's hand.

"You must take your medicine, Gideon," Jane said firmly.

"All right, nanny." He opened his mouth and swallowed the tea, making a face at its bitter taste. "Ugh. Nasty."

"I know, but it will make you better."

Gideon smiled, a happy, innocent smile, one no one in the room had ever seen on his face before. Wherever Gideon's mind had journeyed, had he gone too far away to return to them?

Amelia stared at him, at Gideon as he must once have been. She was sure that she was hearing him as a young child, in the happy years before she had ever known him. In the grip of fever, he seemed to have returned to those days he could not remember when awake.

Still smiling, he turned on his side and tucked his hand under his chin. It was an oddly appealing gesture in such a big, dark man. "Sing to me, Mama," he said again.

Amelia seated herself on the bed and stroked his head softly as she sang the "Coventry Carol," the only lullaby she could think of.

"No, not that one. Mine. Sing my song," he ordered.

Amelia looked around helplessly. "He said his mother had a special song she sang to him, but he could not remember what it was," she whispered to Sir Richard and Jane, who stood watching her, mesmerized.

"You know," Gideon said. "You know it. Sing it!" His voice had risen, and Amelia feared that he might have an adult-size temper tantrum if she could not think of some song.

To her surprise, he smiled that childlike, seraphic smile again. "You forgot, Mama," he said. Then he began to hum in that same cracked but childish voice. It was a simple melody, but one Amelia had never heard before. When he began to hum it again, she joined in a little hesitantly, wanting him to have the comfort his delusion of his mother singing him a special song seemed to give him.

Caught up as she was in Gideon's world, she was taken by surprise when she felt Sir Richard's hand clamp around her arm. She was raised to her feet and set aside between one breath and the next. Stunned, she looked at the colonel.

He was leaning over Gideon, a grim expression on his face that Amelia could not read but that rendered him all but unrecognizable. "Where did you hear that song? Where? How do you know that song?" His voice was a harsh, accusing whisper. "Tell me, you damn gypsy brat!"

Amelia stood paralyzed for a moment, staring at this man she had thought she knew as Gideon's friend. Then she took hold of his arm and tried to pull him away from Gideon. She might as well have tried to pull a tree away from where it was rooted with her bare hands.

Jane was more ruthless. She slapped the colonel smartly across the cheek. "Richard! Stop it! Gideon is delirious! He can tell you nothing. Get hold of yourself!"

He shook his head as if awakening from a heavy sleep and looked at Jane. His expression changed and cleared. "I—I am sorry. I did not mean to—" He broke off as Gideon again began to hum the little melody. "I am sorry. I think I badly need some air." With that, he strode out of the room.

Jane looked after him for a moment then shrugged and turned back to her patient, though she spoke to Amelia. "The colonel has been under a severe strain for the past several days. It is the only explanation I can give for that outburst." She took Gideon's wrist in her fingers. "His pulse is a little quieter. It is a good sign. Whatever its effect on Richard, that queer little lullaby seems to make Gideon feel calmer."

For a few moments the two women stood looking down at the peacefully sleeping captain. Then Jane turned worried eyes to the door. "If you can stay with him for a few minutes, I would like to speak to the colonel. He may need a little laudanum, or perhaps some brandy and milk."

"Of course." Amelia had no intention of leaving the room until she was sure that Gideon was out of danger. She seated herself once again on the edge of the bed and began to stroke his thick black hair as Jane hurried out of the room.

Jane found Sir Richard, not in the library where she had thought he would be, but on the terrace just outside. He stood bathed in the cold moonlight, with nothing but a light coat on against the icy chill. A cigar glowed once or twice as he drew on it. Jane stood by the open French doors and hesitated. Despite their desperate flight to the Abbey and the confidences they had shared on the way, she did not know this man very well. He might not welcome her company at this time. He might—

"I know you are there. Come out and join me, Jane."

Did his voice hold a smile? She didn't know, but he wanted her with him so she stepped out into the darkness. "I cannot stay long. A fever this high is very dangerous."

"He had better not die until he has told me what I want to know." Richard threw his cigar away half smoked. It arched through the darkness in a trail of insubstantial sparks.

"Do you mind telling me what this is all about?" She hesitated to question him, his temper seemed on a very short leash, and she had no right to delve into his life. "You and the captain were friends, I thought. And he is in the grip of a high fever. Yet you seemed so angry with him."

"Yes, I am angry. That young man has pretended to be my friend, and now I find he has knowledge of my family—knowledge he has withheld from me—" He turned away from her, took a few quick steps, then turned back. He found her standing quietly, her hands folded at her waist, looking neither avid nor expectant.

He could speak or not as he chose. He sighed. "I told you about my family. About my nephew, Francis."

Jane did not speak, she only nodded.

"That song that Falconer was humming upstairs. That song—" He stepped up to her and took her by her arms. "My sister-in-law wrote that song, Jane. She wrote it for Francis. She never wrote it down, and no one else ever sang it. No one."

Jane stared into the colonel's furious hazel eyes and said, "I don't understand, Richard. What do you think it could mean?"

"I don't know, but I damn well mean to find out! How in the hell did Gideon Falconer learn that song? He must have encountered Francis somewhere in his dirty gypsy past. And he had better not die until I find out where!" He released Jane's arms so suddenly, she had to take a step backward to regain her balance.

"After that," he finished as he stalked back into the house, "if he doesn't die of his wounds, I may kill him myself."

Chapter Fourteen

Jane followed him back inside, grateful for the cheerful fire that burned on the library's hearth. She went to stand facing Sir Richard across the expanse of the fireplace.

Of all the questions that filled her mind and despite her worry about her patient, she wanted to know only one thing. "I thought you were friends. That you despised the prejudice about Gideon's origins that kept so many doors shut against him." She could not hide the disappointment she felt. "I thought you felt as Amelia and I do."

As all right-thinking people do. He heard the words as clearly as if she had spoken them.

Distractedly Richard ran his hand through his already disordered hair. Where was the cool, sardonic humor that kept the world and its emotions at bay? Gone, with the sound of a child's lullaby.

"It is not that," he murmured. "Not quite that. But why is he alive and Francis not? Why has he never spoken to me of Francis?"

"Richard, do but think," Jane said. She closed the space between them and took his hands in hers. "Gideon is delirious. He has no idea of what he is saying."

"But he knows that song. He heard it somewhere. It did not just spring into his head when he was shot."

"He heard it sometime in the past, but it may be a memory he will not recall when he is awake. I have encountered many such cases in treating fevers and head wounds." Jane looked up at him earnestly. Her glowing topaz eyes entreated his understanding.

"You mean he may never be able to recall where he learned it?" Disappointment swept through him. Once again, his every path to his family was blocked. He longed to put his sister-in-law's torment to rest, and his father's. Sir Richard knew himself to be an unsatisfactory heir, but in some fashion he felt he would redeem himself if he could produce an explanation for Francis's disappearance.

"I mean, we will have to wait until he has recovered to ask him."

"But if you are right and he does not remember when he is awake, then we should ask him now. Find out now, while he can still remember." It was an exciting idea—perhaps now was the very time. Sir Richard longed for action, and this was something he could do immediately. He was still holding Jane's hands. Now he pressed them in an attempt to convey his urgency. "Please let us try. If it disturbs him, I promise I will stop questioning him."

Jane looked at him with doubt clear in her eyes. "I should return to him now in any case. Come with me, and we will see."

Sir Richard bent and would have kissed Jane's hands, but she pulled them away and hurried out of the room ahead of him.

Amelia had not moved since they had left her alone with Gideon. She still sat on the side of the bed and stroked his hair. He lay as if unconscious, his chest barely registering breath.

"Has he awakened at all?" Jane moved to the bed and laid a hand on Gideon's brow.

"Briefly. He still seemed to think he is with his mother." Amelia blinked tears from her eyes.

Her heart had been cracked open with love and pity when she heard that childish voice coming from her intrepid Gideon. This, she was sure, was the memory of his life "before," when he had been warm and loved. Whoever and wherever his mother was, Gideon still loved her. And the memory of her love for him was still alive, although it had been buried for years.

"I need to talk to him, Lady Amelia." Sir Richard stood leaning over her, frowning down at the figure in the bed.

Amelia rose and glared at him. "You may not speak to anyone in my house in the kind of language you used before toward him. If you cannot keep your bigotry under control, I will have to ask you to leave."

He gave her a pained half smile. "I am sorry, ma'am. I forgot myself. It is just that he clearly has some knowledge that he has never shared with me."

For the first time Amelia truly focused on what he was saying. "Knowledge? What kind of knowledge?"

"About my family. He knows something of my nephew." Sir Richard looked at her squarely. "It is of the utmost importance to me and to my sister-in-law that I discover what Falconer knows. And how he knows it."

Amelia began to speak then paused, struck by Sir Richard's words. "What do you think Gideon knows, Sir Richard?"

Impatiently Sir Richard said, "That song he was singing. It is one my sister-in-law wrote for Francis—my nephew. I need to know how Falconer knows it."

Amelia stared at him for a moment, trying to understand. Gideon was ill, wounded, and Sir Richard wanted to wake him up to ask about a *song*? "You cannot be serious. Jane, tell him that Gideon needs rest, not to be questioned about some song!"

"It is very important to Sir Richard, Amelia, and the captain may not remember when he awakes."

"And that is more important than making sure he *does* awake? I begin to think you are as mad as Sir Richard." Amelia felt herself begin to shake with anger. Was she the only person here concerned about Gideon and not some aristocratic nephew of the heir to a marquessate? It was intolerable!

"It will not harm him, Amy," Jane said, placing a soothing hand on her friend's arm. "You know I would not risk it if I thought there was danger. If Sir Richard upsets him, I will not allow him to continue."

"It is monstrous! I cannot think what has come over you both. Who cares about a song? Gideon risked his life for me today as he has for you more than once, Sir Richard. And now you will chance his recovery for a little useless information?"

She sat back down on the edge of the bed and took Gideon's hand, which was curled up clutching something, in both of hers. "Very well. Ask your questions." She glared up at Sir Richard, feeling like a lioness guarding her wounded mate. *Jackal,* her gaze said, *do your worst.*

Sir Richard once again leaned over the bed. He could not get too near Gideon because Amelia sat squarely in the way. Nevertheless, he was close enough to see any expression in the captain's eyes once they were open.

"Falconer," he said, his voice low but commanding, "look at me. It is Colonel Sinclair. Open your eyes."

Gideon groaned, and Amelia's gaze flew to Sir Richard's, all but ordering him silently to stop the questioning before it began. He ignored her.

"Falconer, it is time to wake." The tone was insistent, and Gideon tossed on the pillow but then slowly opened his eyes and stared at his superior officer.

"Sir," he said, his voice a croak. "Do we ride?"

"Not yet. First I need to ask you something."

"Yes, sir." It was the response of a wounded officer, who was still under orders, though he might be dying. Amelia clutched his hand harder.

"You were singing. A lullaby."

"A lullaby, sir?" Gideon's frown was puzzled. Then his face cleared, and once again wore the look of childlike peace Amelia found so unbearably touching. "My mama's lullaby?"

A spasm of pain crossed Sir Richard's face for a moment. "Did your mother teach it to you?"

"Yes, sir." Again that puzzled frown. "I think so. It was long ago."

"Did your mother tell you where she learned that song?" Sir Richard leaned forward. Amelia thought he was willing Gideon to answer.

"She did not learn it," Gideon responded.

Sir Richard looked angry. "What do you mean she didn't—"

"How did she know the lullaby, then?" It was Jane's calm, nurse's voice that asked the question. She laid her hand on Sir Richard's sleeve, and he responded by folding his lips into a tight line and saying nothing.

"She made it up," Gideon said simply, and closed his eyes again.

"That is impossible," Sir Richard said. He turned away from the bed and went to stand by the window. "His mother must have lied to him and told him that. She may have heard it somehow. There were gypsies camped somewhere nearby that summer, and they were everywhere. One of them could have heard the song, I suppose." He shrugged and put a hand on the cold windowpane. "It is always like this. We get what we think are solid clues, and they turn out to be as insubstantial as smoke."

Amelia sat as if turned to stone. "Clues to what, Sir Richard?"

"It is a family mystery, Lady Amelia. One I do not talk about."

"Well, you have talked about it now and have accused Gideon of being somehow involved. I think you had better tell us the rest."

Sir Richard ran a distracted hand through his hair. "Jane already knows the rest."

"And I do not. Pray enlighten me. I have a reason to inquire."

A chief judge could not have sounded more compelling. Richard believed her. "I had a nephew who died at a very early age. My sister-in-law has never accepted his death, and as a result I have attempted to track down any hint of a connection with Francis. I hope to find confirmation of his death."

"Tell me, Sir Richard, if he had lived, would your nephew be your father's heir?" She was frowning at him, a look that might have been distrust in her eyes.

"Yes. He was the son of my older brother, Lionel."

"Who also died?"

"Yes."

"Accidentally?"

"Yes."

A decisive nod. Lady Amelia rose, laying Gideon's hand tenderly on the coverlet. "I would be obliged if you would leave now, Sir Richard. When Gideon has recovered, you may talk to him again, but in his present state you have him at a disadvantage."

Amelia hoped she sounded convincing. Sir Richard's anger at Gideon, his insistence that Gideon knew something about the death of his nephew years before, frightened her. There was a mystery here, but she was afraid Sir Richard was trying to tie Gideon to it for his own reasons.

"I only wish to get answers to a few questions, that is all. If Falconer has nothing to hide, he has nothing to fear from me."

Jane, who had been following the conversation almost as if it were a game of battledore and shuttlecock, looked closely at Gideon. "I believe he will sleep for a while. Richard, perhaps you would be good enough to wait for us in the library."

"Jane, I do not believe I deserve to be treated as if I were a criminal simply because I asked Falconer some questions. If Lady Amelia would explain exactly what—"

"Wait for us, Richard." Jane's look was beseeching, but her tone was adamant.

"Very well." He left with visible reluctance.

"Now, Amelia," Jane said as the door closed behind him, "you had better tell me what is on your mind. You looked at Sir Richard as if you thought he was a murderer."

Amelia bit her lip. "While we were prisoners, Gideon talked a bit about his childhood. The time before he was apprenticed to the sweep. He seems to remember a time when he was not with the gypsies. I did not question him about it. Just thinking of that time made him unhappy. But he remembers a large house, and a woman who sang to him. Who sang that song."

"That is remarkable. We must tell Richard. It could be that Gideon isn't a gypsy, that he is the son of a servant or even a tenant on the estate."

"Oh, Jane, perhaps that is it, but I must think for a moment!" In her agitation Amelia began to pace across the room, back and forth in front of the fireplace and foot of the huge four-poster bed that faced it. Perhaps if she told Jane some of the thoughts that rioted in her brain, they would come clear. "Sir Richard's nephew dies. Then his brother meets with a fatal accident. Now he is his father's heir."

"What in the world are you implying, Amelia?" Jane was clearly horrified. "That Richard wants to be a marquess? You are quite out there, you know. He dreads the thought."

"And you know that because—" Amelia stopped in front of

Jane and broke off her thought, wanting the truth to come out of Jane's own mouth.

"He told me so. We talked a great deal about his family on the way here."

"But that was only today. And he is the only one to swear he has always had that attitude." Amelia was growing colder by the minute. What was she thinking? That Sir Richard had somehow contrived his brother's and his nephew's deaths so that he would become the marquess when his father died? Surely not. And that now he was going to try to tie Gideon to his nephew's death somehow? Why? To avert suspicion? To lay the question of the little boy's death to rest at last?

Whatever the reason, if it was true that Sir Richard was trying to blame Gideon for something to do with his nephew's death, Amelia was going to fight to preserve Gideon's good name. He had earned it entirely by himself, and no one was going to take it away from him while he lay helpless. Not if she could prevent it.

She looked down at him as he slept, his hand still curled up under his chin. Smiling, she smoothed back his thick, dark hair. The petticoat bandage they had contrived for his head had been replaced by Jane's neat white square. Love for him swelled her heart. He had endured so much in his life and had come through it all with his gallantry and, she was sure, his honor intact. How could Sir Richard, or anyone who knew Gideon think for a moment that he would hurt anyone intentionally? That was the reason he had run away from the man who made him fight—Gideon could no longer go on fighting other homeless boys just like himself.

"What exactly are you saying, Amelia?" Jane's voice was that of the schoolmistress demanding an explanation from pupils who arrive without their workbooks.

"I do not know. I do not know, Jane." Amelia sat down in the small brocade armchair that sat to the side of the fireplace. She put her head in her hands. "I only know that Sir Richard is now the heir to his father's title and estates and that he sees some connection here between himself and Gideon that I do not understand."

"They are comrades in arms. And Sir Richard has stood Gideon's friend when he determined to gain an entrée into the ton." Jane's disapproval of Gideon's social life in recent weeks was very apparent.

"Gideon only did that for me. He has no interest in being a part of Society." Amelia smiled at the memory of Gideon standing grim and sentinel-like at musicales and routs. "He and Sir Richard were friends then, it was clear to see. That is what makes Sir Richard's attitude tonight so strange. I cannot believe that he really thinks that a boy of five or six—Gideon must have been about that age when Sir Richard's nephew disappeared—could have done anything criminal."

"Amy." Gideon's voice was hoarse and weak.

She rushed to his side. "Yes, Gideon. What can I get you? Would you like a little barley water?"

"Please." She moved to the mahogany chest beside the window where a carafe and glass awaited her. She poured his drink and took it over to the bed.

"Just sip it slowly, Gideon. Don't gulp it down." She held the glass and tried to hold him up to drink.

"I can sit up, Amy. I'm not dead yet. For God's sake, do not fuss!" He hauled himself to a sitting position while Amelia hastened to pile pillows behind him.

"Was Sir Richard here?" Gideon asked, frowning as he waved away any more barley water. "I thought I heard him speak to me, but it is all rather fuzzy still."

"Yes, Sir Richard and Jane came out from the city to help us."

"Where is he?"

I ordered him to leave the room because I think he may have murdered his brother and his nephew, and is trying to make you responsible somehow. To give it voice even in her thoughts made Amelia blush. Whatever had she been thinking of? True, Sir Richard was behaving oddly, but that was hardly a reason to accuse him of murder. She hoped that Jane did not believe her to be totally deranged from what she had said.

"Amy, where is Sir Richard? Why are you standing there

looking guilty?" Gideon's voice was still a rasp, but his eyes were very clear and bright, and he was completely conscious.

"He seemed to be upsetting you with his talk, so I asked him to leave while you rested." It was close enough to the truth. "I will ask him to visit you later if you like."

The door opened, and Sir Richard, his face wearing a bland smile, strolled into the room. "I have returned. A cold collation is awaiting you ladies in the breakfast room. A maid is bringing up a tray for Captain Falconer and me. I will sit with him while you refresh yourselves downstairs."

"Where is Eustace?" Amelia was not sure she really wanted to know, but she would have to deal with him sooner or later.

"He and Blakeley are being kept in separate rooms in the dower house. Hugh Sidley and others will keep watch on them until you have decided what is to be done with them."

Amelia thought for a moment but could find no fault with this arrangement and dismissed it from her mind. She had more pressing concerns.

"You will not disturb him unduly, will you, Colonel?" There was steel in her voice.

"I will endeavor not to do so, Lady Amelia." There was ice in his.

A footman arrived with a laden tray, and Amelia reluctantly left the field to the colonel. "Are you sure Gideon is up to a meal, Jane?" she said as soon as they were out of earshot.

"I told Richard to make sure that it was light, invalid fare. He has not eaten since before he left London. A little poached chicken and some soup can only help him. Remember, too, he is a soldier and has been in worse cases than this."

"Yes, I know, but I worry that the colonel will upset him with his questions about Gideon's childhood."

Amelia noted that the staff had provided much more than the cold collation Sir Richard had spoken of. There was a raised ham pie and a sweet omelette as well as cold beef and salad.

Much to her surprise, Amelia found that she was starving. She dug into the meal with zest. She refused a restorative glass of claret in favor of tea, because she fully intended to stay awake and sit with Gideon through the night. Still apprehensive about Sir Richard, she rose abruptly while Jane was peeling an apple for dessert and said, "I will just go up and see if Gideon needs anything. Do not hurry. I can get him anything he needs."

Jane looked at her and sighed. "Amelia, you are behaving very strangely. It is not to be wondered at after what you have been through today, but you seem to have some very odd ideas about Richard."

"I am sorry you feel that way." Amelia was halfway out of the room before she finished speaking.

Something drove her up the stairs and into the ducal bedchamber at what was almost a run. When she opened the door, she knew her instinct had been correct. Sir Richard was again standing over the bed. As Amelia entered, he wrenched something out of Gideon's hand.

"What have you got there?" Sir Richard's voice was harsh, accusing.

"Give it back! You have no right! It's mine!" Once again, Gideon's words were almost childlike. But this time the fury in his voice was fully adult. He reared up out of the bed and grabbed Sir Richard's arm with both of his. "Give that to me, you bastard. No one takes that away from me. No one!"

Despite his weakness, Gideon hung onto that arm with bulldog tenacity. But Sir Richard had superior strength and position, and easily threw Gideon back onto the bed. He bent over the small object in his hand and turned it this way and that while Gideon tried to raise himself up again to take back his treasure.

Amelia flew across the room and launched herself at Sir Richard. All her distrust, all the fear she had felt this day and the pity that she felt for Gideon when he had told her of his life rose up and lent her strength. She grabbed the small iron ball out of Sir Richard's hands and put her own fists behind her back.

"You dare to take this!" she said, panting and backing away from the anger in Sir Richard's face. "This has belonged to Gideon as long as I have known him. He is wounded and ill, and you simply cannot stop hounding him. Get out of my house this instant and don't come back!"

Sir Richard took a deep, gasping breath and stood stock-still. He closed his eyes and passed a shaking hand over his face. The silence lengthened and grew thicker as Amelia and Sir Richard stared at each other and tried to calm themselves. Gideon lay sprawled on his side, his face white and his eyes shut.

At last Sir Richard broke the silence, speaking calmly but clearly with great effort. "If you will twist the ball, the top half to the right and the bottom half to the left, you may see something that will explain my actions."

Still suspicious, she took the small iron ball out from behind her back and did as he suggested. Slowly the two halves of the ball began to separate, and after spending some minutes twisting them, they at last came apart.

"Oh," Amelia exclaimed. "Look! It is gold inside. And there is some kind of inscription on one side of it and a crest or something very like it on the other."

"May I see?" said Sir Richard, his voice still calm but his eyes bright with excitement.

Reluctantly Amelia handed the two pieces to him. He came closer and stood beside her. "You see here on this side is the inscription, *amor vincit omnia.* It is very faint now. The second marquess had it inscribed. This was a gift for his wife. And on the other side is the Southbridge family crest. Again, it is scarcely discernible after all these years."

Amelia stared at him. "*Amor vincit omnia.* That means love conquers all, doesn't it?" Sir Richard nodded. "Is it yours?"

"No. It is always a gift to the heir when he reaches five or six years of age. A tradition that the second marchioness began, I believe, because her son, also named Francis, loved to play with it."

He looked at Amelia, his expression grave and somehow fearful. "It was given to my nephew only two days before he disappeared." His gaze traveled down to the small keepsake in his hand. "So you see, I badly need to know how this came into Captain Falconer's possession."

"Gideon?" Amelia looked at him. He still lay sprawled on his side, but his bandage was now red with blood. "Gideon!"

Chapter Fifteen

Amelia took a shuddering breath and ordered her heart to slow down and her brain to function. "I must ask you to help me. But after I repair the damage you have done—if I can—you will leave this house and not return! Now, get me the pile of bandages from the chest in the corner, Colonel." She was pleased that her voice was calm. "And then go and fetch Jane."

"I will do all I can to help. But, Lady Amelia, there is more involved than you know, and I cannot and will not leave until I resolve it." When he handed her the bandages, she looked up at him briefly and paused, wondering why Gideon's sudden relapse should affect him so deeply. He had been fighting over that silly ball, and now he looked stunned, as if he were faced with something totally unexpected. For a moment he stood looking down at Gideon as if he had never seen him before.

"Jane," Amelia reminded him. He left without a word.

Amelia turned to Gideon, pressing a thick pad to the wound and holding it there, hoping to slow the loss of blood. She wouldn't risk examining the wound by herself. If Gideon's struggle with Sir Richard had pulled Dr. Leverett's stitches loose, Jane and she would have to act together to repair them.

Jane entered the room and moved quickly to Amelia's side. "Let me look." Amelia stepped aside, and Jane carefully removed the doctor's bandage, now soaked with blood. She wiped the blood from the wound and examined the stitches.

"Did he pull them out?"

"Not quite." Jane reached out a hand, and Amelia placed another bandage in it. "How did this happen? When I left he was quiet."

"Ask your friend Richard," Amelia said bitterly. "Another of his outbursts. This time he wanted Gideon's little iron ball. The one he fiddles with when he is nervous. Gideon fought him for it."

Jane was busy wrapping Gideon's wound and did not look up. "Who won?" she asked.

"I did." Amelia gave her a brief smile. "I snatched it away from Sir Richard."

"Clever Amelia. I should have guessed." Jane finished and turned to her friend. "Someone should stay with him tonight. Not you," she added. "You are exhausted, and no wonder." She hesitated a moment. "Would you object if Richard and I took turns?"

Amelia stared at her in shock. "Of course I would object. I forbid it! I would as soon have Eustace remain on watch alone than that madman. What has happened to you, Jane? You were always so calm and rational. Yet you know how your friend Richard treats Gideon, and you still calmly suggest that he remain in this room alone with him?"

"I am sure there is some explanation for Richard's behavior." Jane's mouth was set in a stubborn line.

"Oh, I have no doubt. He is quite mad, that is the explanation!" Amelia crossed her hands across her chest and glared at Jane with equal stubbornness. "And I will remain with Gideon tonight. All night," she added defiantly.

"Well, at least have a bath and get into the warmest clothes you can find. Then, if you want to take the first watch, I won't object."

"Very well. I will return in half an hour. Please do not leave the room."

"I will be here." Jane drew a small upholstered chair up to the bed and sat down.

Amelia went to her bedchamber and rang for a bath. Jane's suggestion had been most welcome. She had been going all day on nervous energy, but her reserves were almost depleted. The kidnapping and escape and subsequent adventures had left her more exhausted than she had ever been in her life. Now she looked around the familiar room she had occupied from the moment she was old enough to leave the night nursery, and smiled. From the white coverlet on the four-poster bed to the flowered chintz covering the small slipper chair and the windows, everything spoke of a time when she had been sheltered, protected, loved. A time when her world was bounded by her father and Gideon. Her eyes filled when she contemplated the changes her father's death had wrought in her life.

"Papa," she whispered, "I need you. I'm not sure I can do what needs to be done by myself."

Resolutely she told herself that her father would expect more of her than to lapse into self-pity. She dashed the tears from her eyes and summoned up her reserves of courage and strength. Gideon needed her.

When the tin slipper tub had been set before the fire in her room and footmen had come and gone with their cans of steaming water, Amelia undressed and sank into the tub. She had refused the services of one of the housemaids as a temporary abigail. At her stage of fatigue, solitude was balm to her battered spirit. Slowly she relaxed. The warmth of the water and the flickering of the fire sent her into a state that lay somewhere between waking and sleeping.

Gideon. Always her thoughts returned to him. Something teased at her brain. Something he had said. Something she had thought. For a few minutes she chased the elusive idea around her mind, but to no avail. Yawning, she reached for the soap.

Clean and warm and dry—and safe. Amelia tied the sash of the warm woolen dress she had found in her closet and luxuriated for a few moments in those mundane blessings. Blessings she had wondered if she would ever see again. The terror she had felt at many points during the day and night she had been held captive came back in retrospect. Perhaps, she thought as she made her way down the hall to the room where Gideon lay, she could afford to feel those emotions now that their cause had been vanquished. She had held terror at bay, never fully surrendering to it while the events that caused it had been going on. Now that she was safe, she found herself shaking with reaction.

Jane sat where Amelia had left her. She was leaning forward, her fingers on Gideon's wrist. She smiled at Amelia as she entered. "Ah," she said, "I am glad you took my suggestion. You must feel a great deal better after your bath."

"How is he?" Amelia took up her position on the side of the bed.

"His pulse is normal, and I think his fever is down as well. A good night's sleep, and he should be well on the road to recovery. It was not a serious wound, and if not for the previous harm to his head, I doubt he would be in as bad a case as he is." Jane spoke in her authoritative, teacher's mode, and Amelia was cheered by her conviction.

"I will remain with him for a while, Jane." She leaned over to smooth the unruly dark hair back from Gideon's forehead. "You might as well go to bed. Or better yet, seek out Sir Richard and try to bring him to his senses. A little of your brisk common sense will go a long way toward that end, I am sure."

"I think I understand his feelings about his nephew, but I will talk to him about his treatment of Gideon." The look on Jane's face told Amelia that her friend was not looking forward to the interview. "I will be back to take my turn in an hour or so."

"I will stay. You may think Sir Richard has reason to behave in that extraordinary manner, but I do not. And I will not have him waking Gideon up so they can talk about children drowning."

"Drowning?" Jane said. "Who said anything about drowning?"

"I don't know." Amelia put her hand to her head. She was too tired to remember what had put the idea in her head. "I thought Sir Richard did."

Jane frowned as if trying to remember. Then she shrugged and left the room.

Alone with him at last, Amelia looked at Gideon, trying to decide if he did look better than he had when first brought into the Abbey. She took his hand in both of hers and gazed down at his sleeping face, her heart in her eyes.

"I love you, Gideon Falconer," she whispered. "And I always will. And just in case you were thinking you could wiggle out of marrying me even though you promised me you would, I have every intention of spending this night with you as well."

With an impish grin, she slipped off her shoes, slid under the covers and settled a pillow against the headboard. Leaning back against it, she opened the book she had thought to bring with her and pulled the candle on the table next to the bed a little closer. She knew her behavior was outrageous, but she simply could not bear to be separated from him by so much as an inch.

The day had brought such pain and fear as she had never endured. The only thing that had kept her from shattering into useless, hysterical terror was Gideon. His bravery and humor had kept the worst fears at bay, and his belief in her own courage had buoyed her when she needed it most. He was her best friend as well as her love, and she needed to be near him. Unconsciously she snuggled a little closer to him.

There was also the unaccountable behavior of Sir Richard. She did not understand it, and by now her head felt as if it were stuffed with cotton. The book slid from her fingers to rest face-down on her lap. If for some reason the colonel took it into his head to try to accost Gideon in the night, she would be here to prevent any further harm.

So she would just sit here next to him and read. And perhaps every now and then she might stroke his hair, just a little, to reassure herself that he was here and alive and would be none the worse for his adventures.

She picked up her book again and resolutely began to read. But Gideon's body was warm next to hers, and the single candle on the table next to the bed cast only a dim and flickering light. Inexorably her eyes drifted shut, and she slept.

A vagrant sunbeam that crept from between the heavy velvet window curtains awakened Gideon some hours later. He ached in every muscle and nerve. It must, he thought fuzzily, have been quite a battle. Odd that he was so comfortable. One did not usually find feather beds in one's billets after a battle. Nor did one usually find such a soft, warm body next to—

"Amelia!"

"Wha—what?" She shot upright as if someone had poured cold water over her. "Gideon!"

"What are you doing in this bed?" He was horrified. Surely he hadn't—they didn't—she wouldn't—

"Sleeping," she responded with a sunny smile in which he could see no trace of guilt. "And making sure that you did not open your stitches during the night."

He hauled himself painfully to a sitting position and glared at her. "Well, would you be so good as to remove yourself from my bed at once? I cannot begin to think what your father would—"

She interrupted him with a peal of laughter. "Gideon, you sound exactly like Miss Goodacre when I tried to paint a mural of the Battle of Bosworth on the schoolroom wall. You even purse up your mouth the way she used to. You missed your calling, my friend. You should have been a governess." She chuckled, and Gideon couldn't help smiling back at her. Amy's laugh, her tousled curls, the smile in her eyes evoked feelings that no one else ever aroused. With Amy he felt himself at home, warm and comfortable and yet excited and alive.

He loved her. He had known it forever, but after their adventure, the danger they had shared, the confession of his love, he could not deny it, did not want to deny it. Nothing could come of it, Amy would not want him once the adventure ended. But he would never change. His feelings had grown too strong for him. Seeing her yesterday, afraid but pitting herself against all enemies, ready for any challenge had only added one more layer to his love. She was not only beautiful and good, intelligent and kind—she was pluck to the backbone! What a soldier's wife she would make. If only—

Amelia had placed one cool hand on his forehead and had picked up his wrist with the other. "I believe your fever is gone," she announced with a frown between her brows, "but your pulse is more rapid than I think is good for you."

"I am not surprised," Gideon responded dryly. "I do not usually awaken to find a beautiful woman in bed with me. When I do, my pulse has a tendency to behave in an irregular manner." He grinned at her. "It is considered quite natural, I believe. So if I were you, I would get out of this bed as fast as I could."

"Or . . . ?" She grinned back at him. "What might happen were I to fail to heed your advice?"

He looked into her mischievous eyes and was lost. He leaned over her. "This," he said, and took her mouth with his. Instantly her arms went around his neck, and she drew him even closer. He couldn't help himself. He was drowning in the sweetness of her kiss, the feel of her body pressed against his as they slid slowly down into the bed. She was his. There was no mistaking the quality of her surrender, the passion she didn't even try to hide.

Struggling to control his own desire for one more moment in her arms, Gideon did not know whether to laugh or curse when he heard the door open. He looked up and slowly withdrew from his love's embrace.

"Good morning, Miss Forrester," he said formally.

"Captain." Her tone was neutral as she came into the room and kicked the door shut behind her. She was carrying a breakfast tray, which she set down on the table next to the bed. "Amelia. I think that you may have about thirty seconds to get out of that bed and into the chair. Take the book with you, and try to look as if you spent the night reading and dozing."

"As indeed she did," said Gideon.

Amelia didn't move. She looked defiant, and she gave both her friends a hard look. "I do not see any purpose to be served in pretending I did not spend the night in Gideon's bed, since I did." She silently dared either of them to object.

"Amy, stop trying to ruin yourself so I will marry you. No one but Jane will know that you fell asleep where you did, or that I took shameless advantage of you and kissed you."

"For which forbearance I am supposed to be grateful, I gather." Mutiny was in her eyes.

Gideon sighed. "Amy, angel, we really cannot discuss this now. Please get out of this bed and have some tea. You have to see Eustace this morning, and you had best be fortified."

Amelia's face fell. She had been primed for a battle royal over her behavior, but Gideon refused to gratify her. He had kissed her as if he loved her, and then ordered her to ignore her feelings and prepare to cope with life. Sighing inwardly, she faced the fact that she had other, more practical problems to deal with.

"Eustace," she said, a little residue of fear tingeing her voice. "Yes. I had forgotten." Quiet now, all mischief and passion extinguished, she slid from the bed, her fingers trailing reluctantly from Gideon's arm. "I will return in a few minutes."

By the time Amelia had washed and brushed herself, she was feeling more like a daylight person, brisk and tough as old boots. Ready for anything. Even Eustace. But not for Sir Richard, who had taken up his position in front of the fireplace in Gideon's room when she returned. She did not think she could face another scene with the colonel, and she almost considered escaping to the kitchen and eating with Cook, something she used to do as a child when she had tried Miss Goodacre's patience too far.

"Lady Amelia." He inclined his head, but the look in his eyes was absentminded. His thoughts were elsewhere.

"Sir Richard." He looked grave, she decided, as if there were some momentous problem to be solved.

"Have you looked in on my naughty cousin this morning?" she asked. She knew she sounded flippant and light-minded, but it was either that or quail at the thought of having to see that monster.

Sir Richard frowned. "Naughty?"

"It is just Amy's kind of Dutch courage," Gideon said. He sat up against a pile of pillows with a tray across his legs. He looked bright and amused and ready for anything. Only the lines of strain around his eyes revealed the toll yesterday's actions had taken. "She belittles what she fears."

"I would like to get your opinions of what I should do with regard to Eustace," Amelia said, ignoring Gideon's last comment. He was right, and it shook her that he knew her that well and took that knowledge so casually. "I have determined that he should go abroad. But I need the means to keep him there."

"A credible threat," Sir Richard murmured.

"Yes," said Amelia. "But what would that be?"

There was silence for a few minutes until Gideon smiled a thin, knowing smile and said, "A confession. Make him sign a confession that he kidnapped Amelia and meant to force her to marry him and later that he was going to kill us both. If he signs it, and Amelia deposits it with her banker or lawyer, with orders to reveal it if he ever dares to return, that should keep him removed permanently."

"Excellent idea," said Sir Richard. "If he balks, you can simply threaten to inform the authorities."

"But he will know I would not willingly risk our family name that way," Amelia objected.

"Nonsense." Jane looked up from the knitting with which she occupied her hands. "Eustace will believe that you will do anything for Gideon. If he thinks you want him out of the way to protect Gideon from harm, he will believe that you are capable of anything and he will sign the paper."

"She is right," Sir Richard said, a slight smile curving his lips. "If you would like, I will undertake to draft such a document."

Gideon remained silent. Amelia looked over at him, but his face told her nothing. Their passionate embrace might never have happened. Everyone seemed to know how she felt, but even she did not know how Gideon truly felt about her. She knew Gideon's deep-rooted aversion to being thought a fortune hunter, preying on the daughter of the man who took him in and sponsored him. That and their frantic declarations of love when death stared at them. But what did he really feel, now that they were free and safe? When they were in dire circumstances, he cared enough to grant her her heart's desire. But was it his desire as well? She did not know.

You cannot think about that now. You cannot give way, she told herself. *You have other problems, my girl, and you could use some advice about them.*

"Do you think I had best speak to him myself?" she asked, trying to hide her craven desire not to do so.

"I do not think you can afford to wait until your solicitor or man of business can come here, even if you feel you can confide in them," Sir Richard said. "If you like, I will talk to the duke with you." He sounded oddly diffident, a great change from the furious, driven man of the previous night.

Amelia was still reluctant to accept any help from Sir Richard. His remarks about Gideon had infuriated her, and she did not relish being in his company, still less in his debt.

"That is kind of you, Sir Richard," she said, her voice cool, "but Eustace is my cousin, and I should speak to him alone."

"I would be happy if you would allow Sir Richard to accompany you, Amy. And to draft the document, so that you need not wait for a solicitor to do it." Gideon sounded tired. She looked over at him. He was still wooden-faced, but she could see concern in his eyes. He knew how Eustace had reacted to her yesterday.

She could deny him nothing. "Of course, Gideon, if you wish it. Sir Richard, thank you. I will accept your help."

She could tell by the faint tightening of his lips that the colonel was fully aware of her reluctance to do so. It was only because she dreaded seeing her cousin even more that she had acceded to Gideon's request. He nodded curtly and went back to writing at the table by the bed.

As they left the room to go down to the library, where Hugh Sidley had taken Eustace, Sir Richard frowned and looked down at the figured carpet in the hallways as if it held the answer to a fascinating riddle.

"Lady Amelia, I am sorry for my behavior yesterday with respect to Captain Falconer." He spoke without looking at her. "I was—overset, and I spoke without thinking. I have since thought a great deal, and I ask only that you refrain from judging me until I have had a chance to speak to Captain Falconer. I believe that there is an explanation—" He broke off impatiently. "Let us get this unpleasant task over with, and if you will stay with Captain Falconer while I talk with him, then you will understand us both a bit better."

Amelia was puzzled by the colonel's cryptic speech and the air of preoccupation and suppressed excitement that radiated from him. "Of course, Colonel. If it meets with Gideon's approval, I will stay."

"Thank you."

They had reached the library. Amelia found herself unable to take the first step over the threshold. She simply could not make her feet move. Sir Richard took her elbow and led her over the sill and into the large, paneled book-lined room that her father had loved more than any other place in the world. And now it was being defiled by the presence of his heir and successor. Once he had helped her enter, Sir Richard left her side and went to sit unobtrusively at the desk. Amelia saw him take up one of her father's quills before her attention was drawn to Eustace, her cousin and her enemy.

"Good morning, coz." Eustace was striving for jauntiness and insouciance. But as she looked into his face, Amelia could see the ravages the past few days had taken on him. He was unshaven, unkempt, and one corner of his mouth jerked spasmodically. His eyes were dull, and he refused to meet her gaze.

"Well, coz?" he said with an assumption of bravery. "What have you to say to the head of the family?" He tried to grin, but it was a ghastly travesty.

Her carefully prepared speech outlining her demands went out of her head. "Why, Eustace? Why did you do it?"

He shrugged, and Amelia noticed for the first time that his wrists were not restrained. She stepped back in instinctive alarm. "Because I needed your money, coz. Why did you think?"

"And you were willing to kidnap me and kill Gideon to get it? Eustace, we are blood relations! How could you?"

Eustace's dull eyes gleamed suddenly with malice. "Because I thought you deserved it, you mealymouthed little puritan. And because it would have given me great pleasure to have gotten the best of you and had you and your money in my power." His hatred was palpable and drove Amelia back another step before she stiffened her spine and determined to hold her ground.

"I'm sorry I asked. I should have known the answer." She remembered her mission and laid out her proposal in quick, clear sentences.

As he listened, Eustace's bravado evaporated. When she finished, all he said was, "A confession? Surely you don't require that. My word should suffice."

One look at Amelia's face should have told him her response to that assertion, but his sense of grievance was so strong, he missed the anger in her eyes. It was only when Sir Richard spoke for the first time that he understood.

"Your word is not worth as much as Blakeley's. You will sign the confession or risk being hanged for attempted murder."

Eustace seemed to shrink before Amelia's eyes. "Very well," he said. "Have some scrivener write it up, and I will sign."

"I have taken the liberty of drafting something," said Sir Richard, picking up the papers he had written. "If Lady Amelia will examine it and initial it, you can then sign it."

Amelia skimmed the document. Unable to read of the events of the past days without feeling ill, she took a pen from the desk and quickly scribbled her initials. Then, without looking at him, she handed the sheets to Eustace. He studied them carefully for a few minutes, then shrugged and signed the last page.

"There, dear Amelia, is your revenge. When can I have my money?"

"You may draw it at my banker's the day after tomorrow. I would like you gone before Christmas, if possible. Your mother may go with you or stay and make her home on one of the estates, as she chooses."

"You always were too good to be true. I suppose now you're going to marry that misbegotten gypsy."

Glad to feel anger once again instead of sick revulsion, Amelia said only, "If he'll have me," and swept out of the room.

Chapter Sixteen

As they walked back upstairs, Amelia felt reaction setting in. She had managed to push Eustace's part in yesterday's terrifying scenes to the back of her mind while she was dealing with the results. But now she felt once again the force of her cousin's hatred beating against her mind.

"Why does he hate me so?" she wondered aloud.

"Evil and weakness always hate strength and goodness. It is a law of nature." Sir Richard spoke matter-of-factly, as if what he'd said was too obvious to need explanation.

Amelia considered Eustace's lifelong malice, directed not just at her father and Gideon, but at anyone luckier or more gifted than he. There was a sort of peace in thinking that there was nothing she could have done to deflect that hatred, that it was rooted in his character and was not the result but the cause of the dislike she in turn had always felt for him.

When they reached Gideon's room, Amelia straightened her shoulders and pasted a smile on her face. She would not reveal how shaken she still was by what Eustace had done. Gideon had enough to do just to recover.

"Eustace has agreed," she said as she entered. "He will sign, and then he will be on his way to the Continent or perhaps to the antipodes. It scarcely matters. He will be gone."

Gideon looked at her from the bed, his eyebrows raised at her lighthearted tone. "Did it go as easily as she says, Sir Richard?"

"Not altogether, but Lady Amelia refused to give way and the duke was forced to agree." Sir Richard went to assume his usual position in front of the fireplace. He frowned down into the flames for a moment. Then, as if he had reached a decision about something, he straightened and turned to face Gideon.

"There is something I think you and I need to discuss," he said without preamble.

Jane began to gather her knitting together, but Amelia pulled the other small armchair closer to the bed and sat down with a resolute air. She would not leave unless Gideon requested it.

Sir Richard looked at Jane as she rose and unobtrusively walked toward the door. "I would ask that Miss Forrester stay if you have no objection, Captain."

"Since I am not entirely sure what you wish to discuss, I have no reason to exclude anyone." Gideon gestured to the chair with a smile. "Come and sit down, Miss Forrester. If things get too racy, you may cover your ears."

She inclined her head in agreement and sat down again. All three gazed at Sir Richard, waiting for him to begin. He frowned and was silent for a full minute before he looked up at Gideon and said, "I need to ask you about your life before the gypsies sold you to the chimney sweep."

"No!" Amelia's involuntary protest sounded like a pistol shot.

Gideon shook his head. "No, no, Amy. It is clear that the colonel thinks I know a great deal more than I do about his family. I am not altogether clear about what he thinks he learned from me yesterday." He grinned at Amelia, his mask as the cold-blooded cavalry officer firmly in place. "I was not at my best when we talked. In fact, I believe I was off my head. Perhaps if we go over it now, we can all come to some conclusion." His grin faded, and his expression was almost grim as he looked Sir Richard in the eye and said, "Proceed, sir."

Sir Richard stood on the hearth, facing all three of his companions. He planted his feet firmly, about shoulder width apart and clasped his hands behind his back. "Before I begin, I must apologize for my behavior yesterday. Jane knows a little about my family, but I fear that you, Falconer, as well as Lady Amelia must have been shocked by my accusations.

"I have spent years trying to trace my nephew, Francis. He disappeared one spring day when he was six and has not been seen since. His mother has never been able to face his death and insists that he is still alive, that she would somehow know if her son were dead. So she has entertained charlatans and cranks of every description, not to mention every vagabond and criminal who bears even the slightest likeness to Francis. None has ever come close to convincing her. She is sure she will know her son at a glance, even after twenty-one years.

"I am very fond of Serena, and I hate seeing her suffer, her whole life concerned with nothing but finding her son. I would like to be able to give her incontrovertible proof that Francis is dead." Looking down, he seemed to study his boots for a moment before adding, "At least, that is what I wanted until this morning."

Gideon was listening politely, but something about the colonel's voice had captured Amelia, and now she leaned forward, certain that what was to follow would be important.

Sir Richard appeared uncharacteristically nervous. He looked at Gideon with what seemed to Amelia to be almost a pleading expression—if that were not completely out of the question. She was sure Sir Richard Sinclair had never pleaded with anyone for anything in his life.

"I have to ask you some questions about your life before the gypsies sold you to the chimney sweep."

Gideon's face instantly assumed the shuttered, impervious expression he wore whenever anyone brought up the subject of his childhood. Amelia saw it and moved imperceptibly closer to him, as if to protect him from his painful memories.

"Why do you find this necessary?" Gideon's voice was chilly yet impassive, as neutral as if they were discussing the weather. "I thought you would want to know about the gypsies. The usual information. I do not like to talk about it, but in your case, I am willing to make an exception. I do not understand why you want to know about—before. Surely if I knew your nephew, it was after that."

"I believe the reason for my interest will become clear as we proceed." Strain was evident in the rasp of Sir Richard's voice.

"You will forgive me if I find that assurance insufficient." Gideon turned his head away, dismissing the colonel as clearly as if he had shown him the door.

"Please, just indulge me for a few moments. I understand that this is difficult for you—as it is for me. But I cannot tell you what I hope to learn without prejudicing the outcome."

Sir Richard was pleading now, Amelia thought. There was no doubt about that. Coupled with the tension that seemed to radiate from him, it made her even more convinced that Gideon needed to answer his questions.

Gideon shrugged. "You are not the first to want to know the dirty gypsy brat's origins." His tone stung Sir Richard, as Amelia knew it was meant to do. She could see the colonel flinch. "Go ahead." Now Gideon sounded merely bored. "I will answer."

Sir Richard's tension seemed to grow even more pronounced, and Amelia found herself leaning forward, awaiting his questions as if she herself were going to have to answer.

"What are your first memories?"

Gideon stared at him. This was not what he expected, and he answered without the sarcasm or other defenses he usually assumed. "I—I don't know. Sunlight through white curtains. Laughter. Warmth. A woman singing. Nothing more concrete than that."

"Do you remember what she was singing? That lullaby perhaps?"

Gideon's frown was formidable. Anyone less determined than Sir Richard would have stopped. But the colonel ignored the storm signal. "I tell you again, I need your answers."

"Yes, I remember the lullaby. There were other songs as well, but I remember that one in particular." Gideon felt as if he were being stretched on the rack. To remember was bad enough, but to talk about the dreams that had kept him company through the bad years was torture.

"Do you remember anything at all about the woman who sang?"

Gideon took a moment to respond. When he did, his voice was thick and his throat worked spasmodically. "She had a very sweet voice, and she smelled of flowers." He stopped, then spoke in a low, choked voice. "She had dark hair."

Sir Richard's hands clenched. "And next, the silver ball."

Amelia could see he was as tense as a strung bow. "Where did you get that ball?"

"It is iron, not silver, and I have always had it. I had it in the gypsy camp."

"If you polish it, you will find it is silver. Like the song, the ball came from the time before." It was not a question. Sir Richard seemed to assume the truth of those facts.

"Yes. I have said all this, but you refused to believe me. You seem to think I had something to do with your nephew's death. You tried to take my ball from me." Gideon seemed to draw himself together, as if gathering his forces to face an enemy whose strength he could not yet gauge.

"I—I am sorry." Sir Richard cleared his throat. "I have said so before, and I will repeat it as often as necessary. Yesterday I thought that you were hiding something. I believe now that your answers are all completely truthful." He drew in his breath and seemed to stand even straighter than before. "I need to know one last thing."

Amelia sensed the anguish behind his simple words. This was what the colonel had been driving at all along, she knew. She reached out for Gideon's hand, and he clamped his over her fingers with a viselike grip.

"How did you get to the gypsy camp?"

"What do you mean?" Gideon's eyes were wary and a little wild. This was not something he wanted to deal with, Amelia knew. This brought back the nightmare of drowning.

"What happened to you? Why did you leave the house with the white curtains and the singing woman?"

"I don't know. I don't remember." Gideon spoke quickly. Sweat began to bead his brow.

Amelia's hand moved under his in protest. He did remember at least some of it. He had told her about it only yesterday.

Sir Richard saw Gideon's instinctive response. "I think you do. Tell me," he commanded. "I must know."

Gideon closed his eyes. "I used to have a nightmare. It comes back sometimes even now. Before a battle. When I was wounded. I do not want to think about it." He opened his eyes and faced his inquisitor.

But it was Jane who answered him. "I think it might help you to answer. The nightmare may lose its power over you if you speak of it, and perhaps together we can make some sense of it." She smiled encouragingly at Gideon. "I have seen it happen sometimes, Captain. To look at a nightmare in the daylight can weaken its hold. We are your friends—even Sir Richard is, I am sure."

Gideon still sat silent, his usually healthy tan pale under his bandage, his hand gripping Amelia's until the knuckles showed white.

"I think Jane is right, Gideon," Amelia said. Her heart aching for his pain, yet she was sure that he had to go back to that time. "Try to remember the river."

"River!" Sir Richard exclaimed.

"Yes." It was Amelia who answered. "Tell him, Gideon."

"If nothing else, it will end his attempt to bully you and blame you for his nephew's disappearance," Jane added in her schoolmistress voice. Sir Richard started to smile at her.

"He disappeared?" Gideon said, suddenly alert.

"I think we had better share our memories and dreams," Sir Richard said, his smile gone. "Jane is right. The truth uncovered in the sunlight may set us all free. And it will end my attempts to force you to remember what you so clearly do not wish to. I promise you that."

"Very well." Gideon drew a deep breath and pulled Amelia's hand closer to his chest. The movement lifted her out of the chair, and once again she took up her position on the edge of the bed, guarding Gideon from any threat.

"I remember running water . . . and sunlight upon it. It seemed to me that I knew that stream or river well. But in my dream the water changes and swirls and eddies, and my mouth is full of water and my nose, too." Gideon spoke faster and faster, as if trying to get rid of the words as quickly as possible so he could be done with reliving the pain and loss of that time. "I cannot breathe. My eyes sting, and I cannot see. I try to breathe, but there isn't any air. Just water. Then there is a great flash and a burst of pain in my head. And then I see white light everywhere, and the pain in my head and in my lungs starts to go away."

His hand squeezed Amelia's so tightly she had to fight not to cry out. She could see his eyes grow wilder and more frightened with every word. "After that, I don't remember anything until I woke up with the gypsies. I was under a wagon, covered with rags, and I could hardly breathe. My head hurt, and my chest ached. I didn't know where I was or why I hurt." Gideon sighed and leaned back against the pillows, closing his eyes. "And that is all I remember."

There was silence in the room. Gideon's tortured voice had held them all spellbound, each one trying to picture what could have caused such a reaction.

Jane spoke first, her matter-of-fact voice defusing the unbearable tension. "I think perhaps you fell into a swiftly moving stream and could not swim. And then the flash and pain and waking up much later, still confused, make me surmise that you hit your head on something."

Gideon shrugged, as if anxious to put the whole topic behind him. Amelia could see the sheen of perspiration gleaming on the part of his chest exposed by his nightshirt as well as on his face. The hand that held hers had grown cold as he talked. The white lines around his mouth had grown deeper. He was just about at the end of his tether, she thought.

Sir Richard turned away from the other three. He stood alone in front of the fireplace, isolated in his deep concentration. His frowning face seemed carved from stone, a face that would never smile again.

At last he looked around, and when he spoke it was in the tone of a barrister summing up before the jury. "I have thought about this a great deal. I have come to a conclusion, but I understand that the rest of you do not know what I know. So let me go over the facts." He began to tick off points on his fingers. "First, Gideon Falconer is about the age my nephew Francis would be if he were alive. Second, Gideon Falconer knows the private lullaby that only Francis and members of his immediate family could know. Third, when Francis disappeared he had in his possession the silver ball he had received for his birthday shortly before. Fourth, that ball is now in Gideon Falconer's possession."

"It is iron," Gideon said stubbornly. "It is black iron."

"It is silver," Sir Richard responded in the same tone. "Badly tarnished silver."

"I will see to it that it is polished," Amelia said, striving to keep her tone calm. "Then we will know."

"In any case," Sir Richard continued, "there are a great many coincidences in these two stories. Too many to be accepted as *just* coincidences. I believe there is a pattern."

Amelia tensed. If he was going to insist again that somehow Gideon had known Francis and taken his keepsake and stolen his song, she was not going to order him out of her house again. She was going to get Hugh Sidley and one of the farmers to escort him bodily off the premises!

"Then there is the matter of the river." Sir Richard stepped away from the fireplace and fixed Gideon with his gaze. "A river runs through our estate. Francis used to play there with some of the tenants' children. He was playing there the day he disappeared. Everyone always thought he went into the river somehow. Francis could swim, but not very well. We all believed he drowned." He looked at Gideon with something very like wonder in his gaze. "Just as you remember doing."

Gideon could not seem to stop staring at Sir Richard, as if he were trying to decipher the message contained in his eyes. At last he spoke. "Are you saying once again that I knew Francis? Perhaps that I killed him for his possession?" He threw his chin up and stared defiantly at the friends who looked back at him with worry and fear in their eyes. "It happened more than once on the streets. I can tell you I did not harm anyone to steal from them, but I have no way of proving it. I can say that I never met anyone named Francis, but we all took whatever names we wanted, or were given, on the street. If I did know him, he could have been called anything."

Sir Richard moved as if on marionette strings to stand by the bedside, looking down at Amelia and Gideon.

"I think he was called Gideon," he said.

"Yes," Amelia breathed. It fit. It answered the nagging questions she had asked herself about the song and the iron ball. It explained Gideon's nightmare. "It could be."

Gideon stared at Sir Richard. "You do not think I harmed him? Your nephew?"

There was a long pause, heavy with expectation. Sir Richard extended his hand, and a painful half smile crooked his mouth. At last he spoke. "I think you *are* my nephew," he said. "I think you are Francis, that you fell in the river, cracked your skull, and were fetched up out of the water by the gypsies. Why they did not recognize you as the grandson of the 'seigneur' of the neighborhood I do not know. Perhaps because in your plain breeches and shirt you looked like anyone's child. They must have hidden you under the wagon and covered you with rags so you wouldn't be discovered when our men were out searching for you.

"By that time they must have known who you were and feared being accused of hitting you over the head and kidnapping you because you had been missing for so long. I remember they left the area not long after you were lost. They must have taken you with them so they would not be pursued for kidnapping a peer's child, which would have happened if they had left you behind to be found."

Gideon released Amelia's hand and ran his hands over his face. "No. I do not remember anything like that—and I would remember. I did not know the secret of the ball. I do not remember you or—or my parents. It is just a dream of running water. I must have found the iron ball somewhere. I am not your nephew. I am not some long-lost scion of a noble house! I would have known! I would have remembered." His voice grew hoarser and more tortured as he spoke, and Amelia thought she could see the glitter of tears in his eyes.

"I am convinced that it *is* true. There is no other explanation that covers all the facts." Sir Richard reached into his pocket and pulled out a small, flat case covered in worn petit point embroidery. He flipped a hidden latch and opened it up to reveal two miniatures. One was of a small boy with unruly black hair and a mischievous smile. The other picture was of a beautiful young woman with the same tumbled black curls and smile.

"That is Serena. She has dark hair, as you said of your mother."

"Of the woman who sang," Gideon corrected. He drew back from the open case as if afraid it might harm him. "I do not know if the woman I remember was my mother."

Amelia picked up the case and looked at the smiling child. "Oh, Gideon, that is just the way I imagined you must have looked in the years before I knew you!"

Gideon looked away, as if her words pained him. Immediately Amelia reached for his hand. She had not meant to hurt him, but she was more and more convinced that Sir Richard was right.

Sir Richard turned away, fighting some emotion of his own. It could not be easy for him, probing like a surgeon at the painful boil of Gideon's past, Amelia thought.

"I am convinced of who you are," Sir Richard said. "I know that this is sudden for you and that you are having some difficulty with the idea."

"I am not having any difficulty." Gideon spoke in the cold, controlled voice he used when he was tamping down any emotion, fighting to keep it under control. "I reject the idea. I cannot believe that a small toy and a song can have truly led you to this mad notion."

Sir Richard turned back to face his adversary. He spoke as if Gideon had said nothing. "I want you to come home with me, to Southbridge. For Christmas. If we wait here for a few more days, you will have recovered enough to travel. Christmas isn't until next week." Sir Richard held out his hand, but Gideon ignored it. "If you prefer, I will introduce you simply as my fellow officer, Gideon Falconer. But I want to see you there, and I want you to see it. Once you are there, you may remember something more of your past."

Gideon looked up, and after hesitating a split second, took Sir Richard's hand. "And to see if your sister-in-law has an infallible vision that I am her son? It is very kind of you to overcome your distaste for my origins and try to claim me. I do not know your sister-in-law, but I do not want to play guessing games with her about her loss. It would be unfair to her and to me. I make no claim of being anyone's heir."

Amelia had sat silent, unwilling to utter so much as a word if it would lead Gideon to one reaction rather than another. She wanted to know how he felt, what he believed about himself. For years he had been at odds with Society because he was an outcast who through luck and grit and hard work had made a precarious place for himself in the world. He had despised those who despised him either because of his supposed origins or because he had no origins at all. But he had also rejected any attempt to accept him. He had refused Amelia's love because he felt unworthy of her, for no reason other than his lack of known parents.

Now he was faced with another possibility—that he had been born into the highest levels of the very Society which had scorned him, and which he, in turn, had scorned. Now he had an opportunity to be accepted into those previously closed circles solely on the basis of his ancestors. No wonder his instinctive reaction had been to flee and reject this gift that demanded he turn his back on what he had made of himself in order to become what he had been born to be. Amelia sighed. One way or the other, Gideon's life would never be the same.

Sir Richard looked down at her and smiled. "Will you spend Christmas with me at Southbridge, Lady Amelia? If you come, I feel sure I can persuade Gideon, no matter what his feelings about my ideas of his family. Will you come?"

She answered from her heart, without thinking. "Yes," she said.

"Amy!" Gideon looked at her as if she had betrayed him. "How can you?"

"I have no plans for Christmas, nowhere to go. I do not want to stay here or return to London. Not yet. Not until Eustace has gone." She tried to smile, but the truth of her words pierced her heart. "I do not want anyone's sympathy, Gideon," she hastened to add, despising the idea of being seen as pitiful. "You must make your own decision, but if there is any possibility that Southbridge is where you were born, I want to see it. So thank you, Sir Richard. I accept with pleasure."

The colonel turned to Jane, sitting silent and watchful, a little apart from the others. "Miss Forrester?" he said. "Will you do me the honor of accompanying us to Southbridge for Christmas?"

She shook her head and smiled. "I do not belong at your family reunion, Sir Richard," she said formally. "But I thank you for including me in the invitation. I have work awaiting me in London. Christmas is one of the busiest times of the year for me."

Richard smiled at her. "Lady Amelia is not a relation so far as I know, and Gideon refuses to acknowledge even the possibility of belonging to my family. At least you own yourself my friend. That puts you in a very small group." Looking down at her, he locked his gaze with hers. "Please come, Jane. Surely someone else can take over your work. What would they do if you were ill?"

Jane hesitated. Amelia could see that she truly wished to go but was held back by some apprehension. She couldn't allow her friend to give in to fear. Or Gideon to do so either.

"I wish you would come, Jane. I would like you to be there with me. And you, Gideon. Would it not be better to face the past than to hide from it? Whatever you find at Southbridge cannot change the man you have become."

"Very well, Amelia." Jane's voice was uncharacteristically soft, and she looked at Sir Richard as she spoke. "I will go."

"Outspoken as always, Amy." Gideon's smile was forced, but he raised their clasped hands to his lips. "You win. We will all journey to Southbridge for Christmas."

Chapter Seventeen

Three days later, they set out for Southbridge. Gideon had spent the intervening time sleeping and trying not to think of what Sir Richard had told him. As he had done when hurt fighting other boys years before or when wounded in battle, he set himself the task of healing as rapidly as possible, and managed to convince Amelia and Jane that he was ready after only three days.

After spending the better part of the day in the carriage with the ladies, Gideon insisted on riding the last few miles. He needed the open air and the feel of a horse underneath him when he saw Southbridge for what he insisted to himself was the first time.

The seat of the Marquess of Southbridge was a graceful stone castle, the major part of which dated from the time of the seventh Henry. It fit so perfectly into the woods and rolling lawns surrounding it that it almost seemed to have grown there. When they rounded the last turn in the long, rhododendrum-lined avenue, and the mellow golden stone could be seen for the first time, glowing in the pale sunlight of a December afternoon, Gideon and Sir Richard instinctively reined in their mounts.

"There it is," Sir Richard said.

"It is lovely." Gideon refused to surrender to the surge of emotion that swept over him at his first glimpse of Southbridge Castle. It was mere apprehension, he told himself, akin to the surge of energy one felt just before a charge. It was not recognition, not hope.

"I trust that the groom arrived in time to warn Serena." Sir Richard smiled. "They do not entertain much at Southbridge."

"And did you tell them to kill the fatted calf for the prodigal, Sir Richard?" Gideon asked, his unease finding release in sarcasm.

"They always do that when I come," his host responded. "I am the prodigal, you see."

"Ah. And I am your protégé, I assume."

"I could not very well convey my belief that you are Francis in a message delivered by a groom, Gideon. I will tell the marquess and Serena this evening, with you in attendance. It seems only fair."

Fair! Gideon thought. What in his life had ever been fair? Recently he had begun to remember more about the early days in the gypsy camp. It seemed to him that on first awakening, sick and confused, he had somehow expected to be taken home to find his family again. But in the days and weeks that followed, he had learned that nothing that happened to him had anything to do with fairness or goodness, but only with chance and what he could make of it.

"Shall we go on?" Sir Richard looked at his home with what Gideon thought was wary affection. "The coach will not be far behind us."

"Let us wait for Amelia and Miss Forrester," Gideon said, conscious of a cowardly desire to have Amelia by his side when he met the unknown people who might be his family.

The two men sat silent, looking down on the house below them, each lost in his thoughts. In a few moments Lady Amelia's traveling coach approached and drew to a halt.

Sir Richard leaned down and smiled in at the two ladies within. "We waited for you. Serena is not used to guests, and having two of them young ladies will make it easier for her."

"Oh, dear, Sir Richard, you should have said something. We did not mean to impose." Amelia was mortified. It had never occurred to her that a country house at Christmas would be anything but filled with relatives, friends, and neighbors. As the Abbey always had been.

"Nonsense. It is good for the marquess and Serena to have

guests. Otherwise they might simply ignore the day as they have grown to do over the years." He clicked his tongue and urged his mount forward. "We'll meet at the door. Come on, Gideon, let us lead the way."

When the carriage reached the door, an elderly man in a butler's livery was already out on the steps, directing several footmen to take the riders' saddlebags into the house. He greeted Sir Richard with what appeared to be real affection.

By the time the carriage came to a stop in front of the massive oak door, a dark-haired woman dressed in black had come out to greet the visitors. Amelia had an immediate impression of both warmth and sadness in her eyes as Serena, Lady Mountjoy, greeted her. Sir Richard had explained that the heir to the Marquess of Southbridge was the Earl of Mountjoy. He himself refused to use the title that had belonged to his brother, and Serena continued to be the Countess of Mountjoy.

"Lady Amelia," the countess said in a quiet, sweet voice, "I am so glad that you have come to share the season with us. We have a very quiet Christmas, which I am sure will suit you since your loss is so recent."

"Thank you very much, my lady." Amelia could not help staring a little as she tried to decide if the lady resembled Gideon in any way. Their coloring was the same, she decided, but Gideon's vigor and strong personality were nowhere in evidence.

Lady Mountjoy ushered them all into the main hall of the castle. As they went in, Amelia could hear Gideon's sudden intake of breath as he saw the double staircase that ascended from each side of the hall and met in an elaborately carved balcony that led into the hall above.

"The double stairway," she whispered to him.

The look he gave her in return would have frozen a lesser woman. "Please do not do this, Amy," he said. "Do not try to make this mad escapade real. Many homes have similar staircases."

She bowed her shining head, and Gideon could have kicked himself. The only person in the world who truly cared about him, and he seemed unable to treat her as she deserved. Perhaps what he had endured as a child on the streets had hardened him to the point that he could not respond openly even to the one person he loved, the one person he was sure loved him.

Steeling himself, he turned to the woman Sir Richard thought was his mother and looked her in the eye. "Lady Mountjoy," he said, bowing over her hand. "It is very kind of you to welcome me here on Sir Richard's account."

"Any friend of Richard's is welcome at any time," she said, smiling up at him. As he held her gaze, Gideon became aware of a puzzled look in her eyes. "We have not met before, have we, Captain?" she said, uncertainty in her voice.

"No, my lady. I do not believe so. I have never been in this neighborhood, and I understand you are seldom in London." Gideon betrayed no emotion other than formal politeness.

"No, I never go there. In fact, it has been years since I have left Southbridge and Papa." She shook her head and smiled ruefully. "I must have windmills in my head. Of course, we have not met."

The guests were escorted to their chambers, down a rabbit warren of halls and corridors. Gideon tried not to think, not to ask himself if any of what he saw was familiar. He had felt a jolt when he had seen the countess. Was it just because Sir Richard had told him that she might be his mother, or did he remember her?

So many questions. He sighed. Jane and Amelia were shown into their rooms and disappeared. He felt a stab of loss. He was alone now. Sir Richard had vanished earlier, into a room on the first floor that might have been a library. He was going to greet the marquess. Gideon would meet him this evening, when they gathered in the drawing room before dinner.

At last the footman stopped and stood aside for Gideon to enter a room. He went in, saw his worn saddlebag deposited with care on the floor before a large bed. The bed hangings and curtains were of deep crimson velvet and a dark blue and crimson carpet lay on the shining floor. Everything was clean but worn-out and tired-looking. There was a sense that nothing had been changed in the room in many years, that not so much as a candlestick had been moved even an inch.

Later, as he made his way downstairs to the drawing room, Gideon noticed that the entire house seemed to have that same look of having been frozen at some point in time. He entered the drawing room to find Sir Richard there before him, together with Lady Mountjoy and a tall, spare older man who Gideon decided must be the marquess, Lord Southbridge, Sir Richard's father. Gideon stood a little straighter as he walked slowly over to meet the man who might be his grandfather. He could feel himself stiffen and become cold and formal as he always did when he encountered people who might snub him. After all, if they knew anything about him, it would have to be the story everyone else knew, the story Sir Richard had believed until yesterday. He was never sure how people would welcome a jumped-up gypsy brat with ideas above his station.

The marquess surprised him. There was a look of baffled hurt in his eyes as if life had dealt him more blows than he knew how to deal with. He greeted Gideon with gentle courtesy, the same courtesy he would have used to greet the Archbishop of Canterbury, Gideon was sure. Or the devil himself. Like the late Duke of Doncaster, the Marquess of Southbridge was a true gentleman.

After offering him a glass of Madeira, the marquess said, "My son tells me that you are a good man to have beside him in a battle. From Richard that is high praise indeed."

"Sir Richard is the bravest man I know." Gideon was surprised that he was able to say such a thing to someone he had only just met. But it was true, and the old man before him was the sort of person who valued the truth. Gideon was not sure how he knew that, but he did.

Sir Richard approached, a glass of amber liquid in his hand. "You found your way down without help, Gideon? I asked one of the footmen to go up and lead you back here."

"Yes," said the marquess, "you must have quite a bump of direction. We sometimes have to leave a trail of string, like Theseus in the labyrinth, so our guests can find their way around this old pile." He spoke with obvious affection for his home.

Gideon smiled. "I have always had that knack."

"Unusual, in this place," Sir Richard said, looking down into his glass and refusing to meet Gideon's eyes. "It has been rebuilt and added on to so many times that occasionally I am not sure I know where every room is."

"It was partially burned during the Civil War," the marquess said.

"The fourth marquess failed to turn his coat in time to avoid Cromwell's troops," Sir Richard noted. "The main hall was rebuilt during the Restoration. That's when the staircase was added."

"Let's play Cavaliers, Drake. You can be the general, and we will be your troops."

"Yes, Drake. We will fight the Roundheads off and save the castle."

Where had that picture come from? And who was Drake? Why did that name sound familiar? Those dirty, happy little boys forming into a ragged army behind the one they called Drake, the one who looked like—Gideon blinked and the picture was gone.

"Captain Falconer?" It was Lady Mountjoy's voice, and her hand that lay on his sleeve. "Are you all right?"

He stared down at her for a moment, mesmerized by the concern in her voice. Resolutely he thrust the thought of those little boys aside. "Yes," he said at last. "I am quite all right. This is truly excellent Madeira, my lady."

She smiled at him and removed her hand. "Thank you. I had nothing whatever to do with acquiring it, so I feel perfectly at liberty to agree with you about its excellence."

Before Gideon could think of a reply, Amelia and Jane entered the room. By the time they were introduced to the marquess, offered glasses of sherry or ratafia, asked about their comfort and the adequacy of the fire in their rooms, the butler entered and announced dinner.

Somehow Gideon found himself escorting Lady Mountjoy, while the marquess took Amelia's arm. That left Sir Richard and Jane to bring up the rear.

"You are comfortable, Jane?" Sir Richard asked. "And not missing your friends and activities at home too much? I am afraid that we are somewhat neglectful of Christmas here."

Jane looked around. "Yes. I can see that you do not favor holly or bows or a kissing bough. Do you not have a yule log in that enormous fireplace in the hall?"

"I cannot recall. I am not often here at Christmas."

"Well, now that you are, perhaps we can all help to make it a merrier one than you are used to."

Sir Richard's face grew serious. "If I am right in my deductions, Jane, this is going to be a far happier Christmas than anyone in this house has had for a good many years."

Impulsively she took his hand. "You must not expect things to go as you might wish them to, Richard. Sometimes people do not react as you believe they will."

He looked down at her. "You are warning me not to hope for too much. I will try not to, but it is hard when I have seen Serena bowed down by sorrow for so long."

He stood behind her chair as Jane seated herself. "You care for her very much, do you not?" she asked.

"Of course. Serena is the sweetest person I have ever known." Richard took his seat halfway down the enormous mahogany table, and footmen began to bring in the removes. Jane found that she was not very hungry after all.

Watching Jane toy with her food through two interminable courses, Amelia was struck by the strangeness of this dinner party. She looked at Gideon, who had been seated at his hostess's right and was struggling not to stare at this woman who might be his mother. Amelia smiled at him encouragingly. Considering what he had been through in the past few days, he looked remarkably fit and handsome. He was carrying off what must be the most difficult hour of his life with great aplomb. And now that she saw him seated next to Lady Mountjoy, the resemblance between them was so obvious that she wondered if she was the only one who noticed it.

She turned her head to look at Sir Richard, and saw him staring with the same arrested look she was sure was on her face. Almost dreading what she might see, Amelia turned to look up to where the marquess was sitting, at the other end of the table. When she noticed the epergne, she breathed a little easier. Surely he could not see over the huge silver piece. But then, the marquess was tall, easily as tall as Sir Richard or Gideon. And yes, he was looking at Gideon with a frown. His hand was clenched on the stem of his wineglass.

As Amelia looked on, her heart in her throat, he turned to his son. "Who is he, Richard?" The old man's voice was harsh with strain, and his eyes dark with some emotion Amelia could not read. "Who is Gideon Falconer?"

"Someone I thought you should meet, sir," Richard responded evenly.

His father's fork clashed to the plate. "I had not thought you would fall prey to this foolishness—seeing Francis in every face. I have grown used to it from Serena. I understand her need to hope. But you—! How could you, my boy?"

"Wait until you have all the facts before you judge me, sir." Richard's look was implacable. "I think you will understand."

Lady Mountjoy rose, a signal for Amelia and Jane to do the same. "Do not dare to discuss this without us, Father," she said, her voice sweet but somehow commanding. "I will not say what I think until you have joined us in the drawing room. I suggest you all hurry with your port."

The marquess threw his napkin down on the table. "I think we will all need brandy this evening, Serena. And we will drink it in the drawing room with you ladies. And then, Richard," he said, turning his icy gaze to his younger son, "I will expect a complete explanation from you."

"What is there to explain, Father?" Serena said. The room stilled as she turned to Gideon with a smile that was like a sunrise. "Richard has brought Francis home to us."

Chapter Eighteen

It looked like a scene from a bad melodrama, Amelia thought some ten minutes later. The marquess was standing facing Richard across the expanse of the drawing room fireplace. She and Jane were seated unobtrusively on a settee while Lady Mountjoy sat looking up at Gideon, her face still wreathed in that beatific smile.

And Gideon stood alone in the center of the room. Amelia longed to go and stand beside him to face down this unknown family with him. But for the first time she was unsure of her welcome. He had thrown Sir Richard's claim back in his teeth, proudly insisting on his gypsy heritage. She feared he would do the same with her friendship, simply because he felt he had to stand alone. But how did he really feel? No matter who they were, he had to want to know his kin. He had to be curious about where—and who—he came from.

Sir Richard was finishing his brief narrative of how he had come to believe Gideon Falconer was Francis Sinclair. The marquess stood, as he had since his son had begun speaking, silent and frowning down into his brandy glass.

"And the silver ball was the final link in the chain," Sir Richard was saying. "According to Lady Amelia, Gideon has had that token since she has known him."

The marquess looked up at last. He ignored his son and looked squarely at Gideon. When he spoke, his question took Gideon by surprise. "How do you feel about this, Captain Falconer?"

The words sounded merely curious, not accusatory, and Gideon felt his shoulders relax a bit. "I do not know, sir," he replied as honestly as he knew how. "I am used to thinking of myself as a foundling, probably a gypsy. I gave up wondering about my real family—if I ever had one—a long time ago. The Duke of Doncaster and Lady Amelia have been my family, and as long as I had them, I never felt the need for more."

Out of the corner of his eye, he could see Amelia smile. She must have known how he felt, but he could not remember telling her as clearly as this how much she and her father had meant to him. He was a little ashamed to note that she looked surprised, as if she had expected him to reject her as he had Sir Richard. Could Amy really doubt his feelings for her and her father after all this time? The marquess's voice pulled him back from this uncomfortable thought.

"You never wished to know where you came from? Who your people were?" The marquess appeared to find this remarkable. His voice held surprise and a hint of disbelief.

It was all Gideon needed to set the spark to his temper. "I know who I am. That is all I have ever had, and it has been enough."

To Gideon's surprise, the marquess smiled. "That sounds remarkably like Lionel speaking." To Gideon, he added, "Your—Francis's father."

The words hit him broadside. *Your father.* He had remembered the dark-haired woman, and despite his words to Sir Richard, he had always thought of her as his mother. But a father—

"I do not have a father," he said in a voice like flint. A father! Someone strong and brave, someone who would fight for you, defend you, protect you. Gideon almost laughed. Where had his father been when he was lying under the gypsy wagon, sick and afraid? Or sent scampering up into the tight, filthy confines of a London chimney, with a fire at his back if he balked?

"I do not need a father. It is too late for that, my lord." He could hear the accusation in his own voice.

The sadness Gideon had noticed before in the marquess's eyes seemed to grow deeper. "I am very sorry, my son. Lionel died not long after Francis disappeared. But, of course, you could not know that."

I am not your son, not your grandson. Gideon bit back the words. He did not want to add to the old man's distress. They gazed at each other, and Gideon had the odd thought that they saw and understood the depth of each other's pain in those few charged moments.

"I did not know the secret of the iron ball," he said, apparently at random. He threw the words out defiantly. "Sir Richard had to show me."

"The ball is silver, Gideon. I had it polished before we left the Abbey." Amelia sounded almost apologetic.

"You see!" Gideon said triumphantly. "I did not know. All these years I have thought it was iron."

"You had it in the gypsy camp?" the marquess asked.

For a moment Gideon was tempted to lie, to claim he had found it on the street in London. But then he looked at Lady Mountjoy and changed his mind. He could not lie to her. "Yes. I remember holding it while I was under the wagon. Someone tried to take it from me, but I wouldn't let go, and for some reason they let me keep it."

"You do not remember who you were? They took your name from you?" Lady Mountjoy's voice trembled. She rose and moved toward him.

Gideon restrained himself from backing away. He was afraid of her emotion, afraid of being loved. Teaching himself from an early age to do without ties to a mother, he had unknowingly taught himself not to want them. Now he was faced with a woman who apparently thought she had borne him, and he did not know how to react—except to back away, fearing to accept what he knew he could lose in an instant. Some hint of the pain he had felt as a lost child swept over him as he looked in those soft, caring eyes. Resolutely he shut his heart. It was the only way to survive.

"I was injured, I believe. I don't remember much of what happened right after I—came to the gypsies."

"How did you come to be Gideon?" she asked, laying a soft hand on his arm. "How did you get your name? You did not remember being Fran—having any other name?"

"I don't know. The sweep called me Gideon. I don't

remember if he named me or the gypsies told him that was my name when they sold me to him." He frowned, trying to remember.

"They sold you?" It was a whisper. "Oh, my dear." All the sorrow in the world was in her words.

"It happens." Gideon hoped he sounded matter-of-fact. He did not feel that way. "The duke managed to rescue a number of boys who had been sold and send them to school. He said I gave him the idea." It was the only good that had ever come of that time, and it sometimes redeemed the pain and shame that were its legacy.

"But you do not remember another name?"

"My lady, I believe I gave up trying to remember anything that bound me to another life." If he was being cruel, it was necessary. He could not take much more of this kind of gentle probing. "It was too painful to remember what I could not have ever again."

The marquess had been standing by the fireplace, tense and unmoving while his daughter-in-law questioned the young man standing alone and proud before all of them. Now he spoke again.

"What is it that you want from us, Captain Falconer? Richard brought you here, obviously believing that you are Francis. Yet it seems you do not wish to believe it. What is it that you do want?"

He seemed genuinely curious, Gideon thought, and there was a kindly look in his eye. As if it really mattered what some unknown cavalry captain wanted.

"I have known for many years that miracles do not happen routinely, my lord. I have had my miracle, and it changed my life." He smiled at Amelia. Her answering smile was full of wonder and love. For a moment Gideon allowed himself to look at her and believe that he could accept her love and give her his. He knew that if that were true, he would not need anything else to make his life complete.

"You refer to the duke and Lady Amelia taking you in?" the marquess asked.

"Yes. All that Sir Richard believes to have been proved is

simply too great a coincidence to be possible. When I was a little boy, I allowed myself to dream that I had a family and that someday they would find me and recognize me. Well, they never did. But I found a family nonetheless, and I would not trade them for any other in the world." Where had these words come from, he wondered. He had never spoken so openly about his feelings even to Amelia. Now to reveal them to strangers—

Where had he found the courage? He looked over at Amelia. From her, of course. She had always been his inspiration, her love and faith in him had always been the key to his success. He knew he could succeed because Amelia believed it so strongly, and he had to succeed for the same reason. Now he had to explore the issue of his birth and possible link to this wounded group of aristocrats.

"So it is the fear that Richard is wrong that makes you think he cannot be right?" Was the marquess actually smiling? Gideon could not believe it.

"You may put it that way if you wish, sir." Gideon drew himself up to his full six feet. He had never liked being laughed at. "I would say rather that I have a normal sense of the way life operates. It does not bestow marquessates on chimney sweeps, or make uncles of chance-met fellow officers."

The marquess shrugged, then turned away from Gideon to Amelia. "What kind of a boy did you find Gideon Falconer to be, Lady Amelia? Was he a little cockney thief? Whining on your doorstep? Begging a crust from you? Playing on your sympathies?"

Amelia stood in one fluid motion and rounded on the older man. "Lord Southbridge, Gideon was the bravest boy I ever saw. He asked for nothing. He was starving, and he would not beg. I found him cold and beaten and hungry, yet he did not ask for anything except not to be taken back to the man that made him fight other boys." Her chin stuck out, and her eyes flashed, but she still looked like a Christmas angel. Gideon grinned at her. She would defend her friends with her last breath.

"How did he speak?" It was Lady Mountjoy's quiet voice that spoke, cutting through the tension with her soft words.

"I beg your pardon?" Amelia was barely polite.

"Did he sound like you?"

Amelia frowned for a moment. Then her brow cleared, and she looked both surprised and excited. "Yes, yes he did. I never thought of it before, but he spoke like an educated child, not a street sparrow."

"So he spoke like a child who had been gently reared?" The marquess took up the questioning.

"Yes. And his grammar was quite good—except for some swearing. And that was hardly to be wondered at," Amelia finished in a defensive tone.

Gideon hid a smile. She would admit no flaw in a friend.

"True. It was not to be wondered at if he were not, in fact, a gypsy child but an aristocrat's son taken by mistake," Sir Richard said and looked around triumphantly, as if he had been vindicated. But his father still gazed at Gideon as if the secret of his grandson's identity could only be solved if Gideon himself unraveled the mystery.

"You still do not believe," the marquess said. "Why not?"

Gideon looked at the old man. He saw hope flare in his tired eyes. He searched his mind and came up with what told him that he was not, in fact, Francis Sinclair. "My name," he said. "When Sir Richard said 'Francis' it meant nothing. I always thought that somehow if I saw my home, heard my name, saw my family that I would know. But although the castle could be familiar and Lady Mountjoy's voice is—somehow—like one I seem to remember, my own name does not tell me anything. I am not Francis."

He looked at Amy then, trying to find his lifeline, the one person there who had known him first as Gideon, a ragged, dirty child of the streets and loved him anyway. He found what he sought in her eyes—encouragement, strength, love, everything that she could offer was there, and he drank it all in. He had denied himself, denied her love, but now he needed it with the same all-consuming desperation he had felt so long ago when he had first looked up and seen her face. And as she had then, she gave now without counting the cost or asking for return.

"Drake?" said a familiar voice behind him.

"Yes, Mama?" he said without thinking.

It was the silence that finally broke through his preoccupation with Amy. Total, breathless silence. He looked around, and then it hit him. He felt disoriented and breathless, as if his horse had just been shot out from under him.

"What?" He looked around him, somehow both terrified and excited, the way he felt just as the charge began and he could feel all the others at his back and beside him riding toward the enemy with him. "What is wrong? What did I say?"

Serena Sinclair, Lady Mountjoy, spoke to her son. "You always hated the name Francis. One of the village girls was named Frances, and you detested having what you called a girl's name. From the time you were three, you refused to answer to it." She gave him a tremulous smile, as if inviting him to share the memory. Gideon felt himself smile in response. *Drake. Yes. That was his name. It fit.*

"Lionel told you that you were named for a famous sailor, Sir Francis Drake. You liked that. You thought about it for a minute, and then announced that your name was Drake. And from then on you refused to answer to anything else."

He looked at the marquess, who smiled at him. Welcomed him.

"Just as you answered now." Sir Richard finished the thought.

"Does the name seem familiar?" the marquess asked.

Gideon didn't answer. He couldn't. *Drake. He was Drake.* He looked at Serena, Lady Mountjoy, and for the first time allowed himself to remember his mother, the dark-haired woman who sang. Her voice, the warmth of her arms. *Serena. Yes. She fit.*

"There were white curtains at the nursery windows," he said. It was not a question.

"Yes," Serena replied. "I used to sit with you in a chair that looked out of the window. I would leave it open because you liked to see the curtains blow in the breeze."

Gideon looked around. Everyone was looking at him, waiting to see what he would do. It was up to him. He could still deny what he knew in his heart. He could refuse to acknowledge this family that was ready to claim him. It was a temptation. He had made a life, an identity for himself, and part of that had been an acceptance of the fact that he had no claim on anyone. Now he realized that it had also meant that no one had a claim on him. Not even Amy, unless he chose to allow one. But there were no blood ties, no one who could demand a part of his loyalty.

He hardly knew these people, yet he could already feel tentacles of love and demand closing around him, binding him. The idea took him back to the days he had lain in the gypsy wagon, feverish and frightened and had wept for his mother. The sweep had beaten that out of him, and from then on he had never looked back. Now all those memories were about to be resurrected, and all he could think of was the pain of suppressing them.

"You do not have to accept us, you know." Finally Serena came up to him. Her eyes were bright with unshed tears, but she smiled at him. "You can leave here if you wish and never return." She put her hands on his cheeks and looked into his eyes. "It will not make the slightest difference. I will continue to love you just as I have for all these years. Only now I will know that you are safe, and successful and, I think, loved as well." Her smiling glance met Amelia's sober gaze. "So I have been given what I needed, my dear. Now I know whom to pray for."

Her lips touched his cheek, and Gideon felt his heart crack open, spilling all the fear and pain. Desperately he clung to his mother. "Where were you?" he cried. "Where were you when I needed you? When I cried for you? When I was hungry and cold? I called and called 'Mama,' and you never came."

By the time he finished, the tears he had suppressed for so long were trickling down his face, which was contorted with pain and anger. Serena took him in her arms and pressed her face to his, mingling their tears.

"Oh, my dear one, I know. I felt your tears, I knew that you were unhappy and in danger. So many times I felt desperation and fear and knew the emotions were yours." Tears choked her voice, but she clung to him and turned her face to his. "I tried so hard to find you. We all did. Your father never gave up, not until the day he died. Because we knew that you could be hurt and in trouble. And you were, you were. Oh, God, and we did not help you. You are right. I did not help." She could not go on.

But Richard marched across the room, took her out of Gideon's grasp, and sat her down. Jane, always ready to help those in pain, came over swiftly and knelt by her chair. Richard held out a glass of brandy, and Jane took it, thanking him with a smile. She held it and told Serena gently to drink. With trembling hands Serena took the glass and sipped.

"I am sorry. I did not mean to break down like this." She looked up at Gideon, her eyes pleading with him. "You will have to forgive us."

"Damn it, we did everything we could to find him. We have never stopped trying." Richard turned from Serena's crumpled figure to Gideon, standing like a statue, looking at nothing. "Serena has spent her life looking for you. It was not her fault the damn gypsies made off with you. She has nothing to apologize for. You are talking like a child."

"I *was* a child," Gideon reminded him, still refusing to look at anyone.

"True. But you're a grown man now, and this woman is your mother. She loves you. She has always loved you." Sir Richard's anger reached out and beat on Gideon's already battered senses in waves. It was more than anger. He could sense disdain as well. "And she deserves more from you than childish recriminations for not being more than human and finding you when no one could. Damn it, Gideon, for once think of someone who loves you instead of yourself!"

"I am sorry if I have not thanked you properly for killing the fatted calf in my honor." Gideon could hear his own voice as if it came from somewhere beyond his body. It was the same unreal sense of himself he had when he was wounded. With calm surprise he noted that the wound in his head had started to throb. He touched the bandage and felt a warm stickiness. He was bleeding, it seemed. "I believe if you will all excuse me, I will say good night." He turned on his heel with military precision, and left the room.

Chapter Nineteen

The evening ended soon afterward. Jane saw Serena to her room and instructed her maid to put her to bed and call Jane if there was any need during the night. She advised a soothing infusion of chamomile tea to help her sleep, and left quietly. Richard awaited her in the corridor.

"Is she all right do you think, Jane?"

"Yes," she said quietly. "I think she will sleep. She is concerned for Gideon, not for herself."

"Yes, that is Serena. Always thinking of others." Richard smiled down at Jane, who was unable to smile in return.

"If you will excuse me—" she said, and tried to slip away without saying anything more. When your heart is breaking, she realized, all you want to do is crawl away and hide like an animal in its burrow. Or in this case, your bed.

Richard took her hand, and she did not have the strength to free herself from that warm clasp. "Yes, Jane, you need a good night's sleep. You have been looking after the Sinclairs for a good while now." His smile turned rueful, and Jane gazed at him helplessly, unable to look away. "I hope that you can spare a little time tomorrow for this Sinclair. It seems an age since I have had a chance to speak to you in private. Perhaps a drive around the estate? I would like to show you Southbridge."

"Perhaps." *Never.* She could not endure any more of his friendship or witness more of his devotion to the beautiful, quiet, ladylike Serena. Serena, who had been his brother's wife and was thus forbidden to him by the church. Serena, whom he clearly adored. Serena, who was everything Jane Forrester was not.

"Good night, Jane, and thank you again for all your care." He raised her hand to his lips, but she could stand no more and snatched it out of his grasp. With cowardice she had not thought herself capable of, she fled down the corridor to the safety and solitude of her room.

Several hours later, after the moon had set and there was nothing but silence in the chill watches of the night, Amelia was lying in bed sleepless when she heard her door open and someone step silently into the room.

She knew immediately who it was, but she lay quietly while Gideon approached the bed. He knelt down and looked at her silently for a long moment. At last he reached out a hand and smoothed the curls that lay tumbled about her head, his touch unbearably gentle.

"Gideon," she whispered.

"I woke you. I am sorry. I meant just to look at you for a moment." He continued to stroke her hair. "I know I should not be here, Amy, but I needed to be near you."

Without conscious thought, she reached the small distance to where his hand lay on her coverlet and took it in hers. "I am glad you came. You were bleeding. Are you all right? I have scarcely had a chance to talk to you since—"

"Since the world turned upside down." His smile was wry. "I am fine. A new bandage and I feel as if only four horses had trampled me, rather than the entire regiment's."

At least he hadn't lost his sense of humor, she thought. For a while this evening, she had thought he was going to bolt—just mount his horse and leave. One of the advantages of being without ties except to your regiment and one lone female who would not leave you alone is that you could bolt, she thought. Now he was to some extent tethered, at least for a while. He did not look happy about becoming a marquess's heir.

"How do you feel about it all, Gideon?" she asked.

"Right now all I feel is cold," he responded. "There is a damnable draft around this floor, Amy."

"Well . . ." She debated inviting him into her bed. She

wanted to, there was no doubt about that, but she had compromised him enough already. Not just at the Abbey when they were alone, but in an effort to protect him from Sir Richard. Here, with his family gathered around, was not the place to put him under an obligation to marry.

"If I make up the fire and pull that chair up before the fender, I can wrap us both in your quilts." He looked at her hopefully. "I would like to hold you, Amy. I need you."

And, of course, that was enough. She rose and donned a warm wool robe while he put another log on the embers of her fire. A quilt in her arms, she went to the big wing chair that stood by the fire. Gideon held out his arms, and she went to him like an arrow to the target. He wrapped them both together and sat down with her on his lap, her head cradled on his shoulder.

"Oh, Amy, it feels as if I have held you like this forever." He rubbed his cheek against the silk of her hair. "You are the only sane thing in my life right now. The only person who still feels about me the way you did the day before yesterday."

"Your friends feel the same, Gideon." Amelia allowed herself to snuggle against him, needing his warmth and closeness for as long as she could have it.

"My friends do not yet know of the elevation of my fortunes. When they do, it will change how they feel about me. For better or worse, they won't feel the same about Lord Whoever—"

"Mountjoy," Amelia murmured. "I think it is the marquess's secondary title. Sir Richard refused to use it, I believe."

"Yes, he was knighted for his merits, and only uses that title." Gideon rubbed his forehead absently.

"You could do the same," Amelia suggested.

"I could, but since my entire name would be different, I do not think it would help. Francis Sinclair is not Gideon Falconer." He rubbed his head again, and Amelia reached up to stroke the bandage with cool fingers. He smiled.

"Actually he is. That is what you must remember. You are the same person regardless of your name or title and how many marquesses you are related to."

He smiled into her hair. "I love you, Amy. You always see things so clearly."

"What?" She jerked out of his arms and turned to look up at him, surprise dark in her cornflower eyes.

"You see things clearly. You understand how difficult it is for me to believe that I am the same person. I feel as if I do not exist. That Gideon and Francis are both just suits of clothes, not men at all."

He said I love you, she thought. He could say it just like that and then go on to discuss how he valued her advice!

"Damn you," she said, beginning to struggle out of his arms.

"What?" He held her where she was and looked at her in consternation. Clearly he had no idea of what he had said.

"You cannot just say 'I love you' and then go on to other subjects that apparently interest you more." She pushed hard against his chest, but his arms tightened in response. "I know you have had a difficult time recently, even though there are many people who would think you should be grateful to have fallen into a tub of butter."

"And is that what you think?" he asked, his frown formidable. "That I am the most fortunate of gypsies and should keep my tongue behind my teeth and enjoy my good luck?" He almost spat the words.

Had Amelia been less angry herself, she might well have wondered at her foolhardiness. She was sitting on the lap of a very angry man. But she did not care. She answered in the same style. "Do you love me? Or are you just using those words to mean you are fond of me, or happy to have me as your friend? Because if you do not mean them—"

He jerked her against the hard wall of his chest and took her lips with his in a devastating kiss. It wasn't meant to hurt or overpower, it simply told her what she wanted to know. He wanted her, he delighted in her, he desired her—body and soul. When his lips freed hers, her head was spinning and her heart sang.

"Of course I love you." He still frowned, and his voice was exasperated, as if she should have known how he felt. And she had known that he cared for her, that he desired her. But love—love had to be acknowledged. What he had said in their dark dower house prison was not necessarily true at Southbridge

Castle. What the foundling felt might have been gratitude. What did the earl feel?

"I have loved you from the first moment I saw you. But I have always thought I did not deserve you." A smile played at the corner of his lips for a moment. "You deserve nothing less than a royal duke."

Amelia gave a gurgling laugh. "Which of Prinny's brothers do you fancy in the part, pray? Cumberland perhaps? Or York?"

At the thought of his Amelia legshackled to any of the fat and foolish royal dukes, Gideon had to smile himself. "A fairy-tale prince, then. Do not make fun of me, Amelia. I felt my ineligibility very keenly."

She leaned her elbow on his chest and looked him sternly in the eye. "And now you think that as an earl and the heir to a marquess you are acceptable? Is that it? You still believe that people are to be judged by their ancestors? I am ashamed of you, Gideon!"

"No, angel, that is the amazing thing. That is what I have come to tell you." He pulled her back into the warmth and safety of his arms. "Now I know that it does not matter at all. I will be who I am regardless of my circumstances. And I will love you until the day I die and very possibly beyond that, so it will do me no good not to claim you. And I do." He kissed her again, and this time it was passion unleashed. It left Amelia spent, shaking and wanting more.

Gideon's voice shook, and his hand trembled a little as he ran his fingers down her cheek. "Now I know that you were right all along, and your father and I were wrong. So, angel, I must ask you—"

"My father?" Amelia felt a chill to her bones. "My father never believed that you were unworthy of me. He more than anyone believed in you. He knew—he—"

But the look in Gideon's eyes told her she was wrong, that somehow she had known her father less well than she had believed.

"Gideon? What makes you think this? Did he say anything to you?"

"Damn my tongue that gets ahead of my brain," he muttered.

"Gideon?"

"You are not going to let this go, are you?"

"No. What did my father say to you?"

"Amy, you must understand. He was very kind. He was only trying to spare both of us pain. He talked to me very fairly on several occasions so I would know how the world would view your marrying a—a mongrel."

"That was his word?" She was horrified. "He called you a mongrel?"

"No, no! It was just an example of the kind of talk I would expose you to if I were to presume upon our childish friendship."

He was quoting the duke, she was sure. She could hear her father in the measured words. "Presume? Presume to marry me? Is that what he said?" The idol she had made of her father had feet of clay. Feet! He was made entirely of clay.

"Do not be angry with him, angel. He meant it for the best. Truly."

"How can you say so, when he talked to you as if you were not quite human? Or at least not as human as he and I were!" She was furious. She had always believed that her father felt as she did. Her belief in his devotion to the principles of equality had been a part of the fabric of her life. Now it was being ripped apart.

"Your father believed as you do, angel, but he loved you more than he loved some abstract idea. He did not want to see you hurt by marrying someone unacceptable to the world you lived in." Gideon heard his own words and almost smiled. He believed them, but it had taken him years to come to terms with the duke's hypocrisy. Now he loved Amy enough not to want her belief in her father shattered.

She leaned back against him, and he could feel her draw strength from his words. She would learn to see her father as a man rather than a stainless hero, and that would be a good thing. Perhaps when they had children of their own—

"Amy, will you marry me?"

She looked at him with doubt in her eyes. "Are you sure it

isn't because you and my father think it is seemly now where it was not before?"

"I have told you that I know you were right. I know I am still the same person I have always been. Gideon Falconer and Francis Sinclair are only names." He gazed down at his indomitable, adorable Amy. "I need you beside me, whatever I am called."

"I have never made a secret of how I feel about you." For a fleeting moment Amelia wished she had behaved as Society would have had her do—been contrary and coy, flirted with a fan, and flaunted the admiration of other men. Gideon had always been so sure of her regard. He had never had to try to win her. He had only to be who he was, and she was his.

"It is the only thing that has seen me through sometimes," Gideon said, burying his lips in her hair. "No matter what happened, or what others said about me, I knew that you loved me. You had taken one look at a beaten, bloody, ugly little ruffian, and decided to care for him. That was the miracle, Amy. Not your father's acceptance or the school. Not even the food or the warmth. It was you." His voice, which had grown lower and lower as he spoke, cracked on the last words. "You have always been my miracle."

Amelia's heart seemed to melt within her, and love flooded her body. Gideon had finally uttered the words she had longed to hear for so long. He loved her. And her love, which had sometimes seemed such a burden to her and even to him, had in fact been cherished from the first moment she had bestowed it on him.

"It was always a gift, Gideon. My love was never meant to tie you down or coerce yours in response to it. But I am so glad that you felt it, too, at that very first moment." She raised her face and took his between her hands. "That is the miracle of both of us, perhaps."

"Will you—can you—take a chance on me, Amy? I don't know if I can be a marquess. Or a landowner. I don't even know if I can be a son and a grandson. I'm not sure I can be a good husband or father." He took her shoulders in his hands and gazed down at her. The quilt fell off them and pooled on the floor. "But I can't do any of it without you."

"You can do anything you want to do, Gideon." She slid her hands up to cup his cheeks. She was so sure of the truth of what she was telling him. He had to believe her. "You have always done what you had to do. Now you have a choice, and you can make it and make it work."

He shook his head, and she saw apprehension in his eyes. "No, I haven't a choice, not really. If I accept the name and the title, there are responsibilities that go along with it." There was a bit of the trapped, frightened little boy she had first encountered in his face. "I don't know how to be a marquess, Amy."

"There are many different kinds of marquesses. Some of them never see their estates or their families. They're in London writing laws or in Arabia buying horses or—" She smiled and kissed him. "You can be your own kind of marquess."

"Just as I was my own kind of foundling?" A faint half smile gave her hope.

"And your own kind of gypsy." She smiled at him, her faith in him so strong she was sure he could feel it through her hands that still bracketed his face. "You can be the marquess of cavalry!"

He laughed then, and she breathed deeply, sure that it would be all right, whatever they decided to do. "Not without you. Will you marry me, Amy? You say you love me, but you haven't said yes."

"Wellll . . ." She pretended to consider for perhaps five seconds. "I do love you, but I have been thinking. Perhaps you're right, and I should try to take the Duke of York away from Mary Ann Clarke. He is a royal duke, after all. I'm not sure I want to settle for a mere marquess!"

He stood then, with her still in his arms and whirled her around, while he laughed. "Have you forgotten how thoroughly you were compromised at the Abbey? I thought you were going to insist that I save your reputation after spending all that time alone with you. And you in only your petticoats!"

He stopped short and let her slide through his hands until she was standing on the floor, her head spinning a little from love and happiness. Then, with infinite gentleness and love, he bent to kiss her. His hands skimmed down her body and then gathered her in. Still, his clasp was soft as moonbeams. He would not coerce her. He would not even seduce her. She was free to send him away, to save her love until his ring was on her finger.

As his lips freed hers, she rejoiced in her freedom, in the care and respect that made the choice hers. She looked deep into his eyes for a moment, and then flung her arms around his neck and held him tight.

"I love you, Gideon Falconer—Drake—and I will marry you and love you until the end of my days!" Her arms tightened around him fiercely.

"Thank God for that!" he murmured. "Now I can do anything."

"Anything?" She raised her face to his. The blood was pounding thickly through her veins, and she could feel the heat from his body seeping into hers.

"Anything but leave you." His dark eyes had grown hot and heavy-lidded with what she knew was desire. For her.

She ran her tongue over her lips and pulled his head down for her kiss. "Good," she said. "Then, I won't have to tie you down."

"That is something about which I may never be able to jest, angel," he said. He held her hands and gently caressed the wrists that still bore faint red marks from the bonds Blakeley had tied.

"I cannot be sorry for anything that led me to this moment," she whispered, and he smiled and kissed her again.

Then he laid her on the bed and followed her down, kissing her and caressing her, leaving a trail of fire where his hands touched. She trembled, and he instantly drew back, looking at her in concern. "Are you cold? Am I too rough? I have wanted you for so long," he went on as she smiled and shook her head, "that I cannot trust myself to be as gentle as I would wish. You must tell me if—"

"Stop thinking I am fragile." Her hands came up to caress the skin bared by the open throat of his shirt. "I am not the silly, breakable little thing you think I am."

"I know," he gasped. "Oh, I know. Remember, I saw you with Blakeley. I know what a firebrand you are. Fearless. Beautiful."

He kissed her again, and she found she felt both fearless and beautiful. Her lips opened to his, and the sensations he evoked gave her a further sense of power. This was what she had felt so briefly in the dower house, she though exultantly. This was what she had craved without knowing what it was.

Her arms tightened around him, as his hands began to explore her with such gentle tenderness that she almost wept. He loved her. She had no doubts. His touch told her how he cherished her, adored her. And under those clever hands she began to burn with a passion she would never have believed herself capable of. She craved the touch of his bare skin beneath her hands, and began to work his shirt out of his breeches, until she began to stroke the smooth muscles of his back.

Ah, she sighed. That was it. Closer. Skin to skin. As if he read her thoughts, or shared them, Gideon whipped his shirt off over his head and then gently, holding her gaze with his, raised her night rail and removed it.

They fit. As different as night and day, hard and soft, smooth and rough, still they fit. Nature's comment on the relationship of men and women. The thought drifted across Amelia's brain and was gone in the wake of passion that swept over her with Gideon's hands, Gideon's lips. Oh, God, she was drowning in sensation, and all she wanted to do was sink into it and savor every drop. He stroked her, loved her, readied her, and when at last he entered her, she felt as if she were finally complete. Gently, quietly murmuring of his love all the while, Gideon brought her to a soft, complete understanding of what love was.

Afterward she found her head cradled on his chest, and she listened, half-awake, to the pounding of his heart.

"Amy?" His voice was tentative. She raised her head to look down into his eyes. To her surprise, they were filled with doubt. "Are you all right? I mean, I didn't hurt—"

She understood. "No, no. It was wonderful, Gideon. I thought for a minute that it would never work, but it was—you were—" She groped for a word. "Wonderful," she said again.

He grinned at her, reassured, once again the confident lover. "Thank you, angel. So were you." His arms went around her like a vise, and he hugged her close, his body warming hers. "I hate having to leave you and creep back to my room. Say you will marry me without delay."

"Of course," she said. "We can marry here, as soon as you like. I have no family. None I wish to invite anyway," she added, thinking of Eustace and Hortense. "Jane is the only friend I want to have with me. And your family is here. Perhaps we can be married before we return to the city. That will certainly give the town tabbies something to meow over."

"A splendid idea. I will ask Sir Richard—Uncle Richard, I suppose I must learn to call him—tomorrow morning if there is any way of obtaining a special license, so we do not have to wait for the banns to be read." He leaned over and kissed her, his hand stroking her hair. It was lovely, she decided, lying next to the one you loved, talking like this after making love. She was going to love being married to Gideon.

"Do you dislike it here so much?" Amelia hoped that his transition to Drake Sinclair, Earl of Mountjoy, would be easy. But that wouldn't happen if he left before he'd gotten to know his new family.

"No, it isn't that. Although I do not know what is going to become of me. Once removed from the cavalry and from being Gideon Falconer, I'm not sure who I am or what I will do." He tightened his arm around her. "You are the only constant in my life. Pray God you do not stop loving me."

"Never. Even your terrible condescension when you were fifteen and came home from Eton for Christmas couldn't make me change my mind—or my heart." She turned a little toward him, loving him more in the aftermath of lovemaking than she had ever thought possible. "So you can't expect that a change of profession will do so."

"I hope not." He tucked the sheet and blanket firmly around her shoulders, then, too, her hand. "I don't think I can leave them, Amy. Not after we just found each other. I am beginning to believe that it isn't a dream, that I may really have a family after all."

"I think that will make them very happy."

"And you? Will you be happy here do you think? It won't be London. Though we can go there whenever you want. I don't want to bury you, angel." He smiled at her. "Well, actually I do. I'd like to keep you all to myself forever, but I know that you will want to go to London, see your friends."

"And you? Can you be happy here, Gideon? It will be very different from London and from the regiment." She was a little worried that he was going to be sorry if he changed his life too drastically.

"If you are here with me, I think I will. I think a new challenge is what I need to keep me from becoming bored. And learning about being a landowner with tenants and crops and God knows what else should keep me busy for the foreseeable future." He kissed her and felt her, warm and loving, pressed against his side. "The sun is going to come up in a very short while, angel. I think I hear the clink of coal scuttles already. So unless you want to start life at Southbridge in the midst of a scandal, I had better go back to my room now."

Amelia pouted a little but eventually let him go. She watched with appreciation as he put his clothes on and moved toward the door. He was about to open it when he came back and kissed her once again. "I hate to leave you when you look so rosy and warm and well loved."

"If you don't stop fishing under the covers, I won't let you leave." She pulled his head down for another kiss.

"I am leaving now," he said, grinning at her gasp as he caressed her breast one last time. "Truly." He rose and tiptoed to the door. "I love you. I'll see you at breakfast."

She grinned at him. His face was turned back for one last glimpse of her when he walked into the hall and headlong into Sir Richard.

Chapter Twenty

Sir Richard's eyebrows shot up. "You have just returned from an early morning—or late evening—constitutional with Lady Amelia?"

"My promised bride and I were making—wedding plans." Gideon crossed his arms across his chest and glared. His implacable stance dared Sir Richard to say anything more.

The older man bowed. "My sincere felicitations. She is not only brave and beautiful but kind and loving as well."

Gideon's answering smile was as bright as the dawn. "Yes, she is all that and more. I am the luckiest man in the world this morning."

"What have you decided to do about the other change in your life?" Sir Richard took Gideon's arm. "If you are not still sleepy, perhaps we might cajole a crust and some coffee from Cook. I would like to try to make my peace with you, if I can."

Gideon shook his head. "There is no need. Amy helped me to see that nothing that has happened can change who I am. A name and a title really make very little difference after the streets and the hussars."

They descended the stairs together and made their way to the kitchen. "So long as you do not blame me for catapulting you into a new family and a new life. I never stopped to ask what you wanted." Sir Richard's smile was rueful. "I am glad to have you as a nephew, Gideon. I may have as much trouble thinking of you as Drake as you will."

"No matter what anyone calls me, I am who I am. And," he added with a sheepish grin, "Amy loves me."

He smiled again and knew that his newfound happiness

and satisfaction shined from him. His uncle raised his eyebrows. "Methinks you were doing more than discussing wedding plans, nevvy."

Gideon laughed. "You cannot expect a gentleman to comment on that statement, Sir—Richard. Uncle." He shrugged. "I don't know what to call you."

"Richard will do. Let's see what Cook has ready for the staff's breakfast."

Without thinking about it, Gideon swung open the door into the service area of the castle. "Richard it is. And I can be Gideon or Drake—but not Francis if you please I find I have a rooted dislike for the name."

He stopped short at the doorway to the kitchen when he heard a gasp and the crash of falling crockery.

"Colonel Richard, is this the young man—" a woman's voice broke off, and Gideon looked down to see a small, white-haired, pink-cheeked whirlwind as it raced to embrace him. "Master Drake, it is you. I would know you anywhere. Do you remember me? I was only the undercook when you left, but many's a tart you finagled out of me. I am—"

"You are Dulcey." Gideon's voice was thick. "I remember you. You made the most delicious apple tarts."

"Lord bless the boy!" She reached up and pulled Gideon's head down and gave him a kiss. "He does remember me! I said he would! I told them so last night. He might forget others in all the years, but he won't forget Dulcey!"

"And he didn't." Sir Richard cleared his throat. "Do you suppose we could get a bit of breakfast, Dulcey? Once you finish drowning the lad, that is. And choking him."

Dulcey laughed and wiped her eyes on her apron. "I'll just get right to my pans, then, Colonel," she said, and did so.

Gideon and Sir Richard sat at the scrubbed pine table in the kitchen while Dulcey ordered the other servants about and insisted on cooking their breakfast herself.

"It is coming back to you now that you are here, isn't it?" Sir Richard asked in a low voice.

"Yes. I had made myself forget, but now it is coming back in bits and pieces." Gideon looked around him at the large kitchen, now the scene of more and more activity.

"But you do know that you are Fran—sorry, Drake." There was a note of anxiety in Sir Richard's voice.

"Yes, you and Lady Mountjoy—my mother—were right. I am Drake. I can remember her very clearly now."

Platters of eggs and bacon and fried bread were placed on the table, and large mugs of sweetened tea followed. Gideon found that he was ravenous and had no trouble helping his uncle clean every dish.

Once they had finished and been thoroughly greeted and made much of by those of the staff who were around, they went back to the breakfast room to see if anyone else had arisen. There they found Lady Mountjoy and Jane making a spartan meal of toast and tea. While Serena and Gideon found that they felt quite comfortable in each other's presence, Jane and Sir Richard seemed unaccountably ill at ease. In a remarkably short time, Jane made her excuses and left the room in what seemed to Gideon to be a tearing hurry. To his surprise, Sir Richard followed her almost immediately.

"What in the world is the matter with them?" he asked his mother, as casually as if they had been breakfasting together for years.

"Well," Serena answered, unable to stop smiling at her son, "I believe that Richard is in love."

"With Jane?" The idea had never occurred to him, but Gideon found that it seemed quite logical. "Yes, that could be. How can you tell?"

"I have known him for years. And she does not seem indifferent to him, but something seems to be holding her back. She is avoiding him." Serena sat back and sipped her tea for a few moments. "You should ask Lady Amelia."

"About Jane?"

"That and also to marry you. You are in love with her, aren't you?"

Gideon stared at his mother. "How did you know? You haven't known Amy for years. And truth to tell you haven't known me as an adult."

"A mother's instinct. And does she love you, Gideon?"

He smiled at her. "You called me Gideon."

"It is your name. I am not sure that we can legally change Francis to Gideon, but you must certainly be called what you wish to be called." She laid a soft hand on his. "Just as you were as a child."

So it was going to be that easy, Gideon thought. His mother was ready to accept him—whatever he chose to call himself—and his chosen bride. Like Dulcey, she welcomed him and asked no questions.

"I have asked Amy to marry me, and she has accepted, Mama."

Serena's eyes filled when she heard that name from Gideon's lips. He smiled at her. "I know who you are. I think I knew from the moment I saw you. You are Mama, and I love you very much."

The tears spilled over then, healing and soothing. Gideon rose and went to put his arms around his mother and hold her near. The bitterness of the lost child seemed to fade, and the tight, old scars around his heart softened and eased as he held her.

"Mama," he said at last, as her tears subsided. "I think that we don't need to cry anymore. I think we can let the laughter start now, don't you?"

Serena nodded and smiled through her tears as she groped for a handkerchief. "Yes, darling, of course you are right. And the very first thing we're going to do is celebrate Christmas. Really celebrate it, the way it hasn't been done here since—since you went away."

"A splendid idea!" said a voice from the doorway as Amelia, looking radiant despite her lack of sleep, entered the room.

Congratulations and hugs, tea and a few random tears of joy all mingled for the next few minutes. Then Amelia said, "What has happened to Jane and Sir Richard? I looked out my window and saw Jane headed for the woods and Sir Richard following her as if he were about to arrest her." She looked even more puzzled when both Gideon and Serena began to laugh.

* * *

"Jane," he called out. "Wait for me!"

She must not have heard him, he decided, for instead of turning around and greeting him, she increased her pace and made a sharp turn toward the woods. She might be tall for a woman, but she was no match for his long stride, and it took him less than half a minute to overtake her.

"Jane, did you not hear me?" She turned to face him, and he was dismayed by her look of stark misery. "What has happened to upset you?"

"Nothing," she muttered, and turned away, pulling the hood of her cloak up around her face, hiding it from his view. "I came outside for a walk. A solitary walk," she added.

Sir Richard only smiled and walked in front of her so he could see her face. "And I am spoiling your solitude, am I not?" He could not be sorry; he was so glad to be with her. "But I have some very welcome news for you."

She smiled with a visible effort. "And I for you. I believe Lady Mountjoy will be none the worse for the excitement of last evening."

"Yes, she looked well at breakfast." Serena was not the topic he wanted to discuss. "I am not surprised. Happiness is seldom the cause of lasting illness, I find. And my news is even more welcome. Gideon has told me that he and Lady Amelia are to wed."

Jane's smile seemed more genuine this time, though he was still concerned by the tired, almost hopeless look in her eyes. Jane was never hopeless. The very idea was contrary to her nature.

"I am very happy for them," she said. "Although if he overcame his scruples only because he is now the heir to a marquessate, I will be very disappointed in him."

"No, from what he said to me, I believe that he and the lady have agreed that no matter what his name or station in life, they are made for each other."

Jane seemed relieved. "Then, I am glad. Amelia deserves every happiness, and she has always found that in Gideon."

Sir Richard took her arm as they entered the woods. He wished he had thought to take her inside to the conservatory.

There roses bloomed and there were wrought iron settees, where they might be both comfortable and private. Fleetingly he thought of taking her there now, but he could not wait another minute to put his fate to the touch.

"Jane," he said, and then stopped, unsure of quite how to proceed.

"Yes?" She walked beside him but still did not look directly at him.

"I want to ask you something." He stopped beside a holly tree whose glossy leaves and red berries shone brightly against the bare ground of December.

"Yes?" she said again, still walking on. There was mistletoe, he noted, in the tree above her head.

"I do not know quite how to begin." He caught up with her and took her elbow.

"What is it?" she snapped. "What is so important that you must accost me when I have purposely gone out by myself? Well?" she demanded when he stood silent, stunned at her angry outburst.

"I've never done this before," he said. "So you must pardon me if I am graceless. But Jane, you must know how I feel about you. I know you are self-sufficient and busy and happy as you are but—do you think that you might possibly—could you consider—perhaps—" He broke off as he saw the look of bafflement on her face. He was making a mull of it, as he had feared he would.

"Not right away, of course," he babbled on haplessly. "I know you will have to grow used to the idea, but after a while, do you think you might?"

"Might what? What idea?" She stared up at him, still confused but somehow less sad than before. His heart lightened just a bit.

"Marry me," he said simply. "Do you think you might grow to care for me enough to marry me?"

Jane looked around as if surprised to find herself in a wintry woods with a madman. "You want to—"

"Marry you. Yes, Jane, I do." For some reason he was encouraged by the fact that she seemed to have lost her bearings.

That did not happen to the supremely competent Miss Forrester very often, he was sure.

He smiled down at her a little tentatively and took her hands. "Surely you knew how I felt. I thought it was painfully obvious. The doubt is all as to whether you are willing to make space in your busy and useful life for me."

She stared blankly at him for another heartbeat and then said, "Why in the world would you want to marry me?"

"Because I love you, of course. Why else?" Really, for an intelligent woman she was being painfully obtuse.

"You love me?"

"Yes, Jane, I love you and want to marry you. Now we can talk about the difficulties of combining the cavalry with your school and other work. Or you can simply tell me you do not love me and do not think you ever can. I need to know. Do you love me?"

"Yes." That was all, but it was enough. He swept her into his arms with an exultant laugh. "Then, kiss me, for everything else will take care of itself!"

When Jane and Richard returned a full half hour later, their arms were laden with holly and mistletoe, and they announced that they had found the perfect yule log. Something in their faces, a secret sparkle that she recognized, led Amelia to tug on Gideon's arm.

"Come with me," she murmured. In the small conservatory that Serena had told her of, she turned to face him, her smile an invitation to share a secret.

"What is it?" he asked, after he had kissed her. "I am always happy to have an excuse to kiss you, angel, but what is the occasion?"

"I want to get some white roses. Your mama told me there were some." Amelia looked around. "Ah, over there. Now, if I can just find some secateurs . . ."

"Here they are, madam." A small, gnomelike man wearing a dirt-stained coverall seemed to appear from nowhere. "How many would you like, Master Drake?"

Gideon smiled. "McGregor, isn't it?"

"Aye. Fancy your remembering me. White roses, is it?"

"Yes. As many as you can spare," Amelia said, smiling as one more piece of Gideon's past fell into place.

"Are you ever going to tell me why?" her betrothed complained.

"It is to celebrate Jane's engagement. I thought it would be a lovely, romantic gesture. I don't think Jane has had many of those in her life."

Gideon stared at her. "I am not going to ask how you know they are engaged."

"Because, my love, I can see in their faces what I see in yours—and in mine when I look in the mirror and think of you!" She pulled his head down for a kiss as McGregor went to cut the roses for them.

The roses and the announcements they heralded marked the start of a concerted effort on the part of everyone to produce a Christmas the likes of which Southbridge had not seen in years. Dulcey and the kitchen staff managed to create plum puddings and mince pies, chess tarts and other treats Gideon thought he could remember from long ago.

Lady Mountjoy, Jane, and Amelia decorated the mantels and tables with holly and red bows. Sir Richard unearthed a kissing bough from the attics, and he and Gideon brought mistletoe to put in it and hung it carefully in the drawing room doorway. The marquess looked on all of the festivity with a serene smile, the look of baffled hurt banished from his eyes by the happiness of his son and grandson, and by the joys of the season.

The only note of harsh reality came with a letter from Amelia's solicitor, who had been briefed to see to Eustace and Blakeley. Eustace and his mother had left for Belgium, and Blakeley had sold his shop and decamped for Canada, where, Gideon said when he read the letter, they could only hope he would freeze to death.

Jane and Sir Richard returned to London before the new year. Jane had her work at the school to take up, and Sir Richard's hurriedly arranged leave from Horse Guards had expired. They planned to return to Southbridge in three weeks' time, to take part in the wedding of Francis Drake Sinclair, Earl of Mountjoy, to Lady Amelia Bradshaw, only daughter of the late Aubrey, Duke of Doncaster.

Gideon had been right. The announcement in the *Gazette* caused quite a stir in the drawing rooms and ballrooms of the ton, but the happy couple stayed far away from London until spring, when Sir Richard Sinclair wed Miss Jane Forrester in another wedding that set the ton a-buzz.

But by the time the next Christmas rolled around and the earl and countess's son, Lionel, had been christened, several new scandals had made the ton forget the one about the gypsy earl and the duke's daughter.